UNSPOKEN

UNSPOKEN

MARI JUNGSTEDT

ST. MARTIN'S MINOTAUR

NEW YORK

This is a work of fiction. All of the characters, organizations, and events
portrayed in this novel are either products of the author's imagination
or are used fictitiously.

UNSPOKEN. Copyright © 2004 by Mari Jungstedt. English translation © 2007
by Tiina Nunnally. All rights reserved. Printed in the United States of America.
No part of this book may be used or reproduced in any manner whatsoever without
written permission except in the case of brief quotations embodied in critical articles
or reviews. For information, address St. Martin's Press, 175 Fifth Avenue,
New York, N.Y. 10010.

www.minotaurbooks.com

Library of Congress Cataloging-in-Publication Data

Jungstedt, Mari, 1962–
    [In denna stilla natt. English]
    Unspoken / Mari Jungstedt ; [translated by Tiina Nunnally].—1st ed.
        p. cm.
    ISBN-13: 978-0-312-36377-2
    ISBN-10: 0-312-36377-X
    I. Nunnally, Tiina, 1952–   II. Title.
    PT9877.2.U64I613 2007
    839.73'8—dc22

                                                    2007019345

First published in Sweden under the title *In Denna Stilla Natt* by
Albert Bonniers Förlag

First U.S. Edition: September 2007

10   9   8   7   6   5   4   3   2   1

To my husband, Cenneth Niklasson—beloved best friend

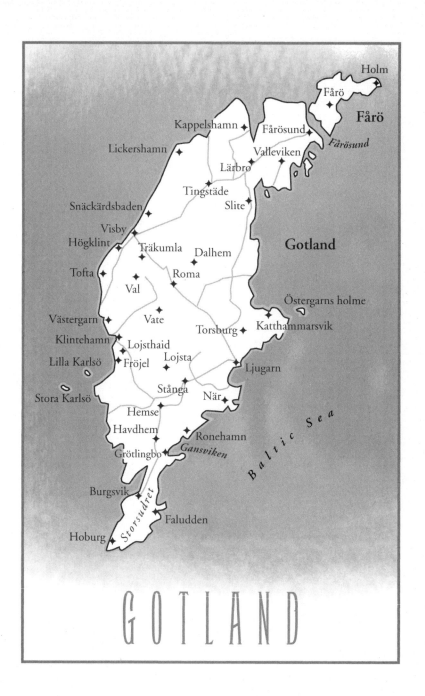

Holm

Fårö

Fårö

Kappelshamn

Fårösund

Fårösund

Lickershamn

Valleviken

Lärbro

Tingstäde

Snäckärdsbaden

Slite

Visby

Gotland

Högklint

Träkumla

Dalhem

Tofta

Roma

Val

Östergarns holme

Västergarn

Vate

Klintehamn

Torsburg

Katthammarsvik

Lojsthaid

Lilla Karlsö

Fröjel

Lojsta

Ljugarn

Stånga

När

Stora Karlsö

Hemse

Havdhem

Ronehamn

Grötlingbo

Gansviken

Baltic Sea

Burgsvik

Storsudret

Faludden

Hoburg

GOTLAND

UNSPOKEN

SUNDAY, NOVEMBER 11

For the first time in a week the sky cleared. The wan rays of November sunshine found their way through the clouds, and the spectators at the Visby trotting track turned their faces with yearning up toward the sun. It was the last race of the season, and there was a sense of anticipation in the air, mixed with a touch of melancholy. A chilly but enthusiastic crowd had gathered in the grandstands. They were drinking beer and hot coffee from plastic cups, eating hot dogs, and making notes in their track programs.

Henry "Flash" Dahlström got out his hip flask and took a good swig of his home-brewed liquor. It made him grimace, but it also warmed him nicely. With him in the stands sat the whole gang: Bengan, Gunsan, Monica, and Kjelle. All of them were rapidly advancing toward various states of intoxication.

The procession had just started. The snorting standardbreds, glossy with sweat, were lined up and prancing forward as the music blared from the loudspeakers. The drivers, with their legs wide apart, were firmly seated in their lightweight sulkies.

The odds were posted on a black tote board out near the track, with the numbers ticking past.

Henry leafed through the racing program. He ought to place a bet on Ginger Star, running in race number seven. No one else seemed to believe in her. She was only a three-year-old. He had followed the horse during the summer races, and even though she had a tendency to break into a gallop, she kept on getting better.

"Hey, Flash, take a look at Pita Queen. She's a beauty, don't you think?" Bengan slurred his words as he reached for the hip flask.

Henry had been given the nickname Flash because he had worked as a photographer for *Gotlands Tidningar* for many years before alcohol took over his life full-time.

"You're damn right. With that trainer . . ." he replied and then stood up to take his racing card to the window.

There was a line of betting windows, all with open wooden hatches. Wallets were eagerly pulled out, banknotes changed hands, and cards were handed in. One flight up was the track restaurant, where invited guests ate steak and drank strongbeer. Honored big-time players puffed on cigars, discussing the current condition of the horses and the technique of the drivers.

The race was about to begin. The first driver politely saluted the judges by giving a brief nod toward the judging tower. Over the loudspeakers the announcer called for the horses to take their places.

After four races Henry had an equal number of wins on his card. If luck was with him, he could win the jackpot with five in a row. Since he had also bet on the long shot Ginger Star in the last race, the winnings ought to be significant. If only she came up to his expectations.

The race began and he followed the sulkies on the track as closely as he could after consuming eight strongbeers and a countless number of shots. When the bell for the final lap rang, his pulse quickened. Ginger Star was running well, damned well, as a matter of fact. With each stride she closed in on the two favorites in the lead, and he seemed to be seeing her more clearly. The powerful neck, the snorting nostrils, and the ears pointing straight forward. She could do it.

Don't start galloping now, do not gallop. He was muttering this plea to himself like a mantra. His eyes were fixed on the young filly, who with furious energy was closing in on the leaders. Now she passed one of her rivals. Suddenly he became aware of the weight of the camera around his neck, and he was reminded that he had planned to take pictures. He snapped several photos, his hands relatively steady.

The red sand of the trotting track spurted up around the hooves that were pounding forward at breakneck speed. The drivers were using their whips on the horses, and the excitement rose among the spectators.

Many in the stands were on their feet, some of them clapping, others shouting.

Ginger Star pulled forward on the outside and was now even with the horse in the lead. Then her driver used his whip for the first time. Dahlström stood up as he followed the horse through the lens of his camera.

When Ginger Star crossed the finish line ahead of the big favorite by a nose, a sigh of disappointment passed through the crowd. Dahlström was aware of scattered comments: "What the hell?" "It can't be true!" "Unbelievable!" "Damn it!"

But he dropped down onto the bench.

He had won all five races in a row.

The only audible sound was the sweep of the broom across the stable floor and the grinding jaws of the horses as they chewed their evening oats. Calm had settled in after the hectic race day. Fanny Jansson was sweeping with brisk, rhythmic strokes. Her body ached after all the hard work, and when she was done, she sank down onto a feed box outside Regina's stall. The horse peered out, and Fanny stuck her hand through the bars to stroke the horse's nose.

The slender, dark-skinned girl was alone in the stable. She had declined an invitation to join the others at a local restaurant to celebrate the end of the season. She could just imagine how rowdy it was bound to get. Worse than usual. She had been there several times before but didn't enjoy it. The horse owners would drink too much and try to hit on her. They called her "princess," pulled her onto their laps, and pinched her on the rear.

Some got bolder the more they drank. They would make comments about her body, both verbally and with their eyes. They were a pack of dirty old men.

She yawned, but she had no desire to bike home, either. Not really. Her mother had the day off from her job, and there was a good chance that she was drunk. If she was alone she would be sitting on the sofa with her mouth turned down in a sullen frown, with a bottle of wine in front of her. As usual, Fanny would feel guilty because she hadn't spent the day with her mother instead of with the horses. Her mother couldn't care less that it was a race day with tons of work to do. Nor did she understand that Fanny needed to get away from home. The stable was her lifeline. If she didn't have the horses, she didn't know what she would do.

Uneasiness seized her as she imagined an even worse scenario: that her mother might not be alone. If her so-called boyfriend, Jack, was there, they would get even drunker, and Fanny would have a hard time sleeping.

Tomorrow she had to be at school early, and she needed to get some sleep. Ninth grade was a torment that she wanted to get through as fast as possible. Fanny had tried to do her best when the term started, but things just kept getting worse. She was having a hard time concentrating, and she had started cutting classes fairly often. She just couldn't face it.

She had enough troubles outside of school.

MONDAY, NOVEMBER 12

A bubble of saliva had formed at the corner of his mouth. With each exhalation it grew bigger until it burst and dribbled down his chin and onto the pillowcase.

The room was very bright. The blinds were rolled up and the dirty streaks on the windowpane were clearly visible. On the windowsill stood a solitary pot with an African violet that had long since perished.

Henry Dahlström slowly regained consciousness as the urgent ringing of the phone cut through the thick silence. The sound echoed off the walls in the shabby two-room apartment, persisting until it finally won out over sleep. Disconnected thoughts popped up in his mind, relentlessly bringing him back to reality. He had a vague feeling of happiness but couldn't remember what it was from.

The headache started the minute he swung his legs over the side of the bed. Cautiously he sat up. His vision blurred the pattern of the bedspread. Thirst made him get to his feet and stagger out to the kitchen. The floor swayed beneath him. He leaned against the door frame and looked at the chaos.

The kitchen cupboards stood wide open and the counter was covered with dirty glasses and plates, as well as scraps of food. There was burned coffee in the glass pot of the coffeemaker. Someone had dropped a plate on the floor. He could make out the remnants of fried herring and mashed potatoes among the pieces of china. On the kitchen table, beer cans were crowded together with liquor bottles, an overflowing ashtray, and a stack of racing cards.

Suddenly he remembered why he should be happy. He had brought home the jackpot as the sole winner of all five races. The sum was breathtaking, at least for him. Over eighty thousand kronor had been paid out to him, in cash, and gone straight into his pockets. He had never before had so much money in his possession.

His eyes flicked anxiously up and down over the half-empty cupboards. Surely he'd had enough sense to hide the money. If only none of the others . . . No, he refused to believe that. Although when it came to liquor or money, you never could tell.

He pushed aside the thought and tried to recall what he had done when he arrived home from the track the previous evening. Where the hell?

Oh, that's right. The broom closet. With trembling fingers he pulled out the package of vacuum cleaner bags. When he touched the bundle of banknotes, he breathed a sigh of relief. He sank down onto the floor, cradling the package in his hands as if it were a valuable porcelain vase. At the same time, thoughts about what he was going to do with the money flickered past. Fly to the Canary Islands and order drinks with little umbrellas. Maybe invite Monica or Bengan to come, too—or why not both of them?

An image of his daughter appeared. He really ought to send some of the money to her. She was grown up now and lived in Malmö. Contact between the two of them had been broken off long ago.

Henry stuffed the package back in the closet and stood up. Thousands of stars danced before his eyes.

The need for a drink became more urgent. The beer cans were empty, as were the liquor bottles. He lit one of the longer cigarette butts from the ashtray, swearing as he burned his finger.

Then he discovered a bottle of vodka under the table, and it turned out to have a decent slug left in the bottom. He greedily gulped it down, and the merry-go-round in his head eased up a bit. He went out to the patio and breathed in the cold, raw November air.

On the lawn lay an unopened can of strongbeer, of all things. He picked it up and definitely started feeling better. In the fridge he found a piece of sausage and a saucepan of dried mashed potatoes.

It was Monday evening. It was past six o'clock, and the state liquor store was closed. He had to go out and find some booze.

Henry took the bus downtown. The driver was nice enough to let him ride free, even though he could now afford to pay the fare. By the time he got out at Östercentrum, he was the only passenger. Rain was in the air, and it was dark and desolate on the streets. Most of the stores were closed at this time of night.

On one of the benches near the Allis hot dog stand sat Bengan with that new guy Örjan from the mainland. An unpleasant type, pale with dark, slicked-back hair and a sharp look in his eye. The muscles of his arms testified to how he had spent his time in the slammer, from which he had recently been released. He had apparently been sent up for aggravated assault and battery. Tattoos covered his arms and chest; part of one was visible inside the dirty collar of his shirt. Henry felt anything but comfortable with him, and things were made only worse by the fact that he always had that growling attack dog in tow. The animal was white with red eyes and a square snout. Ugly as sin. The guy bragged that his dog had bitten a toy poodle to death in Östermalm in the middle of downtown Stockholm. The fucking upper-class dame who owned the poodle went nuts and starting hitting Örjan with her umbrella until the police showed up and took charge. He had gotten off with a warning to buy a stronger leash. The incident was even reported on TV.

As Henry approached, a muted rumble issued from the dog's throat; the animal was lying at Örjan's feet. Bengan greeted him with a wobbly wave of his hand. It was apparent from far away that Henry's friend was quite inebriated.

"Hi, how are things? Congratulations again. It's so fucking great." Bengan gave his friend a befuddled look.

"Thanks."

Örjan pulled out a plastic bottle containing a colorless, unidentified liquid.

"Want some?"

"Sure."

The liquor had a pungent smell. After several sizable gulps, Henry's hands stopped shaking.

"That went down nice, didn't it?" Örjan asked the question without smiling.

"Absolutely," said Henry, and he sat down on the bench next to the other two men.

"How's it going for you?"

"Well, I've got my head up and my feet down."

Bengan leaned closer to Henry and breathed loudly in his ear.

"Shit, what about all that dough?" he muttered. "It's amazing. What are you thinking of doing with it?"

Henry cast a quick glance over at Örjan, who had lit a cigarette. He was staring out toward Östergravar and seemed to have stopped listening.

"We'll talk about it later," whispered Henry. "I want you to keep your mouth shut about the money. Don't tell anyone else about it. Okay?"

"Sure, no problem," promised Bengan. "Of course, buddy." He patted Henry on the shoulder and turned back to Örjan. "Give me a swig." He grabbed the bottle.

"Take it easy, damn it. Pianissimo."

Typical Örjan, thought Henry. *He always has to sound so odd. Pianissimo—what the hell is that?* The dog bared his teeth.

All Henry wanted right now was to buy some booze and get out of there.

"Have you got anything to sell?"

Örjan dug through a worn bag made of imitation leather. He pulled out a plastic bottle containing home-brewed liquor.

"Fifty kronor. But maybe you can afford to cough up more than that?"

"Naw. I've only got a fifty."

Henry handed over the banknote and reached for the bottle. Örjan kept his grip on it.

"Are you sure?"

"Yup."

"What if I don't believe you? What if I think that you've got more and you just don't want to pay more than that?"

"What the hell—let go!"

He yanked the bottle away from Örjan. At the same time he stood up. Örjan laughed and jeered, "Can't you take a joke?"

"I've got to go. See you. I'll be in touch."

He headed for the bus stop without looking back. He could feel Örjan's eyes fixed on his back like needles.

He was sitting in the living room, comfortably leaning back in the only armchair. On his way home he had passed a kiosk that was open at night, and he had bought some Grape Tonic, which he mixed with the booze to make himself a nice, tasty highball. He studied the glow from his cigarette in the dim light of the room, enjoying his solitude.

It didn't bother him that the apartment was still a mess from the party the night before.

He put an old Johnny Cash record on the stereo. The neighbor woman protested by pounding on the wall, presumably because the music was interfering with the Swedish soap opera on TV. He pretended not to notice because he despised everything that had to do with normal Swedish life.

During his professional days he had also avoided routines. As the foremost photographer at *Gotlands Tidningar* he'd had plenty of opportunities to plan his own work hours. When he eventually started his own business, of course, he did precisely as he pleased.

In moments of clarity he surmised that it was this freedom that had spelled the beginning of the end. It created space for his drinking, which slowly but surely nibbled away at his work, his family life, his free time, and finally took precedence over everything else. His marriage fell apart, his clients disappeared, and contact with his daughter became increasingly sporadic and then ceased altogether after a few years. In the end he had neither money nor a job. The only friends who remained were his drinking buddies.

He was roused from his reflections by a clattering sound on the patio. He stopped with the glass halfway to his lips.

Was it one of those damn kids in the area who was going around stealing bicycles and then painting and selling them? His own bicycle stood outside unlocked. They had tried to swipe it before.

Another clatter. He looked at his watch. Ten forty-five. Someone was out there—there was no doubt about that.

Might be an animal, of course, maybe a cat.

He opened the patio door and peered into the darkness. The little patch of grass that belonged to his corner property was lit up in the cold glow of the streetlight. Over by the pathway a shadow disappeared among the trees. Presumably just somebody out walking his dog. Henry pulled the door shut and locked it, just to be safe.

The interruption annoyed him. He switched on the ceiling light and looked around the apartment with distaste. He couldn't stand seeing all the clutter, so he stuck his feet into a pair of slippers and went down to his darkroom in the basement to check on the pictures he had taken during his evening at the harness races. He had taken a whole roll of Ginger Star, and a couple of shots just as she crossed the finish line. Her head thrust forward, her mane flying, and her nose ahead of all the others. What a feeling.

The building superintendent had been kind enough to let him use an old bicycle storage room. He had furnished it with an enlarger, trays for developer and fixer, and a rack for drying the pictures. The basement window was covered with pieces of black cardboard to keep out the daylight.

The only light source was a red bulb on the wall. In the faint glow of this lamp the work could be done without difficulty. He enjoyed spending time in his darkroom. Focusing one hundred percent of his attention on a task in silence and darkness. He had experienced this same feeling of calm only once before, during his honeymoon to Israel. One day he and Ann-Sofie had gone on a snorkeling expedition. As they moved below the surface of the silent sea, it was like being in another dimension. Undisturbed, untouched by the constant noise of the rest of the world. That was the only time he had gone snorkeling, but the experience had stayed with him as a pleasant memory.

He had been working for quite a while when he was interrupted by a discreet knock on the door. Instinctively he froze and listened carefully. Who could it be? It had to be close to midnight.

The knocking came again, slower and longer. He lifted the photo he was working on from the rinse bath and hung it up to dry as thoughts whirled through his mind.

Should he open the door? Common sense told him that it would be best not to. This might have something to do with his winnings. Someone who wanted the money. The news about his win certainly must have spread by now. The sound coming from the other side of the door signified danger. His mouth went dry. Although it could just as well be Bengan.

"Who is it?" he shouted.

The question hung in the darkness. No reply, utter silence. He sank down onto a stool, fumbled for the liquor bottle, and took several quick swigs. A few minutes passed and nothing happened. He sat totally still and waited, though he didn't know what he was waiting for.

Suddenly someone began pounding hard from a different direction, on the windowpane. He gave such a start that he nearly dropped the bottle on the floor. The last of his drunkenness vanished, and he stared up at the cardboard covering the window, hardly daring to breathe.

Then it came again. Hard, loud. As if the person out there wasn't using his knuckles but some sort of tool. The ceiling and walls closed in. Terror seized him by the throat. Here he sat, trapped like a rat, while someone out there was toying with him. Sweat broke out on his forehead, and his guts turned over. He needed to go to the toilet.

The pounding changed into a rhythmic thudding, a monotonous banging against the basement window. No one in the building would hear his cries for help. Not in the middle of the night on an ordinary weekday. Could the person or persons out there break the window? It would still be impossible to get in because the window was much too small. He had locked the door—he was sure of that.

All of a sudden there was silence. Every muscle in his body was on edge. He listened for sounds that weren't there.

For almost an hour he sat in the same frozen position before he dared to stand up. The hasty movement made him dizzy, and he staggered and saw flashing white stars in the dark. He had to go to the bathroom right now; he couldn't hold it any longer. His legs could barely support him.

When he opened the door he realized instantly that he had made a mistake.

Fanny studied herself in the mirror as she ran a comb through her shiny hair. Her eyes were dark brown, and her complexion was also dark. A Swedish mother and West Indian father. Mulatto, without having a trace of typical African features. Her nose was small and straight and her lips narrow. Raven-black hair that reached all the way to her waist. Some people took her to be Indian or North African, while others guessed that she came from Morocco or Algeria.

She had just stepped out of the shower and put on underpants and a big T-shirt. Freshly scrubbed with the stiff brushes that she bought at Åhléns department store. They tore at her body and made her skin tender. Her mother had asked her what she needed brushes like that for.

"For scrubbing myself. They make you a lot cleaner. And it's good for the skin," she replied. She explained that the smell from the horses clung to her. The shower had become her best friend.

She turned sideways and studied her thin body in profile. Her shoulders drooped. If she straightened her back, her breasts stuck out and seemed even bigger. That's why she always walked slightly bent over. She had developed early. By the seventh grade, she already had breasts. At first she had done everything she could to hide them. Big, baggy shirts helped.

The worst was in gym class. Even though she wore a sports bra that flattened out her breasts, they still were visible when she jumped or ran. The changes in her body made her feel sick. Why did everyone get so disgusting when they grew up? She shaved under her arms as soon as the slightest sign of hair appeared. Not to mention her crotch. And the blood that appeared every month, staining her panties and sheet when she bled through during the night. She despised her body.

The fact that she had dark skin didn't make things any better. She wanted to look like all the others. In her class there were only two others who were dark. They were twins, so at least they had each other. Two boys who had been adopted from Brazil. They were the school's best soccer players, and they were very popular because they looked like Roberto Carlos, the famous Brazilian wingback. For them the color of their skin was an advantage. But not for her. She didn't want to stand out.

She longed to have friends, to have her very own best friend. Someone to confide in, to share her worries. In school no one paid any attention to her anymore. Both there and at home, she was always alone. At the same time she was fully aware that this was her own fault. When she started in the ninth grade, kids would sometimes ask her to join them after doing their homework. She always said no. Not because she didn't want to, but because she had to rush home to walk Spot and take care of everything else that had to be done. Inviting a friend home was out of the question. The risk was too great that they would find a messy apartment reeking of smoke, with the blinds down and breakfast dishes still on the table. A depressed mother with a cigarette drooping from the corner of her mouth and a wineglass in her hand. No thanks, that wasn't something she wanted to put herself through, or a friend, either. It would just make everyone talk. How embarrassing that would be. The last thing she needed was more problems.

That was why Fanny was alone. The other kids got tired of asking her, and finally no one even bothered to talk to her. It was as though she didn't even exist.

SUNDAY, NOVEMBER 18

The hail that was ricocheting off the galvanized roof woke Detective Superintendent Anders Knutas at his home, which was a stone's throw outside the ring wall in Visby.

He climbed out of bed and shivered as his feet touched the cold floor. He fumbled wearily for his bathrobe and pulled up the blinds. He peered out in surprise. Hail in November was unusual. The garden looked like something straight out of an old black-and-white Bergman movie. The trees mournfully stretched out their bare branches toward the steel gray sky. The asphalt on the residential street was wet and cold. Off in the distance a woman in a dark blue coat was struggling to cross the street with a baby buggy. Her shoulders were hunched against the wind and the sharp beads of ice that were peppering the ground. Two rumpled-looking sparrows huddled together under the currant bushes, although the sparse branches offered little protection.

Why should I get up at all? he thought as he crawled back under the warm covers. Lina had her back turned to him and seemed to be still asleep. He cuddled up next to her and kissed the back of her neck.

The thought of Sunday breakfast with warm scones and coffee finally convinced them to get out of bed. The local radio station was playing oldies requests, and the cat was sitting in the window trying to catch the drops of water on the other side of the pane. It didn't take long before the children came sauntering into the kitchen, still in their pajamas and nightgown. Nils and Petra were twins and had just turned twelve. They had Lina's freckles and curly red hair but their father's lanky build. They looked alike but were otherwise complete opposites.

Petra had inherited her father's calm disposition, and she loved fishing, golf, and spending time outdoors. Nils was hot-tempered with a bellowing laugh and a talent for mimicry. He was also crazy about movies and music, just like Lina.

Knutas checked the thermometer outside the window. Thirty-six degrees. With a certain gloominess he noted that the crimson days of October were now gone. It was his favorite month: the crisp air, the leaves of the trees blazing with color ranging from ocher to purple, and the strong scent of earth and apples. Glittering bright red rowanberries, and the woods filled with autumn chanterelles. Blue sky. Not too hot and not too cold.

Now October had been replaced with a dirty-gray November, which could hardly please anyone. The sun came up just after seven and went down before four. The days were going to get shorter and darker all the way until Christmas.

No wonder so many people got depressed at this time of year. Anyone who had to be outdoors was in a hurry to go back inside as fast as possible. People hunched their shoulders beneath the wind and rain, not even bothering to glance up at each other. *We ought to hibernate, like bears,* thought Knutas. *This month is just a transitional period and nothing more.*

The summer seemed long gone. Back then the island had looked entirely different. Each summer Gotland was invaded by hundreds of thousands of visitors who came to enjoy the unique nature, the sand beaches, and the medieval city of Visby. Of course the island needed tourists, but the visitors also meant a great deal of work for the police. Hordes of teenagers came to Visby to party at the numerous pubs. Problems with alcohol and drugs increased dramatically.

But this past summer all of that had been overshadowed by a serial killer who had ravaged the island, terrifying both tourists and Gotlanders alike. The police had worked under great pressure, and the enormous scrutiny from the media hadn't made their job any easier.

Afterward Knutas was unhappy about the way things had turned out. He brooded over the fact that the police hadn't seen the connection between the victims earlier and prevented the lives of more young women from being sacrificed.

He and his family had taken a five-week vacation, but when he went back to work, he felt anything but rested.

So far the fall had been uneventful, and that was exactly what he needed.

He had been standing outside the door, ringing the bell for almost five minutes. Surely Flash couldn't be such a sound sleeper? Now he kept his finger pressed on the shiny button, but no one responded inside the apartment.

He leaned down with some difficulty and shouted through the mail slot, "Flash! Flash! Open up, damn it!"

With a sigh he leaned against the door and lit a cigarette, even though he knew that the neighbor lady would complain if she happened to come past.

It was almost a week since he and Flash had met at Östercentrum; he hadn't seen him since. That wasn't like him. They should have at least run into each other at the bus station or at the Domus mall, if nowhere else.

He took one last drag on his cigarette and rang the neighbor's bell.

"Who is it?" squeaked a feeble voice.

"I'm pals with Flash . . . Henry Dahlström next door. I want to ask you a question."

The door opened a crack and an old woman peered at him from behind a thick safety chain.

"What's it about?"

"Have you seen Henry lately?"

"Has something happened?" An inquisitive glint appeared in her eyes.

"No, no, I don't think so. I'm just wondering where he is."

"I haven't heard a sound since all that racket last weekend. There was a terrible uproar. I suppose it was a drunken party, as usual," she snapped, giving him an accusatory look.

"Do you know if anyone else has a key to his apartment?"

"The building superintendents have keys to all the apartments. One of them lives in the building across the way. You can go over there and ask him. His name is Andersson."

When the building superintendent let him into the apartment, they found a chaos of pulled-out drawers, cupboards that had been emptied of their contents, and overturned furniture. Papers, books, clothes, and other junk had been scattered everywhere. In the kitchen the floor was littered with leftover food, cigarette butts, liquor bottles, and other garbage. The room smelled of old beer, cigarette smoke, and fried fish. Someone had also tossed the sofa cushions and bed linens around.

Both men stood in the middle of the living room, their mouths agape. Words came haltingly from the lips of Andersson.

"What the hell happened here?"

He opened the patio door and looked out.

"Nobody out there, either. There's only one other place to look."

They went downstairs to the basement. Along one side of the deserted corridor was a row of doors labeled with various signs: "Laundry Room," "Baby Buggies," "Bicycles." In the middle were the usual basement storerooms with chicken-wire doors. At the far end was an unmarked door.

From the darkroom issued a rotten odor that made their stomachs turn over. The stench just about knocked them to the floor. Andersson switched on the light, and the sight was appalling. On the floor lay Henry Dahlström, drenched in his own blood. He was lying on his stomach, face to the floor. The back of his head was smashed in, with an open wound as big as a fist. Blood had spattered the walls and even the ceiling. His outstretched arms were covered with small, brown blisters. His jeans had dark patches on the seat where he had shit.

Andersson backed out to the corridor.

"Have to call the police," he whimpered. "Do you have a cell phone? I left mine upstairs."

The other man replied only by shaking his head.

"Wait here. Don't let anyone in." The super turned on his heel and ran up the stairs.

When he came back, Flash's buddy was gone.

The gray concrete building made a dreary impression in the November darkness. Anders Knutas and his closest colleague, Detective

Inspector Karin Jacobsson, climbed out of their car on Jungmansgatan in the Gråbo district.

An icy wind from the north made them hurry their steps toward Henry Dahlström's front door. A crowd of people had gathered outside the building. Some were talking to the police. The process of knocking on doors had begun, and the building superintendent had been taken in for questioning.

The apartment building seemed shabby. The outside light was broken, and in the stairwell the paint was peeling off the walls.

They greeted a male colleague, who showed them to the darkroom. When he opened the door to the basement, an unbearable stench enveloped them. The stale, nauseating, cadaverous odor told them that the body had already started to decompose. Jacobsson could feel how perilously close she was to vomiting. She had thrown up plenty of times at murder scenes, but she would prefer not to do so now. She pulled out a handkerchief and pressed it over her mouth.

Crime scene tech Erik Sohlman appeared in the doorway to the darkroom.

"Hi. The victim's name is Henry Dahlström. You probably know him—Flash, the old alcoholic who was a photographer? This was his darkroom. He was apparently still using it."

He tilted his head back in the direction of the basement room.

"His head has been bashed in, and it wasn't just a few blows, either. There's blood everywhere. I just wanted to warn you that it's not a pretty sight."

They paused in the doorway and looked down at the body.

"When did he die?" asked Knutas.

"He's probably been lying here close to a week, I would think. The body has started to rot, not too badly yet because it's reasonably cold down here. If he'd been here another day, the whole stairwell would have stunk."

Sohlman pushed a lock of hair back from his forehead and sighed.

"I've got to keep working. It will be a while before you can come in."

"How long?"

"A matter of hours. Actually I'd be happy if you could wait until tomorrow. We have a lot to do here. It's the same thing with his apartment."

"Okay."

Knutas studied the cramped room. Every inch of space had been put to use. Plastic trays were crowded next to jugs containing chemicals; there were scissors, clothespins, stacks of photographs, boxes and crates. In one corner was the enlarger.

A tray had been knocked over and the chemicals mixed with the blood.

When they exited through the front door, Knutas inhaled the fresh evening air deep into his lungs. It was eight fifteen. The rain pouring down from the dark sky was turning into wet snow.

MONDAY, NOVEMBER 19

The next morning the investigative team gathered at police headquarters on Norra Hansegatan. An expensive remodeling had just been completed, and the criminal division had been assigned new offices. The meeting room was bright with a high ceiling, and it was twice as large as the old one.

Most of the decor was of simple Scandinavian design in gray and white, with birch furniture. In the middle of the room stood a long, wide table with room for ten on each side. At one end was a big whiteboard and a projector screen. Everything smelled new. The light-colored paint on the walls was barely dry.

Both sides of the room were lined with windows. One row of windows looked out on the street, the parking lot at Obs supermarket, and the eastern side of the ring wall. Beyond the wall the sea was visible. The other windows faced the corridor so that it was possible to see who was walking past. The thin cotton curtains could be closed for more privacy—the old yellow curtains had been replaced with white ones in a discreet pattern.

For once Knutas was several minutes late for the morning meeting. An amicable murmuring was going on as he stepped into the room with a coffee mug in one hand and a folder of papers in the other. It was past eight o'clock, and everyone was present. He removed his jacket, hung it over the back of his chair, and took his usual place at one end of the table. Taking a gulp of the bitter coffee from the office coffee machine, he studied his colleagues as they chatted with each other.

On his right sat Karin Jacobsson: thirty-seven years old, petite, with dark hair and brown eyes. On the job she was persistent and fearless, and she could be as irascible as a terrier. She was open and outgoing, but he knew very little about her personal life, even though they had been working together for fifteen years. She lived alone and had no children. Knutas didn't know whether she had a boyfriend or not.

He had spent all autumn without her working beside him, and he had missed her terribly. In connection with the homicides of the past summer, Karin Jacobsson had become the subject of an internal investigation regarding possible misconduct. The investigation was dropped, but the whole thing had taken its toll on her. She had been placed on leave while the investigation was ongoing, and then she had taken a vacation right afterward. He had no idea what she had done while she was away.

Right now she was immersed in a quiet conversation with Detective Inspector Thomas Wittberg. He looked more like a surfer than a police officer, with his thick blond hair and trim body. He was a twenty-seven-year-old playboy who constantly had new girlfriends, but his attention to his job was irreproachable. His talent for making contact with people had been of great use—as the head of an interrogation he was unbeatable.

Lars Norrby, on the other side of the table, was the direct opposite of Wittberg: tall, dark, and meticulous to the point of being long-winded. He could drive Knutas crazy with his fussing over details. At work they knew each other's habits inside out. They had joined the police force at the same time, and for a period they had patrolled together. Now they were both approaching fifty and were as familiar with the criminals on Gotland as they were with each other.

Detective Inspector Norrby was the police spokesman, as well as the assistant head of the criminal investigation unit—a situation that did not always please Knutas.

The technician of the group, Erik Sohlman, was intense, temperamental, and as zealous as a bloodhound; at the same time, he was incredibly methodical.

Birger Smittenberg, the chief prosecutor, was also sitting at the table. He was originally from Stockholm, but he had married a woman from Gotland. Knutas valued his knowledge and his strong sense of involvement.

Knutas began the meeting.

"The victim is Henry 'Flash' Dahlström, born in 1943. He was found dead just after six P.M. yesterday, in a basement room that he used as a darkroom. If you haven't all heard it already, he's the alcoholic who was once a photographer. He used to hang out down on Öster, and the most distinctive thing about him was the camera that he always wore around his neck."

No one at the table said a word. Everyone was listening intently.

"Dahlström was found with extensive contusions on the back of his head. There's no doubt that he was murdered. His body will be transported to the forensic medicine lab in Solna sometime today."

"Did you find the murder weapon?" asked Norrby.

"Not yet. We've searched both the darkroom and his apartment. Those are the only areas that we've cordoned off. Anything else would be pointless since the body has been lying there for a week, and Lord knows how many people have gone up and down the stairs during that time. Dahlström lived on the ground floor in a corner apartment. Right outside is the public passageway to Terra Nova. The whole area has been searched. The dark made our work more difficult, but the search was resumed as soon as it was daylight. Which was just a short time ago."

He looked at his watch.

"Who called it in?" asked the prosecutor.

"The body was discovered by one of the building superintendents. Apparently there are four of them. This one lives in the building across the way. His name is Ove Andersson. He said that a man claiming to be a good friend of the victim rang his doorbell around six P.M. yesterday. The man said that he hadn't seen Dahlström for several days and he wondered where he might be. They found him in the basement, but when the superintendent went up to his place to call the police, the friend took the opportunity to disappear."

"It seems fishy that he ran off. Maybe he was the murderer," Wittberg suggested.

"But if so, why would he contact the super?" objected Norrby.

"Maybe he wanted to get back inside the apartment to get something that he left behind, but he didn't dare break in again," Jacobsson piped in.

"Well, we can't rule that out, even though it doesn't sound very plausible," countered Norrby. "But why would he wait a whole week? There was always a risk that the body would be discovered."

Knutas frowned. "One alternative is that he disappeared because he was afraid of being a suspect. Maybe he was at the party, because it's obvious that a party took place in that apartment. No matter what, we need to get hold of him as soon as possible."

"Have we got a description?" asked Wittberg.

Knutas looked down at his papers. "Middle-aged, about fifty, according to the super. Tall and heavy. He has a mustache, and dark hair pulled back in a ponytail. Dark shirt, dark pants. He didn't notice the man's shoes. I think it sounds like Bengt Johnsson. He's probably the only one of the local winos who fits the description."

"It's got to be Bengan. Those two were always hanging out together," said Wittberg.

Knutas turned to the crime tech. "Erik, you can give us the technical details now."

Sohlman nodded. "We've gone over the apartment and darkroom, but we're far from done. If we start with the victim and his wounds, we need to look at the photos. I should warn you that they're rather nasty."

Sohlman switched off the lights and, using a computer, clicked the digital pictures onto the screen at the front of the room.

"Henry Dahlström was lying prone on the floor with extensive contusions to the back of his head. The perpetrator used a blunt instrument of some kind. My guess is a hammer, but the ME will eventually be able to tell us more. Dahlström was struck repeatedly on the head. The large amount of blood spatter resulted because the perpetrator first knocked a hole in the victim's skull and then continued to strike the bloody surface. Each time he delivered another blow, blood sprayed all over."

Sohlman used a pointer to show spatter that was visible on the floor, the walls, and the ceiling.

"The killer probably knocked Dahlström to the ground and then stood over him and kept striking as he lay there. As far as determining the time of death, I would estimate that the murder took place five or six days ago."

The victim's face was a blotchy yellowish gray shifting to green. His eyes had a dark, brownish-red color, and his lips were black and parched.

"The process of decomposition had begun," Sohlman went on impassively. "You can see the little brown blisters on the body and the corpse fluid that has started to seep out. The same substance is coming out of his mouth and nostrils."

His colleagues around the table grimaced. Jacobsson wondered how Sohlman could always manage to talk about bloody victims, rigor mortis, and decomposing bodies as if he were discussing the weather or his annual income tax returns.

"Everything in the place had been tossed, and the cupboards and boxes containing photos had been searched. The murderer was apparently looking for something. The victim also has defensive wounds on his arms. Here we can see bruises and scratches. So he attempted to resist. The bruise on his collarbone may have been made by a blow that missed its mark. We've taken blood samples, of course. We also found a cigarette butt in the basement hallway, and hairs that don't seem to have come from the victim. Everything has been sent to SCL but, as you know, it will take a while before we get any answers."

He took a sip of coffee and sighed. The response from SCL, the Swedish Crime Laboratory in Linköping, usually took at least a week, more often three.

Sohlman went on. "As far as evidence goes, we've found footprints in the flower bed outside the basement window. Unfortunately, the rain made them impossible to identify. On the other hand, we did get some footprints in the hallway outside the darkroom, and in the best-case scenario they should tell us something. The same footprints were in the apartment—which, by the way, was filled with bottles, ashtrays, beer cans, and a lot of other junk. We've secured quite a few fingerprints, as well as the footprints of four or five different individuals. We also searched the apartment."

The photos of the mess in Dahlström's place sent a clear message: The apartment had been completely turned upside down.

"Dahlström must have had something valuable at home, but I wonder what it might be," said Knutas. "An alcoholic living on welfare doesn't usually have assets of any great value. Did you find his camera?"

"No."

Sohlman cast another glance at his watch. He seemed eager to get away.

"You said that you found a cigarette butt in the basement. Could the murderer have waited outside the darkroom for Dahlström to come out?" asked Jacobsson.

"Quite possibly."

Sohlman then excused himself and left the room.

"In that case, the perp knew that Dahlström was inside the darkroom," Jacobsson went on. "He may have stood in the entryway for hours. What do the neighbors say?"

Knutas leafed through the investigative report.

"We kept knocking on doors until late last night. We haven't got all the reports in yet, but the neighbors in that stairwell confirm, as I mentioned, that there was a party at the apartment last Sunday. A bunch of people came staggering through the front door around nine P.M. A neighbor who encountered them in the entryway guessed that they had been to the racetrack because he heard some remarks about various horses."

"Oh, that's right, Sunday was the last race day of the season," Jacobsson reminded herself.

Knutas looked up from his papers. "Is that right? Well, the track isn't very far away, so they could have easily walked or bicycled home afterward. At any rate, there was a big racket in the apartment, according to the neighbors. A lot of noise and partying, with both male and female voices.

"The woman next door reported that the man who is probably Bengt Johnsson rang her doorbell first, to ask her whether she had seen Dahlström. She referred him to the building superintendent."

"Does her description of him match what the super told us?" asked Norrby.

"Yes, for the most part. An overweight man, younger than Dahlström, about fifty, she thought. Mustache and dark hair pulled back in a ponytail—a biker-type hairstyle, as she expressed it. Wearing shabby clothes, she also said."

Knutas gave a little smile.

"He had on dirty, loose-fitting jeans, with his stomach hanging out. A blue flannel shirt, and he was smoking. She recognized the man because she had seen him with Dahlström several times."

"Everybody knows who Henry Dahlström is, but what do we actually know about him?" asked Wittberg.

"He's been an alcoholoic for years," replied Jacobsson. "He usually hung out at Östercentrum or at the bus station with his buddies. Or at Östergravar in the summer, of course. Divorced, unemployed. He had been living on a disability pension for over fifteen years even though he didn't seem completely destitute. He paid his rent and bills on time, and he kept mostly to himself, according to the neighbors, aside from the occasional party. His friends say that he was utterly harmless, never got into fights or committed any sort of crime. He apparently kept up his interest in photography. This summer I ran into him one day as I was biking to work. He was in the process of photographing a flower near Gutavallen."

"What else do we know about his background?" Wittberg cast a glance at Jacobsson's papers lying on the table.

"He was born in 1943 in Visby Hospital," Jacobsson continued. "Grew up in Visby. In 1965 he married a woman from Visby, Ann-Sofie Nilsson. They had a child in 1967, a girl named Pia. Divorced in 1986."

"Okay, we'll find out more about him today," said Knutas. "And we've got to locate Bengt Johnsson."

He looked out the window.

"Since it's raining, the winos are probably sitting outside the Domus department store, in the mall. That would be the best place to start. Wittberg?"

"Karin and I can go."

Knutas nodded.

"I've started to collate the interviews with his neighbors, and I'd like to keep working on that," said Norrby. "And there are a couple of people I'd like to talk to again."

"That sounds fine," said Knutas, and then he turned to the prose-cutor. "Birger, do you have anything to add?"

"No. Just keep me informed and I'll be happy."

"Okay. We'll stop here. But we'll meet again this afternoon. Shall we say three o'clock?"

After the meeting Knutas retreated to his office. His new office was twice as big as the old one. Embarrassingly big, he might say. The walls were painted a light color that reminded him of the sand at Tofta beach on a sunny day in July.

The view was the same as from their conference room next door: the parking lot at Östercentrum and in the distance, the ring wall and the sea.

On the windowsill stood a healthy-looking white geranium that had only recently stopped blooming in anticipation of winter. Jacobsson had given it to him for his birthday several years earlier. He had brought the potted plant with him from his old office, along with his beloved old desk chair made of oak with a soft leather seat. It spun nicely, and he often made use of that feature.

He filled his pipe, taking great care. His thoughts were on Henry Dahlström's darkroom and what he had seen there. When he thought about the man's crushed skull, he shuddered.

Everything pointed to a drunken brawl that got out of hand and came to an unusually brutal end. Dahlström had presumably taken a buddy down to the basement to show him some photographs, and they started arguing about something. Most cases of assault and battery started out that way, and every year some drunk or addict on Gotland was murdered.

In his mind he thought back, trying to summon up a picture of Henry Dahlström.

When Knutas had joined the police force twenty-five years earlier, Dahlström was a respected photographer. He worked for the newspaper *Gotlands Tidningar* and was one of the most prominent photographers on the island. At the time Knutas was a cop on the beat, patrolling the streets. Whenever big news events occurred, Dahlström was always the first on the scene with his camera. If Knutas met him at private functions, they would usually have a chat. Dahlström was a pleasant man with a good sense of humor, although he had a tendency to drink too much. Knutas would sometimes meet him heading home from a pub, drunk as a skunk. Occasionally he would give him a ride because the man was too drunk to get home on his own. Back then Dahlström was married. Later on he quit his job with the newspaper and started his own company. At the same time, his alcohol consumption seemed to increase.

Dahlström was once found passed out inside the thirteenth-century ruin of Saint Karin's church in the middle of Stora Torget, the central marketplace in Visby. He was lying on a narrow stairway, asleep, when he was discovered by a startled guide and his group of American tourists.

Another time he walked boldly into the Lindgård restaurant on Strandgatan and ordered a real feast consisting of five courses with wine, strongbeer, aquavit, and cognac. Afterward he asked for a cigar imported directly from Havana, which he puffed on as he enjoyed yet another liqueur. When the bill was presented, he openly admitted that, unfortunately, he was unable to pay due to a shortage of funds. The police were called. They took the sated and tipsy man down to the police station, but he was released a few hours later. Dahlström probably thought all the trouble was worth it.

Knutas hadn't seen Dahlström's wife in years. She had been notified about the death of her ex-husband. Knutas hadn't yet spoken to her, but she was scheduled to be interviewed later in the day.

He sucked on his unlit pipe and leafed through Dahlström's file. A few minor misdemeanors, but nothing serious. His friend Bengt Johnsson, on the other hand, had been convicted twenty or more times, mostly on burglary and minor assault charges.

It was strange that they hadn't heard from him.

Emma Winarve sat down on the worn sofa in the teachers' lounge. She was holding her mug of coffee in both hands to warm them. It was drafty in the old wooden building housing the Kyrk School in

Roma. Her mug was inscribed with the words: "World's Best Mom." How ridiculous. A mother who had cheated on her husband and who, for the past six months, had also neglected her children because her mind was always on something else. She was fast approaching forty, and also fast losing all control.

The clock on the wall told her that it was nine thirty in the morning. Her colleagues were already crowding around the table, chatting congenially. The smell of coffee had permanently seeped into the curtains, books, papers, file folders, and the dirty-yellow wallpaper. Emma didn't feel like taking part in the conversation. Instead, she looked out the window. The leaves on the oak trees hadn't yet fallen. They were in constant motion, sensitive to the slightest gust of wind. In the yard next to the school, shaggy gray sheep stood huddled together, grazing. Their jaws were grinding as they ceaselessly chewed their cud. Roma's stone church with eight hundred years of history behind it stood there as steadfast as always.

Everything was going on as usual, no matter what storms might be raging inside of someone. It was incomprehensible that she could sit here, seemingly unperturbed, sipping endless cups of coffee, and no one even noticed a thing. Such as the fact that her mind was in the grip of a psychological battle. Or that her whole life was in the process of going to hell. But her colleagues merely sat around her, carrying on subdued conversations. As if nothing were happening.

In her mind's eye, video clips were playing in rapid succession: her daughter Sara's birthday when all Emma could do was cry; she and Johan rolling around in a hotel bed; her mother-in-law's searching eyes; Filip's cello concert, which had totally slipped her mind; her husband Olle's face when she once again rejected him.

She had gotten herself into an impossible situation.

Six months earlier she had met a man who had ended up changing everything. They got to know each other in connection with last summer's police hunt, when Emma's best friend became one of the killer's victims, and she herself came very close to meeting the same fate.

Johan had stepped into her path, and she couldn't just walk by him. He was so unlike everyone else she had ever known; so alive and intense about everything he did. She had never laughed so much with anyone else or felt so calm, almost spiritual. He made her discover sides of herself that she didn't even know existed.

She quickly fell madly in love with him, and before she knew it, he had totally invaded her life. When they made love she was filled with a sensuality that she had never experienced before. He made her relax. For the first time she didn't give a thought to how she looked or how he might judge her expertise in bed.

To be one hundred percent in the moment was something that she had known only from giving birth to her children.

Yet eventually she chose to break it off with him. For the children's sake, she decided to stay with Olle. When the drama of the serial murders was over and she woke up in the hospital with her family around her, she realized that she lacked the will to go through with a divorce, even though she felt that Johan was the great love of her life. Security counted more, at least at the time. With much anguish she put an end to their affair.

The whole family went to Greece on vacation because she needed to get away and have some distance from everything. But it hadn't turned out to be that simple.

When they were back home, Johan had written to her. At first she considered throwing out the letter, unread. But her curiosity got the better of her. Afterward she regretted it.

It would have been best for all parties concerned if she hadn't read even one line of that letter.

Karin Jacobsson and Thomas Wittberg walked down to Östercentrum as soon as the investigative meeting was over. The pedestrian street between the shops was almost deserted. The wind and rain were having their effect. They hurried into the mall at Obs supermarket and shook off the worst of the rain as they stood inside the glass doors.

The shopping center was quite modest: H&M, Guldfynd, a couple of beauty parlors, a health food store, a bulletin board. Obs with its rows of cashiers, then the bakery and pastry shop, the customer service counter, the Tips & Tobak betting parlor and tobacco shop.

Restrooms in the back, a recycling station for bottles, and the exit leading to the parking lot. Along with weary retirees and the parents of small children, needing to rest their feet, drunks occupied the benches in the mall whenever the weather was bad.

Most of them kept a hip flask in a bag or pocket, but as long as they didn't do any drinking inside, the security guards left them in peace.

Jacobsson recognized two local winos sitting on the bench nearest the exit. They were filthy and unshaven, dressed in worn-out clothes. The younger man was leaning his head against the wall behind him and staring indifferently at the people walking past. He wore a black leather jacket and tattered running shoes. The older man had on a blue down jacket and knit cap. He was leaning forward with his head in his hands. Greasy locks of hair had crept out from under his cap.

Jacobsson introduced herself and Wittberg, even though she was fully aware that the two men knew who they were.

"We haven't done anything. We're just sitting here."

The man in the cap glanced up, his eyes crossed. *And it's not even eleven o'clock in the morning,* thought Jacobsson.

"Take it easy," Wittberg told them. "We just want to ask you a few questions."

He pulled a photo out of his pocket.

"Do you recognize this man?"

The younger drunk kept on staring straight ahead. He refused to give either of the police officers even a glance. The other man stared at the picture.

"Hell yes. That's Flash, of course."

"How well do you know him?"

"He's one of the gang, you know. Usually hangs out around here, or at the bus station. He's been doing that for twenty years. Of course I know Flash, everybody does. Hey, Jonas, you know who Flash is, don't you?"

He poked his pal in the side and handed him the photo.

"What a fucking stupid question. Everybody knows him."

The man named Jonas had pupils the size of peppercorns. Jacobsson wondered what he was high on.

"When did you last see him?" asked Wittberg.

"What did he do?"

"Nothing. We just want to know when you last saw him."

"Hmm, when the hell was it? What day is today? Monday?"

Jacobsson nodded. The man stroked his chin with fingers that had been stained dirty yellow from nicotine.

"I haven't seen him in several days, but sometimes he just takes off, you know."

Jacobsson turned to the other man.

"What about you?"

He was still staring straight ahead. *His face is actually quite handsome, underneath all the dirt and stubble,* she thought. His expression was defiant, showing a strong unwillingness to cooperate. She restrained a desire to stand right in front of him and wave her arms to force him to react.

"Can't remember."

Wittberg was starting to get annoyed.

"What did you say?"

"Why do you want to know? What did he do?" asked the older man in the cap.

"He's dead. Someone killed him."

"What the hell? Is that true?"

Now both men looked up.

"Yes, I'm afraid so. He was found dead last night."

"Are you fucking kidding me?"

"What we need to do now is try to find the person who did it."

"Sure, that's obvious. Come to think of it, I think the last time I saw him was at the bus station about a week ago."

"Was he alone?"

"He was there with his buddies—Kjelle and Bengan, I think."

"How did he seem?"

"What do you mean by 'seem'?"

"How did he act? Did he seem sick, or was he nervous in any way?"

"No, he was the same as usual. He never really says much. He was a little drunk, of course."

"Do you remember what day that was?"

"It was probably Saturday because there were a lot of people downtown. I think it was Saturday."

"A week ago?"

"That's right. But I haven't seen him since then."

Jacobsson turned to the other man.

"What about you? Have you seen him since then?"

"Nope."

Jacobsson suppressed the annoyed feeling that had begun to prickle at her throat.

"Okay. Do either of you know whether he'd spent time with any strangers lately?"

"No idea."

"Is there anyone who might want to harm him?"

"Not Flash, no. He never got into fights with anybody. He kept a low profile, if you know what I mean."

"Sure, I understand," said Jacobsson. "So do you happen to know where his pal Bengan might be? Bengt Johnsson?"

"Is he the one who did it?"

Behind the alcoholic fog, the older man looked genuinely surprised.

"No, no. We just want to talk to him."

"Haven't seen him in a while, have you?"

"Nope," said Jonas.

He was chewing gum so hard that his jaws made a cracking sound.

"The last time I saw him he was with that new guy from the mainland," the older man said. "The guy named Örjan."

"What's his last name?"

"I don't know because he hasn't lived here on Gotland for very long. He was in the slammer on the mainland."

"Do you know where we can find Bengt Johnsson?"

"He lives on Stenkumlaväg with his mother. Maybe that's where he is."

"Do you know the address?"

"Nope."

"All right then. Thanks for your help. If you see or hear anything that has to do with Flash, you should contact the police immediately."

"Sure," said the man with the cap, and then he, too, leaned back against the wall.

Johan Berg opened the morning paper as he sat at the kitchen table in his apartment on Heleneborgsgatan in Stockholm. The apartment was on the ground floor facing the courtyard, but that didn't bother him. The Södermalm district was the very heart of the city, and in his eyes there was no better place to live. One side of the building faced the waters of Riddarfjärden and the old prison island of Långholm with its bathing rocks and wooded walking paths. On the other side the shops, pubs, cafés, and subway were all within easy reach. The red subway line went directly to Karlaplan, and from there it was only a five-minute walk to the editorial headquarters of Swedish TV.

He subscribed to several daily newspapers: *Dagens Nyheter, Svenska Dagbladet,* and *Dagens Industri.* Currently *Gotlands Tidningar* was also in the stack that he plowed through each morning. After the events of the summer, his interest in Gotland had been given a boost. For more reasons than one.

He scanned the headlines: "Crisis in Housing for Elderly," "Police on Gotland Earn Less Than Officers on the Mainland," "Farmer Risks Losing EU Subsidies."

Then he noticed a news item: "Man Found Dead in Gråbo. Police Suspect Foul Play."

As he cleared away the breakfast dishes he thought about the article. Of course it sounded like an ordinary drunken fight, but his curiosity was aroused. He took a quick look at himself in the mirror and put a little gel on his dark curly hair. He was actually in need of a shave, but there was no time for that. His dark stubble would just have to grow out a bit. He was thirty-seven but looked younger. Tall and well built, with regular features and brown eyes. Women were always falling for him—and he'd taken advantage of that fact many times in the past. But not anymore. Ever since six months ago, only one woman existed for him: Emma Winarve of Roma on the island of Gotland. They had met when he was covering the hunt for a serial killer last summer.

She had turned his life upside down. He had never met a woman who moved him so deeply; she challenged him and made him think along whole new lines. He liked himself better when he was with her. When his friends asked him what was so special about Emma, he had a hard time explaining. Everything was just so obvious. And he knew that his feelings were reciprocated.

Things had gone so far that he thought she was actually considering leaving her husband, that it was just a matter of time. He had started fantasizing about moving to Gotland and working for one of the newspapers or for the local radio station. They would move in together, and he would be a stepfather for her two children.

Instead, just the opposite had happened. After the murderer was caught and the case was closed, she called it off. He was completely taken by surprise. His life fell apart. He was forced to take sick leave for several weeks, and when he recovered enough that he could take a vacation, she never left his thoughts for a moment.

When he came home he wrote her a letter. Quite unexpectedly, she answered, and then they started seeing each other again. They mostly met whenever Johan went to Gotland on a story. Occasionally she managed to get away to meet him in Stockholm. But he could tell that she wasn't comfortable with all the lying and that she was struggling with terrible feelings of guilt. Finally she asked for a two-month break. October and November. She explained that she needed some distance and time to think.

Suddenly they had no communication at all. No text messages, no e-mails, no phone calls.

But she had relented once. He was on Gotland on assignment and called her up. She happened to be feeling unhappy just then, and weak, so they met. A quick meeting that merely confirmed how strong their feelings were for each other, at least that's what he thought.

After that, nothing. He had made a couple of awkward attempts, but in vain. She was intractable.

At the same time, he understood. It was difficult for her, since she was married and had young children.

But weeks of restless nights, chain-smoking, and a constant, overwhelming longing for her had taken their toll on him, to put it mildly.

On his way to the subway station, he called Anders Knutas in Visby.

The police superintendent answered at once.

"Knutas."

"Hi. Johan Berg from Regional News here. How are things?"

"Fine, thanks. And you? It's been a while."

"Things are good. I saw an article in the paper about a possible homicide in Gråbo. Is it true?"

"We don't know much at this point."

"What happened?"

A brief pause. Johan could picture Knutas leaning back in his desk chair, filling his pipe. They'd had a great deal to do with each other when Johan reported on the murders from Gotland and then took an active role in solving the case.

"Last night a man was found dead in a basement on Jungmansgatan, in Gråbo."

"Of course."

"His injuries were such that we suspect he was murdered."

"How old was he?"

"Born in 1943."

"Known by the police?"

"Yes, but not because he had committed any crimes to speak of, although he was quite an inveterate alcoholic. He used to hang out downtown, drinking. A so-called local wino."

"Does it have to do with a drunken brawl?"

"It seems so."

"How was he killed?"

"I can't discuss that."

"When was the murder committed?"

"He'd been dead for several days. Maybe as long as a week."

"How could he be dead for so long if he was found in a basement?"

"He was inside a locked room."

"A basement storage room?"

"You could say that."

"Who found him?"

"The building superintendent."

"Had anyone reported him missing?"

"No, but a friend of his contacted the superintendent."

Knutas was starting to sound impatient.

"I see. Who was it?"

"Listen, I can't tell you that. I have to go now. You'll have to make do with what I've said, for the time being."

"Okay. When do you think you might have more to tell me?"

"I have no idea. Bye."

Johan switched off his cell phone, thinking that the murder didn't sound like something that Regional News would report on. Probably just an ordinary drunken fight that got out of hand. The story would be relegated to a few lines.

The Stockholm subway system on a Monday morning in November must be one of the most depressing places in the world, thought Johan as he leaned against the window with the black wall of the tunnel whizzing past an arm's length away.

The car was filled with sallow-faced people, weighed down by worries and the daily grind. No one was talking; the only sounds were the usual clanking and rattling of the subway. A few coughs and some sleepy rustling of giveaway newspapers. People stared at the ceiling, at the ad placards, at the floor, out the window, or at some indefinite point in midair. Everywhere but at each other.

The smell of wet clothing was mixed with perfume, sweat, and the dust burning on the heaters. Jackets were pressed next to coats, scarves next to caps, bodies against bodies, shoes against shoes, faces close to other faces, but without any sort of contact.

How can so many people be gathered in one place without making a sound? thought Johan. *There's something sick about the whole thing.*

It was mornings like this that could really make him long to get away.

When he emerged from the subway at Karlaplan he felt liberated. At least here he could breathe. The people around him were marching like tin soldiers toward buses, offices, schools, shops, the welfare center, a lawyer's office, or wherever they happened to be going.

He set off across the park near the church, Gustav Adolfskyrkan. The kids in the day-care center were outside, playing on the swing set in the biting wind. Their cheeks were as bright as ripe apples.

The huge edifice of TV headquarters loomed in the November fog. He waved hello to the statue of TV star Lennart Hyland before he stepped through the front door.

Up in the newsroom everyone was bustling around. The national morning news program was under way. At the elevators guests were hurrying past, along with anchormen, meteorologists, makeup artists, reporters, and editors—exiting the studios, or going to the bathrooms, or heading for the breakfast table. The row of picture windows offered a view of Gärdet, the big park in Östermalm, swathed in gray fog and swarming with lively dogs from the doggy day care on Grev Magnigatan. Brown, black, and spotted canines galloped around, playing on the big field and unaffected by the fact that it was a dreary Monday in November.

Almost everyone was present for the morning meeting of Regional News: several cameramen, an early-morning editor, reporters, producers, and program planners. It was crowded in the lounge area of the newsroom. After they had discussed the latest broadcast, criticizing some parts and praising others, the editor Max Grenfors presented the day's roster of news stories. The assignments might very well change during the course of the meeting. Some reporter might have his own idea, or the objections to a story proposal might be so strong that it ended up in the wastebasket, or the discussion might take a new direction and lead to a reworking of all their plans. *That's exactly the way things needed to function in a newsroom,* thought Johan, who enjoyed the morning gatherings.

He briefly recounted to the others what he knew about the murder on Gotland. Everyone agreed that it sounded like a drunken fight. Johan was assigned to keep an eye on the situation since he was going to Gotland the next day anyway, to do a report on the controversy regarding a campground that was threatened with closure.

The Regional News editorial offices operated under high-pressure deadlines. Each day they produced a twenty-minute program, basically from scratch. A story that aired for two minutes usually took several hours to film and another two hours to edit. Johan was always nagging his bosses about giving the reporters more time.

He was not in favor of the changes that had been implemented since he had started out as a TV reporter ten years earlier. Nowadays the reporters hardly had time to look over their material before they had to submit it to the editor. This had a disastrous effect on quality. Good images that the cameraman had taken a lot of trouble to capture risked being lost because no one discovered them in all the rush. The cameramen were often disappointed when they saw the final story. As soon as management started taking shortcuts in the use of visual images, which were the real strength of TV, then things were really going downhill. Johan refused to write up his reports or do any editing until he had gone through all the material himself.

Of course there were exceptions. When time was tight and the story was thrown into editing twenty minutes before the broadcast, they still succeeded in putting it together.

Unpredictability was the real draw in terms of working in a newsroom. In the morning he never knew how the day was going to go. Johan worked mostly as a crime reporter, and the contacts that he had established over the years were invaluable for the newsroom. He also had primary responsibility for covering Gotland, which had been placed under the domain of Regional News a little over a year ago. Swedish TV's large deficit meant that they had closed the local office on Gotland and moved the crew from Norrköping back to Stockholm. Johan was happy to take on Gotland, a place that had delighted him since he was a child. And now it was no longer just the island that attracted him.

Spot tugged at his leash. *To think he's never learned to heel,* thought Fanny angrily, but she didn't feel like yelling at him. The streets were deserted in the residential neighborhood where she was walking. A dark mist had settled over Visby, and the asphalt was shiny from the gentle rain. An inviting glow came from the curtain-framed windows of all the houses. How orderly everything was. Flowers on the windowsills, gleaming cars in the driveways, and charming mailboxes. Here and there a well-tended compost pile.

She had a good view inside the homes at this time of the evening, after dark. In one, copper utensils hung on the wall in the kitchen; another had a brightly painted, rustic grandfather clock. In a living room a little girl was jumping up and down on the sofa, talking to someone that Fanny couldn't see. Over there was a man holding a dustpan in one hand. *A few crumbs must have landed on the rug,* she thought and pressed her lips together. A man and woman were standing in another kitchen window; they seemed to be cooking together.

Suddenly the door to a big house opened. An elderly couple came out and went over to a waiting taxi as they chatted merrily. They were well dressed, and Fanny smelled the strong scent of the woman's perfume as they passed quite close to her. They didn't notice that she had stopped to watch them.

She was freezing in her thin jacket. Back home her mother was waiting in the silent and dark apartment. She worked the night shift at Flextronics. Fanny had met her father only a few times in her life, the last time when she was five years old. His band had been playing a gig in Visby, and he dropped by for a brief visit. The only thing she remembered about him was his big, dry hand holding hers, and his brown eyes. Her father was as black as night. He was a Rastafarian and came from Jamaica. In the photos she had seen, he had long tangled locks of hair. They call them dreadlocks, her mother had told her.

He lived in Stockholm, where he played drums in a band, and he had a wife and three kids in Farsta. That was all she knew.

She never heard from him, not even on her birthday. Sometimes she tried to imagine what it would be like if he and her mother had lived together. Maybe her mother wouldn't drink as much. Maybe she would be happier. Maybe Fanny wouldn't have to take care of everything: the cooking, cleaning, and laundry, taking Spot for a walk and doing the grocery shopping. Maybe she wouldn't have a guilty conscience about going out to the stables if her father was around. She wondered what he would say if he knew how things were for her. But he probably didn't care; she meant nothing to him.

She was simply the product of his love affair with her mother.

———

The first thing Jacobsson and Wittberg noticed was the group of sculptures. Almost two meters tall, made of concrete, and gathered in one place on the property. One depicted a rearing horse that was desperately whinnying at the clouds, another looked like a deer, a third was a moose with a disproportionately large head. Grotesque and phantomlike, they stood there in the pouring rain on the flat expanse of lawn.

They dashed from the car to the house, whose roof extended over the simple porch, offering some protection. A typical one-story building from the fifties with a basement and dirty gray stucco facade. The steps were rotting, and there seemed to be an imminent risk that they might put a foot right through them. The doorbell was almost inaudible. After a minute a tall, stout woman in her seventies opened the door. She was wearing a cardigan and a floral-patterned dress. Her hair was thick and white.

"We're from the police," Wittberg explained. "We want to ask you some questions. Are you Doris Johnsson, the mother of Bengt Johnsson?"

"That's right. Has he gotten mixed up in something again? Come in. You're getting soaked."

They sat down on the leather sofa in the living room. The room was cluttered with things. In addition to the sofa group, there were three armchairs, a rustic chiffonier, a TV, pedestals for flowers, and a bookshelf. The windowsills were crowded with potted plants, and every available space in the room held glass figurines in various designs. They all had one thing in common: they depicted animals. Dogs, cats, hedgehogs, squirrels, cows, horses, pigs, camels, and birds. In various sizes, colors, and poses, they were enthroned on tables and benches, in windows, and on shelves.

"You collect these things?" asked Jacobsson, rather foolishly.

The woman's lined face brightened. "Yes, I've been doing it for years. I have six hundred and twenty-seven pieces," she told them proudly. "So what was it you wanted?"

"Well, I'm sorry to say that we've brought some bad news," said Wittberg, leaning forward. "One of your son's friends has been found dead, and we suspect that someone killed him. His name is Henry Dahlström."

"Good gracious! Henry?" Her face turned pale. "He was murdered?"

"Unfortunately, that's probably what happened. We haven't caught the perpetrator, and that's why we're interested in talking to anyone who knew Henry. Do you know where Bengt is?"

"No, he didn't sleep here last night."

"Where was he?"

"I don't know."

"When did you last see him?" asked Jacobsson.

"Yesterday evening. He dropped by for only a minute. I was down in the basement, hanging up the laundry, so I didn't actually see him. He just called down the stairs to me. This morning he phoned to say that he was going to stay with a friend for a few days."

"I see. Who's the friend?"

"He didn't say."

"Did he give you a phone number?"

"No. He's a grown man, you know. I had the impression that he was staying with a woman."

"Why is that?"

"Because he was so secretive. Otherwise he usually tells me where he is."

"Did he call you on your home phone or on a cell?"

"The home phone."

"Do you have caller ID?"

"As a matter of fact, I do."

She got up and went out to the hall. After a minute she came back.

"No, it doesn't show anything. It must have been an unlisted number."

"Does he have a cell phone?"

Doris Johnsson stood in the doorway and gave the officers sitting on the sofa a defiant look.

"Before I answer any more questions, I want to know what happened. I knew Henry, too. You'll have to tell me what this is all about."

"Yes, of course," muttered Wittberg, who seemed to be quite affected by the domineering tone of the stout woman. Jacobsson noted that he used the formal means of address with her.

"Last night Henry was found by Bengt and the building superintendent. He was in his darkroom in the basement of the building where he lives. Someone had murdered him, but I can't go into the details. When the superintendent left to call the police, Bengt took off, and no one has heard from him since. It's urgent that we get in touch with him as soon as we can."

"He got scared, of course."

"That's very possible. But if we're going to catch the perpetrator, we need to talk to everyone who might have seen anything or who can tell us about Henry's actions during the days before the murder. Do you have any idea where Bengt might be, Mrs. Johnsson?"

"Hmm . . . He knows so many people. I suppose I could call around and ask."

"When did you last hear from Bengt, or rather when did you actually see him last?" Jacobsson interjected.

"Now let me see . . . Aside from yesterday evening . . . It must have been yesterday morning. He slept late, as usual. Didn't get up until eleven and then had his breakfast while I was eating lunch. Then he went out. He didn't say where he was going."

"How did he seem?"

"The same as always. He wasn't acting strange or anything like that."

"Do you know if anything unusual had happened lately?"

Doris Johnsson plucked at her clothing.

"No . . ." she said hesitantly.

Suddenly she threw out her hands.

"Well, yes. Henry won at the harness-racing track. He won the five-race jackpot, and he was the only winner, so it was a lot of money. Eighty thousand kronor, I think. Bengt told me about it the other day."

Jacobsson and Wittberg looked at her in astonishment.

"When did this happen?"

"It wasn't this past Sunday, so it must have been the previous Sunday. Yes, that's when it was, because they were at the track."

"And Henry won eighty thousand kronor? Do you know what he did with the money?"

"Bought booze, I assume. Part of it went straight to alcohol. As soon as they have a little cash, they start buying rounds for everybody."

"Who else belongs to his circle of friends?"

"There's a man named Kjell that he hangs out with a lot, along with a couple of girls. Monica and Gunsan. Though I suppose her real name is Gun."

"Last names?"

She shook her head.

"Where do they live?"

"I don't know that, either, but somewhere here in town. Also a man named Örjan, by the way. I think he just moved here recently. Bengt has been talking about him lately. I think he lives on Styrmansgatan."

They said good-bye to Doris Johnsson, who promised to call as soon as she heard anything from her son.

With the information about the track winnings, they now had a clear motive for the murder.

Knutas had brought along a packet of Danish open-faced sandwiches for lunch. His father-in-law had recently paid them a visit and delighted the whole family with the delicacies he had brought from Denmark. The three slices of dark rye bread each had a different kind of lunch meat: liver sausage topped with a piece of pickled squash; sliced meatballs with pickled beets; and his favorite, Danish sausage roll. And an ice-cold beer to go with this glorious repast.

He was interrupted by a knock on the door. Norrby stuck his head inside.

"Do you have a minute?"

"Of course."

Norrby folded his nearly six-foot-two frame into one of the visitor chairs in Knutas's office.

"I've been talking to one of the neighbors, who had something interesting to say."

"Let's hear it."

"Anna Larsson is an elderly woman who lives in the apartment above Dahlström's. On Monday night around ten thirty she heard Flash go out. He was wearing his old slippers, which made a special sound when he walked."

Knutas frowned. "How could she hear that from inside her apartment?"

"I know, that's something you might well ask, but it so happened that her cat was suffering from diarrhea."

"So?"

"Anna Larsson lives alone, and she doesn't have a balcony. She was just about to go to bed when her cat shit on the floor. It smelled so bad that she didn't want to have the garbage bag containing the shit in her apartment. She had already put on her nightgown and didn't want to go downstairs to the trash cans, for fear of running into one of her neighbors. So she put the bag on the landing outside her door for the time being. She thought that nobody would notice if she tossed it out first thing in the morning."

"Get to the point," said Knutas impatiently. Norrby's tendency to present too many details was sometimes annoying.

"Well, at the very moment that she opens her door, she hears Dahlström coming out wearing his slippers. He locks his door and goes downstairs to the basement."

"Okay," said Knutas, tapping his pipe on the table.

"Mrs. Larsson doesn't think any more about it. She goes to bed and falls asleep. In the middle of the night she's awakened by her cat meowing. This time the cat has made a mess on the floor of her bedroom. That animal had a really bad stomachache."

"Hmm."

"She gets out of bed and cleans up everything. She now has another bag of cat shit that has to be put outside on the landing. When she opens the door, someone comes in the entrance one floor down and stops at Dahlström's door. But this time she doesn't hear Dahlström's shuffling slippers; this person is wearing real shoes. She's curious, so she stands there listening. The stranger doesn't ring the doorbell but the door opens and the person goes inside, and she doesn't hear any voices."

Now Knutas's interest was aroused. His pipe froze in midair.

"Then what happened?"

"Then everything was quiet. Not a sound."

"Did she have the impression that someone had opened Dahlström's door from the inside? Or did the person outside open it?"

"She thinks that the person outside opened it."

"Why didn't she tell us about this earlier?"

"She was interviewed on the evening when Dahlström's body was found. She says that she felt stressed and upset, so she mentioned only that she had heard him go down to the basement. Afterward I got to wondering how she could be so sure about it. That's why I went back to talk to her again."

"Good job," Knutas said. "It might have been the killer that she heard, but it could just as well have been Dahlström coming in from somewhere. This was several hours later, wasn't it?"

"Definitely, but it seems quite unlikely that he would have gone out, don't you think?"

"Maybe. Did the woman notice anything else after the person went inside?"

"No, she went back to bed and fell asleep."

"Okay. The question is whether the person had a key—assuming that it wasn't Dahlström, that is."

"There's no sign that the lock was forced."

"Maybe it was someone he knew."

"That seems most plausible."

When the investigative team met again that afternoon, Jacobsson and Wittberg started off by reporting on their encounter with Doris Johnsson and what she had told them about the winnings at the race-track.

"Now at least we have a motive," said Jacobsson, concluding her report.

"That explains why the apartment was ransacked," said Knutas. "The murderer apparently knew that Dahlström had won big at the track."

"The money still hasn't turned up," added Sohlman, "so presumably the perpetrator found it."

"Bengt Johnsson comes immediately to mind," said Jacobsson. "I think we need to put out an APB on him."

"Considering that this involves a homicide, I have to agree." Knutas turned to Norrby. "We've obtained some new information from a witness."

His colleague told everyone about Anna Larsson and her sick cat in the apartment above.

"Damn," said Wittberg. "That indicates that the perp had a key. Which reinforces our suspicions about Johnsson."

"Why is that?" Jacobsson objected. "The perp could just as easily have killed Dahlström, then stolen his keys and gone up to his apartment."

"Or he might have just picked the lock," Sohlman interjected. "Dahlström had a regular cylinder lock on his door. A skilled burglar could have gotten it open without leaving any sign of forced entry. We didn't find any damage on first examination, but we'll take another look at the lock."

"I agree with Wittberg," said Norrby. "I think it was Bengt Johnsson. He was Dahlström's closest friend and it's likely that he had a spare key. Unless it was Dahlström himself who had decided to go out again in the middle of the night. Wearing real shoes this time."

"Sure, that's possible. But if it was Bengan, why would he then contact the super?" said Jacobsson, sounding skeptical.

"To divert suspicion from himself, of course," snapped Norrby.

"If the neighbor woman's testimony is accurate, then Dahlström was alive twenty-four hours after he went to the racetrack and had a party in his apartment," said Knutas. "That means he wasn't killed in connection with the party. The murder most likely took place late on Monday night or in the early hours of Tuesday morning. We'll soon have a more precise determination of the time from the medical examiner."

"By the way, we received another interesting piece of information from a witness," Norrby went on. "I was out there today, talking with all the neighbors for a second time. One of them who wasn't home gave me a call later on."

"Yes?"

Knutas leaned his head on his hands, preparing for another lengthy report.

"It's a girl who goes to Säve High School. She also heard someone in the stairwell late Monday night. She said it was Arne Haukas, the man who lives across from her on the floor below, meaning the same floor where Dahlström lived. Haukas is a PE teacher, and he usually goes out jogging in the evening. Normally he goes out around eight, but on Monday she heard him leave his apartment around eleven P.M. She also saw him from her window."

"Is that so? How can she be so sure of the time and day?"

"Her older sister from Alva was visiting. They were up late, talking, and they both saw him. This girl has been keeping an eye on him ever since she discovered that he's a bit of a Peeping Tom. He always looks in her window whenever he runs past. She thinks he goes jogging in the evening as a pretext for peering in people's windows."

"Does she have any proof for her allegations?"

"No. She actually sounded a little doubtful herself. She said that she wasn't sure about it, that it was just a feeling she had."

"Is this Haukas married?"

"No, he lives alone. And there could be some basis for the girl's uneasiness. I've only managed to make one phone call about the man so far, and that was to Solberga School, where he works. The principal, whom I happen to know personally, told me that several years ago Arne Haukas was accused of spying on the girls when they changed their clothes. The students claimed that he would barge into the locker room to tell them about something trivial. Four of them thought it was so unpleasant that they filed a complaint with the principal."

"What happened?"

"The principal had a talk with Haukas, who denied the allegations, and that was the end of the matter. It apparently never happened again. No other students have complained."

"There seem to be a lot of sleazy individuals living in that building," Wittberg interjected. "Alcoholics, sick cats, Peeping Toms . . . It
makes you wonder what kind of madhouse that place is."

His comments prompted some merriment around the table. Knutas
raised his hand in admonishment.

"In any event, we're not looking for a sex offender; we're looking
for a murderer. But this PE teacher might have seen something since
he was out running on the night of the murder. Has he been interviewed?"

"No, apparently not," replied Norrby.

"Then we need to do that today."

He turned to Jacobsson. "Anything new on Dahlström?"

"We know that he was employed as a photographer at *Gotlands
Tidningar.* He worked there until 1980, when he resigned and started
his own company, called Master Pictures. The business did well for
the first few years, but in 1987 it went into bankruptcy, with major
debts. After that, there's no information that Dahlström had any sort
of job. He lived on welfare until he started receiving a disability pension in 1990."

"Where are his wife and daughter now?" asked Knutas.

"His ex-wife still lives in their old apartment on Signalgatan. His
daughter lives in Malmö. Single, with no children. Or at least she's the
only person listed at that address. Ann-Sofie Dahlström, his ex-wife,
was on the mainland, but she'll be back home later this afternoon. She
promised to come straight here from the airport."

"That's good," said Knutas. "We need to get in touch with the
daughter, too. I want to put out an internal APB on Bengt Johnsson
immediately. We need to ask everyone in his circle of acquaintances
where they think he might be staying. Sohlman, you're in charge of
examining the apartment door lock one more time. The question is:
How many people knew about the money Dahlström won at the
track? Everyone who was at the track with him that evening has to be
interviewed. But did anyone else know?"

"In those kinds of circles, news like that probably spreads like wild-
fire," said Wittberg. "No one that we've talked to in town has said a
word about the money, but they may have their reasons for not talking."

"You'll have to interview them again, along with all the others," said Knutas. "The money throws a whole new light on the case."

If there was one thing that Emma detested, it was sewing machines.

To think that anyone should have to bother with this kind of shit work, she thought, her mouth full of pins. Her sense of irritation was fast becoming a headache. She swore silently. Why should it be so damned difficult to make a pair of pants? When other people sewed in a zipper, they made it look ridiculously easy.

She was really trying her best, and she had armed herself with tons of patience before she started, promising herself that this time she wouldn't give up. She would not surrender to the slightest obstacle, although she had a tendency to do just that. She was certainly well aware of her own weaknesses.

She had been struggling with this sewing project for an hour, and she had already smoked three cigarettes to calm her nerves. Sweat broke out on her forehead as she tried to straighten out the denim fabric under the presser foot. Twice she had been forced to undo the seam when the zipper ended up buckling.

In school she had always hated sewing class. The silence, the sternness of the teacher. The fact that everything had to be so finicky—the seam allowance, the fitting of the pattern, the wrong and right side of the fabric. The only bad grade that she'd ever received on her report card in grade school was in sewing. It was a permanent reminder of her failure to make anything from pot holders to knitted caps.

The ring of her cell phone came like the arrival of a much anticipated guest. When she heard Johan's voice, fire raced through her breast.

"Hi, it's me. Am I interrupting anything?"

"No, but you know you're not supposed to call me."

"I couldn't help it. Is he home?"

"No, he plays floorball on Monday nights."

"Please don't be mad."

A brief silence. Then his voice again, low and gentle. Like a caress on her brow.

"How are you?"

"Fine, thanks. But I was just about to have a hysterical fit and throw my sewing machine out the window."

His soft laugh made her stomach lurch.

"You're trying to sew something? What happened to that vow you made?"

She was reminded of the time last summer when she had tried to mend a hole in his shirt with a needle and thread from his hotel. Afterward she had vowed never to try sewing anything again.

"It went to hell, just like everything else," she said without thinking.

"What? What do you mean?"

He was trying to sound neutral, but she could hear the hope in his voice.

"Oh, nothing. What do you want? You know you're not supposed to call," she repeated.

"I couldn't help myself."

"But if you don't leave me in peace, I won't be able to think," she said gently.

He tried to persuade her to meet him when he arrived in Gotland on the following day.

She refused, even though her body was screaming for him. It was a battle between reason and emotion.

"Don't keep doing this. It's hard enough as it is."

"But what are your feelings for me, Emma? Tell me honestly. I need to know."

"I think about you, too. All the time. I'm so confused. I don't know what I should do."

"Do you sleep with him?"

"You'd better hang up now," she said, annoyed.

He heard her light a cigarette.

"Come on, tell me. Do you? I want to know if you do."

She sighed deeply.

"No, I don't. I don't have the slightest desire to sleep with him. Are you satisfied?"

"But how long can you keep that up? You're going to have to make

up your mind, Emma. Hasn't he noticed anything? Is he that insensi-
tive? Doesn't he wonder why you're acting this way?"

"Of course he does, but he thinks it's a reaction to what happened
this summer."

"You still haven't answered my question."

"What question?"

"What are your feelings for me?"

Another deep sigh.

"I love you, Johan," she said quietly. "That's what makes everything
so difficult."

"But what the hell, Emma. We can't keep going on like this for
much longer. Wouldn't it be better to make a clean break and tell him
how things stand?"

"What the hell do you mean by 'how things stand'?" she roared.
"You have no idea how things stand!"

"Yes, but—"

"But what?"

Her voice was angry now, and she was on the verge of tears.

"You have no fucking idea what it's like to be responsible for two
young children! I can't sit on the sofa and cry all weekend because I miss
you. Or decide to be with you just because I want to. Or need to. Or
have to, in order to survive. Because surely you know that my whole life
revolves around you, Johan. You're the first thing I think about when I
wake up and the last thing I see in my mind's eye before I fall asleep. But
I can't let this take over everything. I have to keep functioning. Take
care of the house, my job, my family. Above all, I have to think of my
children. What would happen to them if I left Olle? You go around over
there in Stockholm with only yourself to think about. A good job, your
own nice apartment in the center of town, and lots to do. If your longing for me starts to get difficult, there are plenty of things to divert your
attention. You can go out to pubs, meet with friends, go to the movies.
And if you're feeling sad and want to cry over me, you can do that, too.
But where the hell can I go? Maybe I can sneak into the laundry room
and cry. But I can't just go into town if I'm feeling unhappy and find
something else to do. Or meet some new people who are fun? Not
likely. Sure, there are plenty of people like that out here!"

She slammed down the phone just as she heard the front door open. Olle was home.

Ann-Sofie Dahlström had the driest hands that Knutas had ever seen. And she kept rubbing them together so that flakes of skin came off and fell onto her lap. She wore her brown hair pulled back and fastened with a plastic barrette at the nape of her neck. Her face was pale and without a trace of makeup. Knutas began by expressing his condolences over the death of her ex-husband.

"We haven't had any contact for a long time. It's been years since we last talked. . . ." Her voice trailed away.

"What was Henry like when you were married?"

"He was almost always working. There were plenty of late nights and working weekends. We didn't have much of a family life. I was the one who mostly took care of our daughter, Pia. Maybe it was partly my fault that things turned out the way they did. I probably shut him out. He started drinking more and more. Finally it got to be intolerable."

How typical for a woman, thought Knutas. *An expert at taking the blame for her husband's bad habits.*

"In what way was it intolerable?"

"He was almost always drunk and started neglecting his work. As long as he had a full-time job at *Gotlands Tidningar,* he managed well enough. The problems began when he started his own company and didn't have anyone looking over his shoulder. He started drinking in the middle of the week, didn't come home at night, and lost customers because he either failed to show up or didn't bother to deliver the photographs he had promised. I finally had to file for divorce."

As she talked, her hands continued their bizarre massage, making a faint scraping sound. She noticed Knutas's glance.

"My hands get like this in the winter, and no lotion does any good. It's the cold. There's nothing I can do about it," she added with a certain sharpness to her voice.

"No, of course not. Forgive me," Knutas apologized. He took out his pipe in order to focus on something else.

"How did his drinking affect Pia?"

"She became withdrawn and uncommunicative. She spent more and more time away from home. Told me that she was studying with friends, but her grades kept getting worse. She started skipping classes and then developed an eating problem. It took a long time for me to realize that it was serious. During the fall semester of her second year, the teachers concluded that she was suffering from anorexia, and she didn't get over it until she finished high school."

"But she stayed in school, in spite of her illness?"

"Yes. I don't think it was the most severe form of the disease, but there's no question that she had an eating disorder."

"What sort of help did you receive?"

"As luck would have it, I knew a doctor at the hospital who had worked at a clinic on the mainland—a clinic for patients with eating disorders. He helped me. I managed to persuade Pia to go over there with me. At the time she weighed only ninety-seven pounds, even though she's five foot nine inches tall."

"How did your husband react?"

"He didn't want to know anything about it. This was toward the end of our marriage."

"What does your daughter do now?"

"She lives in Malmö. She's a librarian at the municipal library."

"Is she married?"

"No."

"Children?"

"No."

"So how do you think she's doing?"

"What do you mean?"

"How is she?"

The woman sitting across from Knutas looked him in the eye without saying a word. Her right eyebrow was twitching. The silence was palpable. Finally it got so oppressive that he was forced to break it.

"How would you describe your contact with each other?"

"Regular."

"And what form does it take?"

"She calls me once a week. Always on Friday."

"How often do you see each other?"

"She usually comes to Gotland for a couple of weeks every summer. But she stays with friends."

"But you see each other?"

"Yes, naturally, we see each other. Of course."

The APB that was issued for Bengt Johnsson on the police-band radio brought results after a couple of hours. Jacobsson took the call from the local police in Slite. A boy who claimed to have seen Johnsson had come into the station. Jacobsson asked to speak to him.

"I think I know where the man is that you're looking for," said a young boy's voice on the phone.

"Really? Where is he?"

"In Åminne, in a cabin. It's an area near here, for summer houses."

"Have you seen him?"

"Yes, he was unloading things from a car outside one of the cabins."

"When was this?"

"Yesterday."

"Why did you happen to contact the police?"

"My best friend's father is on the police force in Slite. I told my friend that I'd seen a suspicious-looking guy out by the summer houses, and he told his father."

"Why did you think the man was suspicious?"

"He was dirty and had on ragged clothes. He seemed nervous and kept looking around, as if he didn't want anyone to notice him."

"Did he see you?"

"No, I don't think so. I was standing behind a tree. I waited to ride my bike past until he went inside the cabin."

"Was he alone?"

"I think so."

"Can you tell me anything else about how he looked?"

"Pretty old, maybe fifty or sixty. Very fat."

"Anything else? What about his hair?"

"He had dark hair, in a ponytail."

Jacobsson felt a vague lurch in her stomach.

"What was he unloading?"

"I couldn't tell."

"How did you happen to catch sight of him?"

"We live right next to the summer-house area. I was on my way home from visiting a friend."

"Could you point out the cabin?"

"Sure."

"Could I talk to one of your parents?"

"They're not home right now."

"Okay. Stay in the house. We'll be there in half an hour. Where do you live?"

Five minutes later Jacobsson and Knutas were in a car, heading east toward Åminne, a popular seaside vacation spot in the summer, located on the northeast side of the island. The local police were going out to the boy's home to await their colleagues.

Outside the car windows, the winter darkness was nearly impenetrable. There were no streetlights, and their only guides were the headlights of cars, as well as reflector posts that appeared at regular intervals. They passed an occasional house, a warm glow coming from its windows. A reminder that people lived out here in the countryside.

When they reached the boy's house, a Slite police car was in the driveway. The boy's name was Jon, and he looked to be about fifteen. Accompanied by his father, he led the way to the summer-house area. It was hard to see the houses in the dark. Without flashlights they would have been fumbling blindly. When they aimed the beams at the cabins, they saw that all of them were a dark Falun red with white trim. Each of them had a yard surrounded by a decorative fence. On this November evening the deserted area seemed almost ghostly. Jacobsson shivered and zipped up her jacket.

Suddenly they saw a light in one of the cabins at the very edge of the woods. It occurred to Knutas that they should have called for backup. Or dogs. Johnsson might not be alone. Knutas put his hand in the inside pocket of his coat, feeling for his service revolver.

Jacobsson was the only one who didn't have a weapon, since the investigation into her potential misconduct during the summer's serial killer case was ongoing, so she had to wait a short distance away. They sent the boy and his father home. The officers stopped before reaching the house and turned off their flashlights so they could discuss how to proceed.

An old Volvo Amazon was parked outside the fence. Knutas crouched down and crept forward, with the other two officers close behind. He paused under a window while the others took up position on either side of the front door.

Not a sound could be heard from inside. Cautiously Knutas stood up enough to peer through the window. In a matter of seconds his brain registered a complete picture of the room: the fireplace with a rocking chair in front of it, the table with four chairs, and an antique lamp hanging from the ceiling. All very cozy. On the table stood several bottles of beer. He signaled to his colleagues. No one there.

At that instant all three of them gave a start as someone moved inside the cabin. Knutas ducked down. The sound of someone clattering and rummaging around penetrated the walls. They waited. Knutas's legs were aching and his fingers were stiff from the cold. Again silence settled over the cabin. Knutas peeked inside and saw the back of a large man now seated in the rocking chair. The ponytail indicated that it was Bengt Johnsson. He had put more wood on the fire, and the flames were dangerously high. He had also moved the table over next to him. On the table stood a whiskey bottle, which looked as if it had been newly opened. Next to the bottle was a glass and an ashtray. The man was smoking as he stared into the fire. Then he leaned forward to take a gulp from the bottle. It was Johnsson, no doubt about it.

Visible to the right of the room was a hallway and part of the kitchen. Knutas had the feeling that Johnsson was alone, but he couldn't be absolutely sure. One of the police officers shifted his feet uneasily. It was freezing cold, and none of them was dressed for standing outdoors for any length of time.

Suddenly Johnsson stood up and looked right at the window. Knutas ducked so quickly that he fell over. Whether Johnsson had seen him or not, it was impossible to tell, but it was now or never.

Knutas took up position in front of the door with his weapon drawn and, after a nod of agreement from the other two officers, he kicked in the door with all his might.

They were greeted by Bengt Johnsson's look of bewilderment. He was obviously drunk, and he was once again sitting in the rocking chair with the glass in his hand.

"What the hell?" was all he managed to say when the three officers stormed in with their guns drawn.

The fire in the fireplace crackled pleasantly, and the kerosene lamps gave off a gentle glow. And there the man sat, peaceful as could be.

The situation was so absurd that Knutas felt an urge to laugh. He lowered his gun and said, "How are things going, Bengt?"

"Fine, thanks," slurred the man sitting next to the fire. "Nice of you to drop by."

Several Months Earlier

He made her unsure of herself. Fanny didn't know how she was supposed to act. He was probably twice her age. She really ought to think of him as a nice old man and nothing more. But there was something about the way he treated her that changed everything. In the beginning, he would grab a lock of her hair and cautiously tug at it, which was both playful and annoying at the same time. She would blush, finding the whole thing embarrassing because she sensed that it meant something more. Sometimes when she met his gaze, he would turn serious, and it felt as if his eyes were stripping her naked. She didn't find it entirely unpleasant. Sometimes she even thought him attractive when she studied him surreptitiously. He was muscular. He had thick, shiny hair with just a hint of gray at the temples. The wrinkles around his eyes and mouth revealed his age. His teeth were slightly yellow and crooked, with multiple fillings.

How could he look at her the way he did when he was so old? she had wondered. If was as if his eyes made her older than she was. Although he didn't always pay attention to her; sometimes he ignored her completely. Then, to her surprise, she would feel disappointed, as if she actually wanted him to notice her.

One time he had asked her if she wanted a lift. She said yes because it was windy and below freezing. He had a big car, and she got in. He put on some music—Joe Cocker. That was his favorite, he told her with a smile. She had never heard of Joe Cocker. He asked her what she liked to listen to. When she couldn't think of anything, he just laughed. It was great to sit there in his warm car and listen to his gentle laughter. It felt somehow safe.

The mere fact that she was sitting in that big fancy car made her feel more important.

TUESDAY, NOVEMBER 20

The morning dawned with a pale white sun that barely managed to rise above the horizon. The sea was still relatively warm, and from the surface a mist slowly lifted upward. The water merged with the sky, and in the haze it was impossible to distinguish one from the other. A seagull shrieked between Visby's medieval merchant buildings on Strandgatan. The rugged ring wall from the thirteenth century that surrounded the town was the best preserved in all of Europe.

From the harbor came the sound of a small fishing boat chugging its way into port with its nighttime catch of cod.

Knutas had just dropped off Lina at the hospital where she worked as a midwife. She started work at seven thirty in the morning, which suited him fine. He could drive her there and still arrive in time for the morning meeting.

They had been married for fourteen years, and he didn't regret a single day of it. They met when he was attending a police conference in Copenhagen. One evening he went to a restaurant on Gråbrødretorv with a colleague. Lina was working there as a waitress while she was studying. It was a warm summer evening, and she had on a short-sleeved blouse and black skirt. She had tried to bring some order to her unruly red hair by fastening it with a barrette, but stray locks kept on escaping and falling into her eyes. She had more freckles than anyone Knutas had ever seen. The tiny spots reached all the way to the tips of her milky-white fingers. She smelled of almonds, and when she leaned over the table, her arm brushed against his.

The next evening they had dinner together, and that was the beginning of a love the likes of which he had never even come close to before. The year that followed was filled with passionate encounters, exhausting good-byes, long nightly phone conversations, an aching sense of longing, and an ever-growing mutual feeling that they had found their partner in life. Lina finished her training, and without further ado she agreed to marry him and move to Gotland. He had just been promoted to head of the criminal division, and that was why they had decided to try living on Gotland.

It had turned out to be a good decision. Lina had no trouble adapting. With her open and cheerful manner she quickly made new friends and created her own life for herself. After only a couple of months she had found a temporary position at Visby hospital. They bought a house, and then it wasn't long before the twins were on their way. Knutas was thirty-five when they met, and he'd had a couple of previous long-term relationships, but he had never known how natural everything could feel. With Lina at his side, he was prepared for anything.

Of course they'd had their crises and arguments, just like everyone else. Lina had a quick temper, and when she started yelling in a strong Danish accent, he had a hard time understanding what she meant. He often couldn't help laughing, which only made her more furious. Even so, their arguments usually ended amicably. There was no sense of competition between the two of them.

Now her birthday was coming up, and he was feeling stressed. She was going to be forty-seven next Saturday, but this year he had no clue what to buy her.

And right now, he had other things on his mind. He was looking forward to the interview with Bengt Johnsson. The man had been drunk out of his mind when they took him in, so the interview had been postponed.

Smittenberg had decided to arrest him, having good reason to suspect him of murder, or at least manslaughter. That was the lowest degree of suspicion, and the evidence against Johnsson would have to be stronger for him actually to be arraigned. The prosecutor had three days to do that. He based the arrest on the argument that there was a risk Johnsson might obstruct the investigation if he was released. He had no alibi for the night of the murder, and he also had a great deal of money in his possession, although he couldn't explain where it had come from. Ten thousand kronor—money they assumed was part of

Dahlström's winnings at the track. The fingerprints on the bills were being examined by the Fingerprint Center in Stockholm, and they expected to have an answer by morning. If it turned out that Dahlström's prints were on the bills, then things didn't look good for Johnsson.

Emma pedaled toward Roma, cursing herself for deciding to ride her bike to work. It was crazy how the cold and wind had picked up as she left the schoolyard and made her way out to the main road. The Kyrk School was located some distance from town. She started biking faster to get warm. On Tuesdays she finished teaching by twelve fifteen. She usually stayed at school to put in a couple more hours of work, but today she was planning to visit a friend. Then she was going to take the children into town to go shopping and stop at the pastry shop, as she had promised. They were in desperate need of new wardrobes.

The main road was quiet and deserted, with very little traffic at this time of year. She passed the lane that led to the cloister ruins where plays by Shakespeare were performed every summer. Then past Roma School and the public baths. Farther along, on the other side of the road, were the ramshackle buildings from the Roma sugar mill, which had been shut down. The windows in the yellow brick buildings gaped darkly at her. The sugar mill had been founded more than a hundred years earlier, but it was closed when profits began to plummet. The now deserted mill stood there as a sad reminder of how times had changed.

She lifted her face to the sky, closed her eyes, and inhaled the air deep into her lungs. Emma belonged to those who appreciated November. It was an in-between month without demands, unlike the summer, with its expectations of barbecue evenings, swimming excursions, and all the visits of friends and relatives. And God have mercy on anyone who wasn't outdoors when the sun was shining.

When the autumn darkness descended, she could retreat inside without a guilty conscience, and watch TV in the middle of the day if she felt like it, or read a good book. She could forget about putting on makeup and shuffle around wearing an old, nubby bathrobe.

In December, new demands appeared as Advent was celebrated, and preparations had to be made for Saint Lucia and Christmas Eve, with all the cooking, baking, buying Christmas presents, and putting up decorations.

For thirty-five years she had outwardly lived a good life. She was married and had two children; she had a teaching job and a great house in the middle of Roma. She had lots of friends and a good relationship with her parents and parents-in-law. Outwardly everything seemed fine, but her emotional life was in chaos. She would never have imagined how much her longing for Johan could hurt. It made her anxious, and it kept her awake at night. She had thought that her feelings for him would diminish with time. Oh, how she had deceived herself. They had seen each other only once in almost two months, and they had known each other for barely six months. By all rights their love ought to be dead. From a logical point of view, at least. But emotions and logic had nothing to do with each other.

She had tried to forget and to move on. She could see an uneasiness in the eyes of her children. Sara was only eight, and Filip was a year younger. Yet sometimes she imagined that they knew what was going on. More than Olle did. He carried on as usual. He seemed to think that they could go on forever, side by side, without touching each other. They were now like a couple of old friends. He seemed to have come to terms with the situation. Once she asked him how he could seem so content, in spite of everything. He replied that he wanted to give her time. Time after the trauma of Helena's death and everything else that followed. Olle was still under the illusion that all this had to do with the aftermath of the events of the past summer. And it was true that she thought often about Helena's horrible death. And she missed her terribly.

At first she had thought that the whole drama was the reason why she had fallen in love with Johan. That she had gone through some sort of emotional shock. But she couldn't stop thinking about him.

She seemed to see his face everywhere she turned—at the Konsum grocery store, in the schoolyard, when she went into town.

Her guilty conscience tormented her. To think she was capable of betraying Olle in such a dreadful way. The phone conversation with

Johan had made her even more confused. Of course she wanted nothing more than to see him. But the consequences of such a meeting scared her to death.

When she looked at Olle she tried to conjure up the image of the man who had once sparked her love. The man to whom she had said yes in front of the altar. He was still the same person, after all. The same now as back then. They were supposed to grow old together, damn it. That's what they had decided long ago.

The throbbing above his temples started as soon as Johan disembarked from the plane. Shit. The last thing he needed right now was a headache. Accompanied by his colleague, cameraman Peter Bylund, he rented a car at the airport and drove straight to the old TV newsroom that was still at their disposal. It was next to the Radio Gotland building, in the middle of Visby.

It smelled musty. Dust bunnies as big as balls of yarn lay in all the corners, and the computers were also covered with a fine layer of dust. It had been a while since anyone had been inside.

The story that was their priority for the day had to do with the future of the Björkhaga campground. It was a classic camping area from the late forties, idyllically located near a sandy beach on the west side of the island. During the summer months it was filled with tourists and Gotlanders alike. Many were regular visitors, who came back year after year because they appreciated a quieter campground, without all the facilities. Now the municipal grounds had been leased to a private individual. The plan was to transform the Björkhaga campground into a modern resort area. Protests from campers and the local inhabitants came quickly.

The story had all the makings of a good TV report: photos from the deserted campground that had given so many families and their children great pleasure over the years, and a fierce conflict in the form of outraged local residents versus a business-minded entrepreneur who had the municipal bigwigs behind him.

An easy job. From Stockholm, Johan had already scheduled the interviews, so it was just a matter of getting started. The biggest challenge for him was to keep away from Emma. Right now there were only a few miles between them.

The interrogation room was sparsely furnished with a table and four chairs. The tape recorder was as new as the furniture. This was the first time it would be put to use.

Bengt Johnsson didn't look as relaxed as he had the night before. Dressed in blue prison garb, he sat hunched on a chair, glaring at Jacobsson and Knutas, who were seated across from him. His dark hair was pulled back into a skimpy ponytail, and his mustache drooped, as did the corners of his mouth.

After the preliminary formalities were taken care of, Knutas leaned back and studied the man who was suspected of killing Henry Dahlström. Every interview had great significance for the investigative work. Establishing trust between the suspect and the interrogator was of the utmost importance. That was why Knutas took pains to proceed cautiously.

"How are you feeling?" he began. "Would you like something to drink?"

"Yes, damn it. A beer would taste good right now."

"Unfortunately, that's not something we can offer you." Knutas gave him a little smile. "How about a soda or some coffee?"

"I'll have a Coke."

Knutas rang for a soda.

"Am I allowed to smoke?"

"Sure."

"Great."

Johnsson shook a cigarette out of a crumpled pack of John Silvers and lit it with a slight tremor in his hand.

"Can you tell us when you last saw Henry?"

"It was the day after he won at the track. Or rather, the evening after. I was in town with a pal and Flash came over to see us. I was drunk, so I don't really remember much."

He was interrupted by the door opening. A police officer came in with the soda.

"What happened?"

"We just talked for a while."

"Who was your friend?"

"His name is Örjan. Örjan Broström."

"What did you do then?"

"Flash didn't stay long."

"Was he on foot when he left?"

"He went to catch a bus."

"And you didn't see him after that?"

"Nope."

"And this was on Monday, November twelfth, the day after you were at the track?"

"Yup."

"What time?"

"I'm not really sure, but most of the stores were closed and it was dark. There were hardly any people around, so I think it was pretty late."

"What do you mean by that? Ten or eleven at night?"

"No, no, damn it. It wasn't that late. Maybe seven or eight."

"And you didn't see Henry again after that night?"

"No, not until we found him in the darkroom, that is."

"The building superintendent says that you rang his doorbell. Is that right?"

"Yes."

"Why did you want to talk to him?"

"I hadn't seen Flash for a while. I get a little worried when a buddy suddenly isn't around."

"Why did you take off after you found him?"

Johnsson was silent for a moment before he resumed talking.

"Well, you see . . . I'd done something really stupid, something damn stupid."

"Okay," said Knutas. "What was it?"

"The whole gang was at the racetrack on Sunday, the last race day of the season, so it was extra festive. I was there with Flash and Kjelle, and two broads: Gunsan and Monica. We went over to Flash's place beforehand to have a bite to eat. And then when he won, he wanted to celebrate and we did, too. So we went back to his apartment afterward. We had a party there that night."

He fell silent. Knutas clearly sensed that this was a turning point in the interrogation. Now it was starting to get interesting.

"Well, Flash had won all this money at the track, eighty thousand big ones, in thousand-kronor bills. He showed me where he hid the money, in a box in the broom closet. Later, when the others were all in the living room, I just couldn't resist. I thought he wouldn't notice if I took a few thousand. I've been going through a real cash crunch, and Flash seemed to be really flush lately, so I thought that . . . well."

He paused and gave the officers a pleading look.

"But damn it, I didn't kill him. No, I didn't. I could never do anything like that. But I did take some of his money."

"How much?"

"I guess about twenty thousand," said Johnsson quietly.

"You only had ten thousand in the cabin. What happened to the rest of it?"

"I spent it. On a lot of booze. This thing with Flash really upset me."

"But why did you run away from the darkroom?" Knutas asked again.

"I was scared that you'd think I killed Flash because I stole his money."

"What were you doing on the evening of November twelfth?"

"What day was that?"

"Last Monday, when you saw Henry at the bus station."

"Like I told you, we were there until maybe eight or nine o'clock. Then I went home with Örjan. We spent the night drinking until I passed out on his sofa."

"What time was it then?"

"Don't know."

"Where does he live?"

"On Styrmansgatan, number fourteen."

"Okay. Then he should be able to back up your story."

"Sure, although we were both pretty far gone."

They were interrupted by a knock on the door. It was about the results from the Fingerprint Center. They took a short break and the officers left the room. Johnsson wanted to use the toilet.

Dahlström's fingerprints had been found on the bills. This finding was of little consequence if the police chose to believe Johnsson's story. Many other prints were also found, but none that matched any in police records.

"What do we do now?" asked Jacobsson as they got coffee from the office coffee machine.

"I don't know. Do you believe him?"

"Yes, actually, I do," she said, looking up at Knutas. "I think he sounds very convincing."

"I do, too. If only there was someone who could corroborate his story, we could release him right away. I think we can disregard the theft of the money for the time being."

"His pal, this Örjan, seems to keep popping up. We need to get hold of him," said Jacobsson.

"I'll talk to Birger about whether we should hold Bengt Johnsson any longer or not. I think we'll stop the interview here. Would you like some lunch?"

The choice of lunch restaurants in Visby during the wintertime was limited. Most of the pubs were open only in the evening, and so they usually ended up at the same place if they wanted a change from the meager offerings in the police department's cafeteria. Of course the lunch was more expensive, but it was worth every öre. The Cloister was furnished in classic inn style and had a well-respected chef. The owner, Leif Almlöv, was one of Knutas's best friends. When Knutas and Jacobsson stepped through the door, they were met by a great bustle and clatter and plenty of hurrying waitresses. All the tables were taken.

Leif caught sight of them and waved.

"Hi, how are things going?"

He gave Jacobsson a hug and shook hands with Knutas as he kept an eye on everything going on around them.

"Good. It's sure crowded in here today," said Knutas.

"There's a convention in town. It was like this yesterday, too. Total hysteria. What would you like to eat?"

"Looks like we're going to have to settle for hot dogs instead."

"No, no, don't even think of it. Of course I'll get you a table. Just wait here. Have a seat at the bar for the time being."

He called to the bartender to give them something to drink, on the house. As they sat down with glasses of light beer in front of them, Jacobsson lit a cigarette.

"Have you started smoking?" exclaimed Knutas in surprise.

"No, not at all. I only smoke when I go to a party or if I'm having problems."

"I see, and what would you call this?"

"The latter. I'm having some personal difficulties."

"Is it something you'd like to talk about?"

"No. Leif is waving to us—we have a table."

Sometimes Jacobsson could really drive Knutas crazy. She was overly secretive about her private life. She might tell him something about her travels, her relatives, or some social event that she had gone to, but he seldom found out anything important.

They didn't meet socially, except infrequently at a party. He had been to her place only a few times. She lived on Mellangatan, in a big three-room apartment with a view of the sea. The only male companion she ever talked about at any length was her large cockatoo named Vincent, who was the center of attention in his cage in the living room. The stories about him were legion: for one thing, he was a whiz at playing Ping-Pong with his beak, and he could scare off unwelcome visitors by growling like a dog.

Knutas didn't actually know very much about Karin Jacobsson except that she was interested in sports. She played soccer in Division Three and was by all accounts very good at it. She could always talk about soccer. She was a midfielder on the Visby P18 team that played in the mainland league, which meant that she often played matches off the island. Knutas imagined that if she operated on the same level as she did on the job, she was undoubtedly a tough player to tackle, in spite of her small size. She shared her interest in sports with Erik Sohlman. They were always talking about soccer.

Jacobsson was from Tingstäde parish in the north of the island. Her parents still lived in the same house on the edge of Tingstäde swamp, practically right across from the church. Knutas knew that she had a younger brother, but she never talked about him or her parents.

Many times he had wondered why she still lived alone. Karin was both charming and nice, and when she first started working with the Visby police, he had been slightly attracted to her. But that was just when he happened to meet Lina, so he had never fully examined his feelings. He didn't dare ask Karin about her love life; her sense of privacy blocked all attempts of that sort. Yet Knutas never held back from telling her about his own problems. She knew just about everything about him, and he considered her to be his best female friend.

Their food arrived, and they hungrily focused their attention on eating as they discussed the investigation. They both agreed that they believed Bengt Johnsson's story.

"Maybe the murder has nothing to do with the money Dahlström won at the track," said Jacobsson. "The perp could have stolen the cash as a diversion. He wants us to think that the murder was the result of a burglary. But then the question is: What was the real motive?"

"Do you know whether he was seeing anyone?"

"Well, that Monica who was at the track with him told us that they sometimes slept together, but it was nothing serious."

"What about in the past? Maybe there's a story farther back and none of his current friends knows anything about it."

"That's conceivable," said Jacobsson, drinking the last of the light beer she was having with her fish. "Do you think it might be about an ex-girlfriend who wanted revenge, or a jealous husband whose wife was sleeping with Dahlström, or some neighbor who got tired of all the coming and going in the stairwell?"

"I think the explanation could be even simpler than that. The most obvious motive is the track money—someone killed Dahlström for the money, plain and simple."

"Maybe." Jacobsson stood up. "I've got to run. We're going to track down Örjan Broström—Bengt's buddy."

"Okay. Good luck."

Most of the lunch guests had left the restaurant, and Leif sat down on the chair that Jacobsson had vacated.

He opened a frosty bottle of beer and took several long gulps.

"What an ordeal. Practically every customer wanted to order à la carte instead of choosing the daily special. The kitchen was an inferno, and the chef has been yelling at everyone. I had to console one of the waitresses who started sobbing."

"You poor guy," said Knutas with a laugh. "Is she cute?"

Leif made a wry face.

"Not much fun when you have to play nanny to every single person. Sometimes this place seems just like a day-care center. But never mind that, a lot of people means money in the bank, and that's what we need during the long, cold winter. How are things with you?"

"Lots of work—just like you. The difference is that the profits are scanty."

"How's the investigation going?"

"We've got someone under arrest, although between you and me, I doubt he's the guy. But I'm sure we'll solve this case, too."

"Wasn't it one of his drinking buddies who did it?"

"That seems the most likely, but we'll have to wait and see," said Knutas.

Even though he and Leif were close friends, he didn't like to discuss an investigation when he was in the middle of it. Leif was fully aware of this and respected his reticence.

"How are Ingrid and the kids?" asked Knutas.

"They're all fine. This morning I went out and bought tickets to Paris. I'm thinking of surprising Ingrid with a week of romance right after New Year's. We're celebrating our fifteenth wedding anniversary."

"Has it been that long?"

"Incredible but true."

"You always manage to come up with such good ideas. I can't think of what to buy Lina for her birthday. Do you have any suggestions?"

"No, you're going to have to think of something yourself. I've filled my quota when it comes to your wife's birthdays. At least until it's time for her fiftieth."

Knutas smiled with embarrassment. When Lina had turned forty they were going through a rough period financially. So the Almlövs had provided the place and the wait staff for the big celebration. Leif also happened to know the members of a band, and they had agreed to play for free. Leif was truly a thoughtful and generous friend. The entire Knutas family had been invited to the Almlöv mountain cabin and to their time-share apartment on the Costa del Sol in Spain.

The two families belonged to completely different economic brackets. This had bothered Knutas at first, but over time he had accepted this difference. Leif and Ingrid had a relaxed attitude toward their wealth, and they never talked about it.

Knutas asked for the bill, but Leif refused to let his friend pay for lunch. Every time Knutas came to the restaurant they had the same argument.

Johan was standing in front of the ATM on Adelsgatan when he noticed her. She came walking from Söderport, holding the hand of a child on either side. She was talking to them and laughing. Tall and slender, with her sand-colored hair hanging straight down to her shoulders. He saw the contours of her high cheekbones as she turned her head. She was wearing jeans and a short, lion-yellow quilted jacket. A striped scarf was wrapped around her neck. And she had on mocha-colored boots with fringe.

His mouth went dry and he turned his back to peer down at the ATM. "Receipt requested?" Should he turn around and say hello? Last night's conversation complicated matters. He didn't know whether she was still angry.

He had never met the children, just seen them from a distance. Would she notice him, or would she just walk past? There was hardly anyone on the street, which meant that she was bound to see him. He felt a slight panic and turned around.

She had stopped to look in a window a short distance away. He gathered his courage.

"Hi!" He looked right into her shining eyes.

"Hi, Johan."

The children looked up at him inquisitively, their cheeks red under brightly colored caps. One of them was slightly taller than the other.

"You must be Sara and Filip," he said, holding out his hand. "I'm Johan."

"How do you know our names?" asked the girl in her lilting Gotland accent.

She bore a striking resemblance to her mother. A mini-version of Emma.

"Your mother told me."

Emma's presence made him feel weak in the knees.

"Johan is sort of a friend of mine," Emma told the children. "He's a TV journalist and lives in Stockholm."

"Do you work for a TV station?" asked the girl, wide-eyed.

"I've seen you on TV," said the boy, who was smaller and blonder.

Johan was used to having children claim they had seen him, even though he knew it was very unlikely. He made an appearance only on those rare occasions when he did a stand-up, when reporters explain something with live video for the viewers.

But he didn't let on.

"Is that right?"

"Yes," said the boy solemnly.

"Next time don't forget to wave, okay?"

The boy nodded.

"How are things going?" Emma's question sounded rather indifferent.

"Fine, thanks. I'm here with Peter. We're doing a story on the Björkhaga campground."

"I see," she said without interest.

"What about you?"

"I'm good. Fine. Just fine."

She glanced quickly around, as if she were afraid that someone might notice them.

"I'm teaching, as usual. I've been really busy."

Johan felt a growing sense of irritation.

"How long are you staying?" she asked.

"I'm going home tomorrow or Thursday. It hasn't been decided yet. It depends."

"Uh-huh."

Silence settled between them.

"Come on, Mamma."

Filip was tugging at her arm.

"Okay, sweetie, I'm coming."

"Could we meet?"

He was forced to ask the question, even though she had already said no.

"No, I can't."

Her gaze shifted away from him. He tried to catch her eye.

The children were tugging at her. They didn't care about him anymore. They wanted to move on.

"Mamma," they both called.

Suddenly she looked him straight in the eye. And deep inside. For a second he felt everything stand still. Then she said exactly what he was hoping to hear.

"Call me."

Örjan Broström's apartment was on the fourth floor with windows facing Styrmansgatan. When they rang the doorbell, a dog started barking wildly. The barking was interspersed with a deep growl. They automatically took a step back.

"Who is it?" a man's voice said from the other side of the door.

"The police. Open up," ordered Wittberg.

"Just a minute," the voice said.

It turned out that Broström was not alone. Two beefy men with shaved heads were sitting in the kitchen playing cards, drinking beer, and smoking. They spoke an Eastern European language. Estonian, guessed Jacobsson.

"Who are your friends?" she asked as they sat down in the living room.

"Some of my buddies from Stockholm."

"From Stockholm?"

"That's right."

Broström gave her a sullen look. He was wearing a black vest that accentuated both his muscular arms and his chalk white skin. Not to mention all the tattoos. To her horror, Jacobsson noted that he had something resembling a swastika tattooed on his shoulder. He had greasy dark hair and a hard expression on his face. He kept one hand on the collar of the snarling attack dog as he lit a cigarette. In silence he peered at them through the smoke. An old trick among criminals was to let the cops speak first.

"Do you know Henry Dahlström?"

"I can't say that I really knew him. But I knew who he was."

"So you know what happened to him?"

"I know that he's dead."

"When did you last see him?"

"Don't remember."

"Think about it. We can always take you down to the station if that might help your memory," Wittberg suggested.

"Hell, that doesn't really seem necessary."

He made a face that might have been intended as a smile.

"Then you'd better start cooperating. You can begin by trying to re-call when you last saw him."

"It must have been in town. That's the only place I ever saw him. We weren't really pals."

"Why not?"

"With that guy? An old drunk? Why would I want to hang out with him?"

"I have no idea, do you?"

Wittberg turned to Jacobsson, who shook her head. She was having a hard time relaxing in the cramped apartment with the dog on the other side of the table. The animal kept staring at her. The fact that he growled every once in a while didn't make things any better, nor did the hair standing up on his back or his stiff tail. She felt a strong urge to light a cigarette herself.

"Could you get rid of the dog?" she asked.

"What? Hugo?"

"Is that his name? It sounds a little too sweet for a dog like that."

"He has a sister named Josephine," muttered Örjan as he took the dog out to the men in the kitchen.

They heard the men exchange a few words and then burst out in raucous laughter. The kitchen door closed. Örjan came back, casting an amused glance in Jacobsson's direction. *That's the first real sign of life in his eyes,* she thought.

"When did you last see him?" Wittberg asked again.

"I guess it was one night a week ago when Bengan and I were at the bus station. Flash came over to talk to us."

"Then what did you do?"

"We just sat and drank."

"For how long?"

"Don't know. Maybe half an hour."

"What time was it?"

"Around eight, I think."

"Can you possibly remember what day that was?"

"It must have been last Monday, because on Tuesday I was busy with something else."

"What?"

"It's private."

Neither of the police officers felt like asking any more questions about that matter.

"Have you ever been to Henry Dahlström's apartment?" asked Jacobsson.

"No."

"How about his darkroom?"

Örjan shook his head.

"But he and Bengan were good pals, and you hang out with Bengan. How come you never went to his place?"

"It just never happened. I just moved here, damn it. I've only lived here for three months."

"Okay. So what did you do after that on Monday night, after Dahlström went home?"

"Bengan and I sat there for a while longer, even though it was fucking cold out, and then we came back here to my place."

"What did you do here?"

"We just sat and talked, watched TV, and drank a lot."

"Were the two of you here alone?"

"Yes."

"Then what happened?"

"I think we both crashed on the sofa. In the middle of the night I woke up and got into bed."

"Is there anyone who can confirm that what you're saying is true?"

"Don't think so, no."

"Did anyone call you during that time?"

"No."

"Was Bengan with you all night?"

"Yes."

"Are you sure about that? You were asleep, weren't you?"

"He passed out before I did."

"So what did you do?"

"Flipped through the TV channels."

"What did you watch?"

"Can't remember."

They were interrupted by one of the skinheads.

"Hey, Örjan, Hugo is getting restless. We're going to take him out for a walk."

Örjan looked at his watch.

"Good, he probably needs to go out. His leash is hanging on a hook in the hallway. And make sure he doesn't eat any leaves—they're not good for his stomach."

Amazing, thought Jacobsson. How considerate.

They left Örjan Broström without making any further progress. He was not someone they looked forward to meeting again.

When Knutas was back in his office after lunch, someone knocked on the door. Norrby's demeanor, which he normally kept under tight control, had now been shattered by an excitement that Knutas hadn't seen in his colleague for a long time.

"You won't believe this," Norrby gasped as he waved a sheaf of papers.

He dropped into one of the visitor's chairs.

"These are printouts from the bank, from Henry Dahlström's bank account. For years he had only one account, and that's where his disability pension was always deposited. See here?" said Norrby, pointing to the numbers on the page.

"Four months ago he opened a new account. Two deposits were made, both of them for the same large amount. The first was made on July twentieth, when the sum of twenty-five thousand kronor was deposited. The second was as late as October thirtieth, and for the same amount of twenty-five thousand."

"Where did the money come from?"

"It's a mystery to me."

Norrby leaned back in his chair and threw out his hands in a dramatic gesture.

"We now have a new lead!"

"So Dahlström was mixed up in some kind of monkey business. I've always had the feeling that this wasn't an ordinary robbery homicide. We need to call everyone in for another meeting."

Knutas looked at his watch.

"It's one forty-five. Shall we say two thirty? Will you tell the others?"

"Sure."

"In the meantime I'll call the prosecutor. Birger should be here, too."

When the investigative team had gathered, Norrby began by telling them about the deposits made to Dahlström's account.

The sense of focus in the room sharpened tangibly. Everyone automatically leaned forward, and Wittberg gave a long whistle.

"Jesus. Can we find out where the money came from?"

"Whoever made the deposit used an ordinary deposit slip. It doesn't give any information about the person. On the other hand, we do have the date of the deposit."

"What about the bank surveillance cameras?" Jacobsson suggested.

"We've already thought of that. The bank saves the tapes from the cameras for a month. The first bank tape from July is gone, but we have the one from October. If we're in luck, we can use it to trace the individual who made the deposits. We're picking it up right now."

"I've talked with the Swedish Forensic Lab. They're working hard on the evidence taken from the darkroom and apartment, and if we're lucky we'll have answers by the end of the week," Sohlman informed the others. "There are also palm prints and fingerprints from the basement window that we checked against the criminal records. We didn't come up with a match, so if they belong to the perp, he doesn't have a police record."

"What about the murder weapon?" asked Wittberg.

Sohlman shook his head.

"So far we haven't found it, but all indications are that it was a hammer, the ordinary kind that you can buy in any hardware store."

"All right. We need to proceed with the investigation as usual, but let's concentrate on finding out what Dahlström was up to. Who else among his acquaintances might know something? What about the building superintendent? Or the daughter? We still haven't had a proper interview with her. We're going to expand the interview process to include anyone who had contact with Dahlström or who may have seen him on the night of the murder—the bus driver, employees in kiosks and stores, more neighbors in the area."

"And the racetrack," Jacobsson interjected. "We should contact people at the track."

"But it's closed for the season," objected Wittberg.

"All the stables are still in operation. The horses have to be exercised, the stable personnel are working, and the drivers are there. It was at the track that he won all that money, after all."

"Absolutely," said Knutas. "All suggestions are welcome. One more thing before we adjourn—this has to do with how we're going to handle the media. So far, thank God, no journalist has published any details—as you know, we never allow that when it's a matter of a drunken brawl. But their interest in the case is going to grow if the news about the money gets out. So let's keep it under wraps; don't say a word to anyone. You know how easily word can spread. If any reporter starts asking you questions about the investigation, refer them to me or to Lars. I also think it's time for us to call in the National

Criminal Police. I've asked for their assistance. Two officers will be arriving tomorrow."

"I hope Martin is one of them," said Jacobsson. "That would be great."

A murmur of agreement was heard.

Knutas shared their positive view of Martin Kihlgård, who had helped them with the investigation in the summer, but his relationship with the man did have its complications. Kihlgård was a cheerful and congenial person who was quite domineering and had an opinion about almost everything. Deep inside, Knutas was aware that his touchiness when it came to Kihlgård might have to do with a little-brother complex in relation to the gentleman from National. The fact that Karin Jacobsson had such an openly high opinion of his colleague didn't make the situation any better.

With a whir and a click the tape slipped into the VCR. Knutas and Jacobsson were alone in Knutas's office. A few seconds of grainy gray flickering, and then the inside of the bank appeared in black and white. They had to fast-forward a bit before they reached the time in question.

The clock in the upper-right-hand corner showed 12:23, and the date was October 30. Almost five minutes passed before anyone made the deposit in Dahlström's account. The bank was quite crowded because it was the lunch hour. This particular branch was centrally located in Östercentrum, and many people liked to take care of their banking at lunchtime. Two windows were open, with a female and a male teller behind the glass. On chairs near the window facing the street sat four people: an elderly man with a cane, a girl with long blond hair, a fat middle-aged woman, and a young man wearing a suit.

Knutas thought to himself that right now he might be looking at the very person who had murdered Henry Dahlström.

The door opened and two more people came into the bank. They didn't seem to be together. First a man who appeared to be in his fifties. He was wearing a gray jacket and checked cap with dark slacks and shoes. He walked forward without hesitation and took a number.

Behind him came another man, very tall and of slight build. He stooped a bit. He apparently already had a number, and he went to stand in front of the teller's window, as if he were next in line.

When he turned and glanced around the bank, Knutas saw that he had a camera hanging around his neck.

They recognized him at once. The man was Henry Dahlström.

"Damn it," groaned Knutas. "He deposited the money himself."

"There goes that possibility. How typical. It was too easy."

Jacobsson turned on the ceiling light.

"He got the money and then put it in the bank himself," she said. "Impossible to trace, in other words."

"Damned rotten luck. But why didn't the person just transfer the money directly into Dahlström's account? If he was so afraid of being discovered, it must have been an even bigger risk for him to meet Dahlström to give him the money than if he had transferred the sum directly."

"It certainly seems strange," Jacobsson agreed. "I wonder what the money was for. I'm convinced the story about the racetrack is true. Dahlström gambled regularly, and the track has always attracted a shady clientele. Something underhanded could have been going on there, maybe a dispute between two criminal elements. Maybe Dahlström was hired to spy for someone and take pictures, so that the person could keep tabs on his rivals."

"You've been watching too many movies," said Knutas.

"Shit," cried Jacobsson as she glanced at her watch. "Speaking of movies, I've got to get going."

"What are you going to see?"

"We're going to the Roxy to see a Turkish black comedy. It's a special showing."

"Who are you going with?"

"You'd really like to know, wouldn't you?"

She gave Knutas an annoying wink and disappeared into the hallway.

"Why are you always so secretive?" he shouted after her.

Several Months Earlier

Fanny had come home from school to an empty apartment.

Her feeling of relief was mixed with a dose of guilt. The less she saw of her mother lately, the better she felt. At the same time, she didn't think it was right to feel this way. You were supposed to like your mother. And besides, she was Fanny's only parent.

She opened the refrigerator and her mood sank. Her mother hadn't gone grocery shopping today, either.

Never mind. Right now she was going to do her homework. She was worried about Thursday's math test; math had never been her strong suit. She had just taken out her books and sharpened her pencils when the phone rang. The sound gave her a start. The phone hardly ever rang in their apartment.

To her astonishment it was him, and he wanted to invite her to dinner. She was both surprised and uncertain. She didn't know what to say.

"Hello, are you still there?" His smooth voice in the receiver.

"Yes," she managed to say, feeling her cheeks grow hot.

"Can you? Do you want to?"

"I've got homework to do. We're having a test."

"But you still have to eat, don't you?"

"Sure, of course I do," she said hesitantly.

"Is your mother home?"

"No, I'm here alone."

He sounded even more determined.

"Well then, it should be fine. If you study for the test now like a good girl, I can pick you up around seven. Then we'll have dinner together and I'll drive you straight home afterward. Surely there can't be any harm in that. And you'll have time to study, too."

He sounded so anxious that she felt compelled to say yes. But what were they going to talk about? At the same time, the invitation to go out to a restaurant was tempting. She could count on one hand the number of times she had gone out to eat. The last time was during a disastrous vacation the previous summer. Her mother had rented a car for a week and they took the boat to Oskarshamn so they could drive around Skåne and stay in youth hostels. It poured the whole time, and her mother drank every single day. On the last evening they went to a Chinese restaurant, and her mother got to talking to a group of Danish tourists. They drank a lot and started making a ruckus. Her mother got so drunk that she fell off her chair and pulled the whole tablecloth down with her. Fanny wanted to sink right through the floor.

She sat down at the kitchen table with her math books, wondering which restaurant they would go to. As long as it wasn't too fancy. What was she going to wear? Now she really couldn't concentrate on her math homework. Why had she said yes? Why was he inviting her out? Even though these thoughts were whirling around in her mind, she couldn't help feeling flattered.

Suddenly she heard keys rattling in the lock and then her mother's voice in the entryway.

"All right, Spot. Good dog. What dirty paws you have! Where's the towel?"

Fanny stayed where she was at the table without saying a word. She counted off the seconds: 1, 2, 3, 4 . . .

Then it came. Four seconds this time.

"Fanny. *Fanny!*"

Slowly she stood up.

"What is it?" she called.

"Could you come and help me, please? My back hurts. Could you rinse off Spot? He's so filthy."

Fanny took the dog by the scruff of his neck and led him to the bathroom.

Her mother kept on chattering. She was clearly having one of her "up" days.

"We walked all the way out to Strandgärdet. I met a nice lady with a poodle. They just moved in. The dog's name is Salomon—can you imagine that? Spot really liked him. We took off their leashes, and they both went into the water, even though it's so cold. That's why he's so filthy, from rolling in the dirt afterward. God, I'm hungry. Did you go grocery shopping?"

"No, Mamma. I just got home from school. We have a math test, and I need to study."

As usual, her mother wasn't listening. Fanny heard her opening and closing cupboards in the kitchen.

"Don't we have anything in the freezer? Oh, look, this is great: fish casserole. I need to eat. How long does it have to be in the oven? Forty minutes. Good God, I'll starve to death. Oh, I really have to pee. Oooh."

She came rushing into the bathroom and sat down to pee while Fanny resolutely rinsed off the dog's dirty paws. Why did her mother always have to announce all her needs loud and clear so that everyone would know how she felt at every second? Her head was pounding with irritation.

"Make sure you dry him off properly so he won't catch cold," said her mother as she wiped off her crotch.

"Yes, Mamma."

How wonderful it would be if her mother showed the same concern for her daughter once in a while.

When Fanny came out of the bathroom, her mother was lying on the sofa with her eyes closed.

"Are you tired?"

"Yes, I need to rest for a while before going to work. Could you put the casserole in the oven when it's preheated?"

"Okay."

She sat down in the kitchen. Her mother seemed to have fallen asleep. *She acts like a big baby,* thought Fanny as she set the table. It was four o'clock. She now had three hours left. Two to study, she hoped, and one to get ready.

"What are you going to eat?" asked her mother when Fanny put the casserole on the table.

"Nothing. I'm not hungry yet. I'll fix something later."

"All right," said her mother, who already seemed to be thinking about something else.

Fanny was on the verge of telling her about the fun theater performance they had seen at school, but she could see that her mother wouldn't be able to concentrate enough to listen. Just as well to keep quiet.

His disappointment over the tape was still bothering Knutas as he drove the short distance home in the evening.

He shivered in the ice-cold car. Lina was always complaining about the fact that he stubbornly insisted on keeping the old Benz, even though they could afford a new car. So far he had managed to fend off her ideas about buying a new one. It was too expensive and too much trouble to have two cars, and besides, there wasn't room for more than one outside their house. And he would have a hard time giving up his Mercedes—there were too many memories and experiences attached to these comfortable old seats. It was as if he and the car felt a mutual affection for each other.

When he parked outside their house, he saw lights on in all the windows. A good sign; it meant that everyone was home. He was looking forward to a peaceful evening at home, but he found anything but an idyllic family scene when he opened the front door.

"Like hell I will! I don't give a shit about what she says!"

Nils pounded up the stairs and slammed his door. Petra was sitting at the kitchen table. Lina was standing at the stove with her back turned, clattering the pots and pans. He could see from the way she stood that she was angry.

"What's going on?"

Knutas asked the question even before he took off his coat.

His wife turned around. Her throat was flushed, and her hair was sticking out in all directions.

"Don't talk to me. It's been a hell of a day."

"So what have you two been up to?" asked Knutas, patting his daughter on the head. She instantly leapt up from her chair.

"What have the two of *us* been up to?" she shot back at him. "You should be asking what *he's* been up to. My so-called brother!"

And then she also pounded up the stairs.

"I had an awful day at work, and this is more than I can stand," said Lina. "You're going to have to deal with it."

"Did something bad happen?"

"We'll talk about it later."

He hung up his coat, took off his shoes, and then took the stairs in a couple of bounds. He summoned both children to the bedroom and sat down on the bed with them.

"Okay, tell me what's going on."

"Well, we were supposed to help set the table, but first we had to empty the dishwasher while Mamma cooked," said Nils. "I took out the silverware basket and started emptying it. But then Petra came and said that she wanted to do it."

"That's not what happened!"

"Quiet! I'm talking right now. That *is* what happened. You yanked it out of my hands even though I had already started."

Petra began to cry.

"Is that true?" asked Knutas patiently, turning to his daughter.

"Yes, but he always gets to do the silverware basket, just because it's easier. I thought it was my turn. I wanted to trade jobs, but he wouldn't. Then Mamma got mad and said that we should stop fighting and then Nils said that I was stupid."

Nils's face flushed with indignation.

"Yes, but I'd already started! You can't just come and yank it away from me! And then Mamma started yelling at me that it was all my fault!"

Knutas turned to his daughter.

"I agree that you can't just come and take away the silverware basket if Nils has already started to empty it. At the same time, Nils, you need to take turns when you empty the dishwasher from now on. And keep in mind that your mother is tired, and it's not much fun for her to listen to you fighting when she's trying to cook. And don't call your sister stupid, Nils."

"Okay, I'm sorry," he said sullenly.

Knutas put his arms around both children and gave them a hug. Petra relented, but Nils was still mad and pulled away.

"Come on, it wasn't that bad."

"Leave me alone," snapped Nils, giving his father an angry glare.

Knutas took Nils aside, and after some persuasion, his son reluctantly agreed to come downstairs for dinner.

Lina looked tired and worn out.

"So what happened?" asked Knutas when peace had once again settled over the household.

"Oh, we had a problem at work. I'll tell you later."

"But we want to hear about it, too," objected Petra.

"I don't know. . . . It's such an awful story," cautioned Lina.

"Please, Mamma. Tell us."

"Well, okay. A woman who was supposed to give birth to her first child came in this morning with labor pains. Everything looked fine, but when she started to push, we couldn't get the baby out. Anita thought we should give the mother an epidural to ease the contractions, but I wanted to wait."

Tears welled up in her eyes as she talked. Knutas reached for her hand under the table.

"Then the baby's heartbeat suddenly got fainter, so we had to do an emergency cesarean. But it was too late. The baby died. I feel like it was my fault."

"Of course it wasn't your fault. You did the best you could," Knutas assured her.

"Oh, that's so sad. Poor Mamma," said Petra, trying to console her.

"I'm not the one you should feel sorry for. I'm going upstairs to lie down for a while." Lina gave a big sigh and got up from the table.

"Shall I come with you?" asked Knutas.

"No, I'd rather be alone."

Usually her work was a source of great joy for Lina, but when things went wrong, she was very hard on herself. She would go over and over everything that had happened, brooding about what they could have done differently, whether they could have done this instead of that.

It wasn't really so strange, thought Knutas. She had to deal with life and death all day long. Just as he did.

WEDNESDAY, NOVEMBER 21

Pia Dahlström was a tall, dark, and very beautiful woman. Completely unlike her parents, both in appearance and demeanor. She was wearing a jacket, black pants, and high heels. Her hair was pinned up in a knot. She had arrived early because she had to leave that same morning. It was only 7:00 A.M., and police headquarters was still deserted.

Knutas had offered her coffee, which he had taken the trouble to make himself. It was rare that anyone bothered to make real coffee, even though the coffeemaker stood right next to the dreary office coffee machine. They chatted while they waited for the coffee to brew. She reminded him of Audrey Hepburn in the old movies from the fifties. Her big, dark eyes were rimmed with dark eyeliner, just like the movie star's eyes.

When the coffee was done brewing, she sat down on his visitor's sofa.

"Could you describe your relationship with your father?" Knutas asked, thinking that he sounded like a psychiatrist.

"We weren't close at all. His alcoholism prevented that. He started drinking more and more the older I got, or maybe I just noticed it more as I grew up."

She gave her beautiful head a slight shake. Not a strand of hair was out of place.

"He didn't care about me," she went on. "He never came to watch any of my riding lessons or gymnastics routines. Mamma was always the one who went to the PTA meetings and the quarterly teacher conferences. I can't remember him ever making a single sacrifice or doing anything for my sake. No, I really couldn't care less about him."

"I can understand that," said Knutas.

"You speak Gotland Swedish, but you sound like a Dane," she said with a smile.

"I'm married to a Dane, so I guess some of it has rubbed off. How did you react when you heard about your father's death?"

"I just felt empty inside. If he hadn't been murdered, he probably would have ended up drinking himself to death. When I was younger I was angry at him, but that feeling is long gone. He chose the life he was living. He used to have everything: a stimulating job, a family, and a house. But he chose booze over me and my mother."

"When did you last have contact with him?"

"The same day I passed my school exams," she said without changing expression.

"But that must be more than fifteen years ago," exclaimed Knutas in surprise.

"Seventeen, to be exact."

"How could it be that the two of you haven't had any contact since then?"

"It's very simple. He never called, and I never did, either."

"And you didn't have any contact with him after the divorce?"

"Sometimes I would spend the weekends with him, but it wasn't much fun. The fact that I was there didn't stop him from drinking. He never had any ideas about what we should do except stay in his apartment, and then his buddies would come over. They'd drink without paying any attention to me. Watch the races and soccer games on TV, or sometimes they'd sit there and look at girlie magazines. It was disgusting. Usually I'd end up going back home after an hour. Then I stopped going there at all."

"What about your relationship with your mother?"

"It's fine. I suppose it could be better, but I think it's at an acceptable level," she said, sounding as if she were talking about stocks and bonds.

She scratched her collarbone and her bra strap was visible for a moment. It was a glossy gold with a nice embroidered edge.

She's undoubtedly just as perfect underneath, thought Knutas, and then he was annoyed with himself for letting her femininity affect him.

"So how are you doing now?" he asked, to change the subject.

"Fine, thanks. I work at the municipal library in Malmö, and I like my job. I have lots of friends, both in Malmö and in Copenhagen."

"Do you live alone?"

"Yes."

"Do you know if your father had any enemies? You haven't had contact with him in so many years, but something from the distant past might also be important."

A frown appeared on her face. "Not that I can think of."

Not much more came out of the conversation. When Pia Dahlström left, a faint trace of her perfume lingered.

Several Months Earlier

"Are we going to eat here?"

She couldn't hide her disappointment. She had thought that they were going to a restaurant.

"That's right. I borrowed an apartment from a friend. The food is ready upstairs. Come on."

He led the way through the front entrance. The building was located on one of those posh streets near Södertorg, inside the ring wall. There was no elevator, so they had to trudge their way up to the fifth floor. When they reached the top landing, she was out of breath and had a growing sense of uneasiness in her chest. She looked at his trousers with the sharp creases. He suddenly seemed so old. What did he want with her here, anyway?

She had an urge to turn around and run back down the stairs, but then he took her hand.

"Wait till you see how nice it is."

He fumbled with the keys.

The apartment was the biggest one she had ever seen. It was on the top floor, with thick beams in the ceiling and a view of the sea. The living room was enormous, with a polished hardwood floor and big, colorful paintings on the walls. In one corner stood a table that was set with plates and glasses. He hurried over to light the candles in a candelabra.

"Come on," he said eagerly. "Come over here and have a look."

They went out on the balcony, which had a panoramic view. She could see the water and part of the harbor, the town, with its labyrinth of buildings, and the tower of the cathedral.

"Let's have some champagne."

He made it sound so natural that she felt very grown up. He came back with a bottle and two glasses. He eagerly filled them.

"Cheers."

She didn't dare refuse. Cautiously she took a sip. It tickled her nose but didn't taste very good. She hadn't tried much alcohol before. Just a couple of times when her mother had urged her to have some wine on a Saturday evening so that she wouldn't have to drink alone. Red wine tasted horrible. This was better. She took another sip.

"So, what do you think? Isn't this grand?" he said, putting his arm around her as if it were the most natural thing in the world. It made her feel uncomfortable. She didn't know how to react.

He drank another toast with her.

"Drink up, little lady. Then we'll go in and eat."

For dinner they first had toast with some kind of topping. She ate carefully, watching him to see what he did. He poured the rest of the champagne and clinked glasses with her again and again. She took small sips but soon began to feel dizzy. The conversation kept stalling. He asked her a number of questions but mostly talked about himself. Boasted about all the amazing trips he had made to exotic places in the world. As if he wanted to impress her.

She listened but said very little. Reluctantly she began to relax. It was wonderful to be sitting in such a beautiful room, feeling the warmth from the candles. To be eating such an elegant dinner with muted music in the background. The main course was pork tenderloin with saffron rice. And red wine with the food, much better than the wine she'd tasted at home. She drank the whole glass. He kept on talking as Fanny devoted herself to studying the movements of his lips. She started getting the giggles.

"Did you enjoy the food?" he asked as he stood up and started clearing away the plates.

"Yes, thank you. It was great." She snickered.

"That's good."

He looked so satisfied that she started laughing even more. To think he could be so pleased just because she was happy.

"Would you like some coffee? Or maybe you don't drink coffee?"

She shook her head.

"Where's the bathroom?"

"It's out in the hall, to the right. It says 'WC' on the door."

He pointed, eager to show her the way. She was in such a hurry to pee that she felt as if she would burst.

The bathroom was just as elegant as the rest of the apartment. It had a light dimmer. She played with the light switch, moving it back and forth. The bathroom was sparkling clean, and it smelled nice. Everything looked new and unused. The toilet paper had a pattern, and it was softer than what she was used to. She smiled at herself in the mirror, then giggled. To think she was allowed to enjoy all this luxury.

When she went back, he had dimmed the lights and was sitting on the sofa. On the low coffee table stood two glasses of wine and a tray with candles of varying sizes.

"Come here," he said softly.

She felt wary, didn't really know what he wanted. She sat down cautiously, some distance away from him.

"You're so beautiful. Do you know that?" he said gently.

He moved closer. Took her hand and played with her fingers. She hardly dared look at him. He put one hand on her leg. It felt warm and heavy through her jeans.

He left it there, not moving.

"You're so beautiful," he whispered.

Cautiously he tugged at a strand of her hair.

"And you have such lovely hair, black and shiny and thick."

He leaned back and stared at her.

"Your body . . . it's perfect. Do you know how sexy you are?"

She felt anxious and uncomfortable but couldn't utter a sound. No one had ever said anything like that to her before.

Suddenly he pulled her close and kissed her. She didn't know what to do, just sat there, motionless. Her head was spinning from the wine. His mouth pressed harder against hers, and he tried to open her lips with his tongue. She let him do it. His hands began groping under her shirt, sliding up toward her breasts. She felt his weight as he bent over her. Then his hand reached one of her breasts. She was frightened by his reaction. He moaned and whimpered. Started getting rough, tugging and pulling at her bra. His tongue whisked around in her mouth. Suddenly her thoughts were crystal clear. The only thing she knew was that she had to get away.

"Wait," she said. "Wait."

He didn't seem to hear but just kept tearing at her clothes.

"Wait a minute. I have to go to the bathroom," she added to make him stop.

"But I just want to touch you a little," he cajoled.

"Please, wait."

He put his hands on her back. They were sweaty now, he was sweaty all over. They sat motionless for a moment, and she listened to him breathing hard.

Then he loosened his grip. It seemed as if he were giving up.

He held her away from him and fixed his eyes on her breasts.

"Do you know how beautiful you are?" he whispered. "What are you doing to me?"

He began groping her again. Even rougher than before.

"No," she said. "I don't want to."

"Just a little. You can just give me a little."

He pushed her down onto the sofa, pulled down her zipper, and took a firm grip on her jeans, pulling them off with a jerk. They were so tight that her panties came off with them. She was completely exposed and realized that she didn't have a chance. She stopped struggling and lay still. He pushed her thighs apart.

Then she started to cry.

"I don't want to," she screamed. "Stop it! *Stop it!*"

All of a sudden he seemed to come to his senses. He let go of her.

When he drove her home, he didn't say a word the whole way. She didn't, either.

Against all odds, Emma had agreed to meet him for lunch. Johan had finished the interview with the county governor, which meant that he was free for the rest of the day. He was supposed to fly home in the morning.

They had agreed to meet at his hotel room. She didn't dare go anywhere else.

Grenfors had called to talk about the story Johan had been assigned to do back in Stockholm; it sounded totally uninteresting.

After the phone conversation, he sat in an armchair and looked at his watch. He had twenty minutes until Emma arrived. Should he order lunch now, to get that out of the way? It was probably a good idea. If the food was delivered faster, they would have more time to themselves. He grabbed the menu and scanned the selections: toast, Caesar salad, sole on a bed of spinach for two hundred and forty kronor—scandalous. Hamburgers with pommes frites—couldn't they just write French fries for once?

What would Emma like? What did she eat? Shrimp, shellfish—no, not shrimp soup. Pasta Bolognese—a fancy way of saying ordinary spaghetti with meat sauce. Something light, but not too light. But maybe she was super-hungry. How about an omelet?

He started to sweat. He would have to take a shower. Without making up his mind, he punched the number for room service. What did they recommend? What's fast, good, not too heavy, and not too expensive? Meatballs with cream sauce and lingonberries—sure, maybe not very elegant, but what the hell.

He ordered two portions and then tore off his clothes. Fifteen minutes left. Would the food come on time, or would they be interrupted in the midst of this longed-for rendezvous? At least *he* had been longing for it—as for her, he had no idea. What if she had agreed to meet him just to tell him that it was over?

As he got out of the shower, there was a knock on the door. No, it couldn't be . . . He needed to get dressed, comb his hair, and put on some aftershave. He stopped. Or was it their food? He crept over to the door with water dripping all over.

"Yes?"

"Room service," said a voice on the other side of the door. Relief flooded over him. Why did everything feel as if it were a matter of life and death?

The waiter started setting the table. No, no, that wasn't necessary, thanks. He couldn't offer him a tip, standing there like that in his underwear with a meager towel held up in front of him as a shield. Two minutes left. He threw on some pants and a clean shirt. Then it was twelve ten and she hadn't arrived. Time for a panic attack. What if she didn't come? Had he missed a text message on his cell phone? It was on the table. No, no messages. She had to come, damn it. He looked at himself in the mirror—pale, helpless, at the mercy of his stormy emotions and the despair that would inevitably flood over him if it turned out that she had changed her mind.

There was a knock on the door. He took such a deep breath that he saw stars. He shook his head. To think he couldn't take control of his own life.

It was unreal seeing her standing there in the corridor. With her dark eyes and rosy cheeks, she looked shamelessly perky and healthy. She smiled at him, and that was enough to make the floor disappear from under his feet.

"Mmmm . . . that smells good. Meatballs," she said without much enthusiasm.

How could he be so hopelessly stupid? Offering a teacher meatballs. That's what they probably had every day at school. What an idiot. They sat down at the table.

"Would you like a beer?"

"Sure, thanks."

What an absurd situation. Here they sat, each of them with a plate of food on the table, in a hotel room with cloudy skies outside, and it was the first time they had seen each other in almost a month. She had put on a little weight, he noticed. It suited her.

"How are you?"

The question sounded as artificial as the flowers on the table.

"Fine, thanks," she replied without looking up from the food. "What about you?"

"Not too bad."

The meatballs felt like cardboard in his mouth.

Silence.

They looked up from their plates at the same time and finished chewing with their eyes fixed on each other.

"Actually, I feel like hell," said Johan.

"Me, too."

"Miserable, in fact. I feel sick all the time."

"Same here. I keep feeling as if I'm going to throw up."

"The whole situation is rotten."

"Rotten to the core," she said, and her eyes danced.

They burst out laughing, but stopped abruptly. She took another bite of her food.

Johan leaned toward her, earnest now.

"I feel as if I'm only half alive. You know—I do all the usual things that I'm supposed to do. Get out of bed in the morning, have breakfast, go to work, but nothing is real. Everything seems to be happening somewhere else. I keep thinking that it's going to get better, but that'll never happen."

She carefully wiped her mouth with the napkin and got up from the table. She had a solemn look on her face. The only thing he could do was sit still. Quietly she pulled him up from his chair. They were almost the same height. She put her arms around him, kissed him on the neck. He felt her warm breath in his ear.

Her strong, hard body against his. They tumbled onto the bed, and she pressed herself against him, their legs intertwined, their arms wrapped tightly around each other. Her lips were soft and warm, her hair smelled like apple. He felt tears stinging his eyelids. Embracing her was like coming home.

He didn't really know what he did, or what she did; he knew only that he didn't want it to end.

It turned out that Martin Kihlgård from the national police did come after all. He was accompanied by Hans Hansson, who was a gaunt and unobtrusive man, compared with his boisterous colleague. Everyone in the criminal division welcomed Kihlgård with open arms. He was a big man whose clothes were always in disarray, but he was a respected and capable detective. There was much backslapping and handshaking all around. Karin Jacobsson gave him such a long hug that Knutas felt a pang of the same irritation he had felt last summer. Those two had gotten along so well that Knutas was jealous, even though he would never admit it out loud. Kihlgård was a big lug, but it was obvious that Jacobsson appreciated his outgoing personality.

When he caught sight of Knutas, Kihlgård's jovial smile got even bigger.

"Well, hello, Knutie," he shouted heartily, slapping him on the back. "How's it going, old boy?"

He sounds like Captain Haddock in the Tintin comics, thought Knutas as he returned the smile. He found it very annoying that Kihlgård had suddenly decided to call him Knutie.

They sat down in Knutas's office and started reviewing the case. No more than ten minutes passed before Kihlgård began grumbling about food.

"Aren't we going to have lunch?"

"Of course, it's almost time for it," said Jacobsson promptly. "Why don't we go to the Cloister? Anders's friend owns the place, and they have great food," she explained, turning to both officers from National.

"That sounds excellent," growled Kihlgård. "You get us a good table, okay, Knutie?"

Lunch was pleasant, in any event. Leif gave them a window table with a view of Saint Per's Ruin. Hans Hansson had never been to Gotland before, and he was impressed.

"It's even more beautiful than in the pictures we see. You live in a regular fairy tale city over here. I hope you appreciate it."

"Normally we don't think much about it," said Jacobsson with a smile. "But a trip to the mainland is always a good reminder. Then I realize how beautiful it is when I come back home."

"Same here," Knutas agreed. "I'd have a hard time living anywhere else."

They ate the grilled lamb and root-vegetable casserole with gusto. Kihlgård had no time to talk while he was eating, except once when he asked for more bread. Knutas was reminded that his colleague apparently had an insatiable appetite. The man was always eating, at all times of the day and night.

The restaurant was furnished in an old-fashioned style, with lighted candles and linen tablecloths on all the tables. The cozy atmosphere was particularly welcome now that it was overcast and cold outdoors. Leif surprised them with the restaurant's specialty, a homemade chocolate cake, with their coffee. Then he sat down to join them for a moment.

"How nice to have new lunch customers. Are you staying for a while?"

"We'll have to wait and see," said Kihlgård. "This is an amazingly delicious cake."

"Please come again, anytime. We're always happy to see all of our customers."

"I suppose it must be difficult in the wintertime."

"Yes, it's tough running a restaurant here that's open all year round. But we've managed to do all right, at least so far. Well, don't let me disturb you anymore."

Leif stood up and left.

"We've gone over the details of Dahlström's life, but what's the situation with alcoholics here on the island, in general?" asked Kihlgård. "For instance, how many are there?"

"I would estimate there are about thirty or so truly hard-core alcoholics, meaning individuals who drink all the time and have no job," replied Jacobsson.

"So they're homeless?"

"We actually don't have any homeless here, like you do in the city. Most of them have their own apartment or else they live in municipal housing for addicts scattered here and there."

"What about violent crime among this sort of people?"

"Occasionally they kill each other when they're drunk. We have a couple of murders a year, on average, that are drug or alcohol related. But usually that happens among the drug addicts. The alcoholics are generally harmless."

It was about time to go back to the office. Knutas waved to Leif to get the bill. The wonderful chocolate cake was on the house.

After seeing Emma again, Johan had a longing for fresh air. He took a walk to distract his thoughts.

Almedalen Park was quiet and deserted. The wet asphalt of the public footpath through the grass glittered in the glow of the street-lights, and he could hear the low quacking of the ducks in the pond, even though they were barely visible in the dark. He turned onto the shoreline pathway that ran from Visby all the way out to Snäckgärds Beach, two miles north. Here the wind picked up, and he turned up the collar of his jacket against the chill. Not a soul was in sight. The waves rolled in to shore, and seagulls shrieked. A large passenger ferry with its navigation lights shining through the darkness was approaching Visby Harbor.

He thought about Emma and couldn't comprehend how he had managed without her for so long. All his feelings had now been reawakened, and he realized that it would be rough to go on waiting. Even though their relationship had now entered a new phase. The anxious waiting was over, and he knew how she felt about him. And knowing this made him feel both calm and strong.

What he needed to do now was to come up with some good story ideas so that he could come back to the island as soon as possible. It was harder for Emma to find an excuse to go to Stockholm.

He passed the Maiden Tower, one of the ring wall's many defensive structures. There was an old legend about this particular tower. In the fourteenth century, King Valdemar Atterdag of Denmark was attempting to capture Visby and strip the city of its riches. A young woman helped him to gain access through one of the gates in the ring wall. The woman had fallen in love with the king, and he had promised to marry her and take her back to Denmark if she opened the gate for him and his men. She did as he asked, and the Danes then plundered Visby. But the king broke his promise and left the young woman to her fate after she had done what he asked. When her role was discovered, the townspeople punished her by walling her alive in the Maiden Tower. According to legend, her cries for help can still be heard. As Johan walked past in the dark, he could easily imagine her inside. The wind was howling, and perhaps it was her desperate cries that he heard in the wind. Even though he was freezing, he was enjoying the weather.

As he passed the Botanical Gardens, the rocks of Strandgärdet appeared, and in the distance shone the lights from the hospital.

Suddenly he heard a shout. A very real shout.

He stepped forward into the darkness and discovered an elderly woman lying on an embankment with a yapping terrier at her side.

"What happened?"

"I fell down and can't get up," complained the woman, her voice quavering. "My foot hurts terribly."

"Wait, let me help you," Johan reassured her, taking a firm grip on her arm. "Careful now, stand up slowly."

"Thank you so much. That was awful," moaned the woman as she got to her feet.

"Are you hurt? Can you put any weight on your foot?"

"Yes, it'll be fine. You're not the kind of man who mugs old women, are you?"

Johan couldn't help smiling. He wondered how he must look, in his black jacket, unshaven, and with his hair disheveled.

"You don't have to worry. My name is Johan Berg," he said.

"Thank goodness. I've had enough drama for one day. My name is Astrid Persson. Do you think you could walk me home? I live over on Backgatan, up there across from the hospital."

She pointed with a gloved finger.

"Of course," said Johan, taking her by the arm. In his other hand he held the little terrier's leash, and together they set off toward Backgatan.

Astrid Persson absolutely insisted on inviting him in for a cup of cocoa. Her husband, Bertil, had started to get worried, and he thanked Johan warmly for his help.

"You're not from Gotland, are you?"

"No, I'm here on an assignment. I'm a journalist for Swedish TV in Stockholm."

"Is that right? Are you here to report on the murder?"

"You mean the murder of Henry Dahlström?"

"Yes, exactly. Do you know anything about who did it?"

"No, we hardly know anything at all about the case. The police aren't saying much. At least so far."

"Ah, so that's how it is."

Bertil slurped his cocoa.

"He was a nice guy, that Dahlström."

"Did you know him?"

"Sure, of course I did. He helped me with some carpentry. He built our carport, and he did a really good job."

"He also did some work on the dormer window," his wife added. "He worked as a carpenter in his younger days, you know. Before he became a photographer."

"Is that right? And he managed to do carpentry work, in spite of his alcohol problem?"

"Oh yes, he did fine. It was as if he pulled himself together while he was working. I did notice that he smelled of liquor one time, but it didn't affect his work. He did the job he was supposed to do, showed up when he promised he would, and so on. Yes, he did an excellent job. And he was pleasant, too, not much of a talker but nice."

Astrid nodded in agreement. Her husband had carefully taped up her foot, which she was now resting on a stool.

"How long ago was this?" asked Johan.

"Well, let's see. We had the carport built several years ago. When was it?"

He looked at his wife.

"Four, maybe five years ago? And the dormer window was done last year."

"Did he help other people with this sort of work?"

"Sure he did. I heard about him from a friend in the local folklore society."

"Have you told the police about this?"

Bertil Persson looked embarrassed. He set his cocoa cup on the table.

"No, why should we? What does it matter that he was here and did a bit of carpentry work? Why would the police care about that?"

He leaned toward Johan and lowered his voice to speak confidentially.

"And besides, we paid him under the table. He was living on welfare and that's how he wanted it. You won't say anything, will you?"

"I hardly think the police would care about how he was paid, given the situation. They're conducting a murder investigation, and this would be important information for them to have. I can't keep it to myself."

Bertil raised his eyebrows.

"Really? But then we risk getting caught for hiring an illegal worker."

He looked upset. Astrid Persson put her hand on his arm.

"As I said, I don't think the police will take that very seriously," said Johan.

He stood up. He wanted to get out of there as quickly as possible.

"But I told you this in confidence," exclaimed Bertil Persson, looking as if he thought his days were numbered.

"I'm sorry, but there's nothing I can do."

The man grabbed Johan's arm, and his voice took on an ingratiating tone.

"But it can't be that important, can it? My wife and I are members of the church—it would be embarrassing if this got out. Can't we forget about the whole thing?"

"I'm sorry, but no," snapped Johan, pulling his arm away, a bit more brusquely than he intended.

He hurried out of the building after saying a rather strained goodbye.

Knutas sank onto his desk chair, holding what he hoped was his last cup of coffee for the day—at least if his stomach had anything to say about the matter. The preliminary autopsy report from the ME showed, exactly as expected, that Henry Dahlström had died as the result of contusions to the back of his head caused by a hammer. The perpetrator had delivered a series of blows, using both the blunt and claw end of the hammer.

The time of death was probably late on Monday night, November 12, or possibly early Tuesday morning. This coincided well with the circumstances known to the police. All indications were that the murder had occurred after 10:30 P.M., when Dahlström's neighbor heard him go down to the basement.

Knutas started meticulously filling his pipe as he continued studying the photos and reading the description of the victim's wounds.

Solving a homicide was like solving a crossword puzzle. Rarely was the solution discovered through direct means. Instead, it required leaving certain details alone for a day while concentrating on others. When he later returned to what he had set aside, new patterns would often emerge. And the same thing happened when he did crossword puzzles: He frequently found it very surprising that a particular problem had caused him so much trouble. When he looked at it again, the solution seemed crystal clear.

Knutas went over to the window, opened it slightly, and lit his pipe.

Then there were the witnesses. Dahlström's friends had nothing of any direct value to report. They had largely just confirmed what the police already knew. Nor had anything new emerged that might reinforce their suspicions about Johnsson, so the prosecutor had decided to release the man. He was still going to be charged with theft, but there was no reason to keep him in custody.

Knutas had practically ruled out the idea that Johnsson was the guilty party. On the other hand, he was giving a good deal of thought to the man named Örjan. An unpleasant type. He'd been in jail for aggravated assault and battery. And he seemed capable of murder.

When Örjan was interviewed he had denied it, of course, claiming that he hardly knew Dahlström. And this had been confirmed by others in their circle. But that didn't preclude the possibility that he might have killed Dahlström.

Arne Haukas, the PE teacher who lived in the same section of the building as Dahlström, had been questioned about his whereabouts on the night of the murder. He claimed that he had simply gone out jogging, as usual. He explained the late hour by saying that he'd been watching a movie on TV, and so he had postponed his run. There was a lighted ski trail nearby, so there was no problem with running at night. He hadn't seen or heard anything unusual.

Knutas's ruminations were interrupted by the phone ringing. It was Johan Berg, who told him about the carpentry work that Dahlström

had done for Bertil and Astrid Persson on Backgatan. Knutas was surprised.

"Strange that we didn't hear about this before. Do you have the
names of anyone else he did work for?"

"No, the old man wasn't happy when I said that I'd have to tell the
police. But you could check with the local folklore society—that's
where he heard about Dahlström."

"All right. Anything else?"

"No."

"Thanks for calling."

"You're welcome."

Knutas put down the phone, thinking about what he'd learned. So
Dahlström had done work for people in their homes. The information opened a whole new avenue. In his mind he sent Johan words of
gratitude.

Fanny went straight home from school. At the door she met her
mother's boyfriend, Jack. He glanced at her but didn't even bother to
say hi. He just hurried past. The door to the apartment wasn't locked,
and Fanny realized at once that something was wrong. She peeked in
the kitchen, but it was empty.

She found her mother stretched out on the sofa under a blanket.
The blanket had slipped to one side, revealing that she was naked. On
the table stood empty beer and wine bottles next to an ashtray filled
with cigarette butts.

"Mamma," said Fanny, shaking her by the shoulder. "Wake up!"

Not a hint of life.

"Mamma," Fanny repeated with a sob rising in her throat. She
shook her harder. "Mamma, please wake up."

Finally her mother opened her eyes and said in a slurred voice, "I
have to throw up. Get me a bucket."

"Which one?"

"Bring the one under the kitchen counter. The red one."

Fanny dashed out to the kitchen to get the bucket, but she didn't
find it in time. Her mother threw up all over the rug.

She helped her mother into the bedroom, pulled the covers over her, and set the bucket next to the bed. Spot had started licking up the vomit. She chased him away and then used some paper towels to wipe up the worst of it. But she could see that the rug would have to be washed. She ran hot water in the bathtub, poured in some laundry soap, and then lowered the rug into the water. She left it to soak in the tub while she cleaned up the living room, collecting all the bottles, emptying the ashtray, and airing out the place. When she was finished, she sank onto the sofa.

Spot whimpered. The poor thing needed to go out. She seriously considered calling her mother's sister to tell her that she couldn't handle things anymore. But she decided that she didn't dare; her mother would be furious. Yet what would happen if she kept on drinking like this? She risked losing her job, and then what?

Fanny didn't have the energy to think about that. Soon she wouldn't have the energy for anything at all.

THURSDAY, NOVEMBER 22

The aroma of freshly brewed coffee and warm cinnamon rolls swept over Knutas as he stepped into the conference room the next morning. Someone had gone to a lot of trouble. He glanced at Kihlgård. It must have been him, of course. Everyone sitting at the table was in a lively mood. Jacobsson was joking with Wittberg, who had evidently been out partying last night. Knutas surmised that he was entertaining Jacobsson with a story about one of his girlfriends. He had a bottle of Coca-Cola in front of him, which was a clear sign that he had a hangover.

Kihlgård and Smittenberg were both leaning over a newspaper. The prosecutor was holding a pen in his hand, while Kihlgård was holding a roll, naturally. Good Lord, they were working on a crossword puzzle! Norrby and Sohlman were standing at the window, looking out at the rain mixed with hail and discussing the weather.

It was a virtual cocktail party. Incredible what effect fresh-baked goods could have.

Knutas took his usual place at one end of the table and loudly cleared his throat, but no one took any notice.

"All right, everyone," he ventured. "Shall we start?"

No reaction.

He gave Kihlgård a surly look. This was so typical of that darn fellow. To come here, all sweet and nice, bringing rolls and causing a disruption. Knutas had nothing against people enjoying themselves at work, but there was a time and a place. Besides, he was in a foul mood after having a big fight with Lina that morning.

It started with her complaining that clothes were scattered on the floor, that the cat hadn't been fed, and that he hadn't run the dishwasher last night, even though it was full and he was the last one to go to bed. Then she found out that, in spite of a solemn promise, he had forgotten to buy a new floorball stick for Nils, who had broken his old one, and he had a game to play tonight. That turned out to be the last straw. She blew up.

The noise in the conference room forced Knutas to get up from his chair and clap his hands.

"All right, could I have your attention?" he shouted. "Shall we get to work? Or maybe you've decided to devote the day to social activities?"

"An excellent idea," exclaimed Kihlgård. "Why don't we stay in, rent a good video, and make some popcorn? It's such awful weather today—I'm freeeeeezing."

His voice rose to a falsetto. He bent his forearms up and shook his palms at the same time as he wiggled his hips. Given the impressive bulk of his body, the dance was extremely funny. What a clown. Even Knutas couldn't help smiling a bit.

He started by telling them about the work Dahlström had done for payment under the table.

"How did we find this out?" asked Kihlgård.

"Actually it was that TV reporter, Johan Berg, who told me. The couple that lives on Backgatan didn't want to go to the police since it was a question of unreported payments."

"It's just amazing how people with money behave," exclaimed Jacobsson, whose expression had darkened as Knutas talked. "It's so damned wrong. People with high incomes who use illegal workers even though they could afford to pay them legitimately. And then when someone is murdered, they won't even go to the police because they're afraid of getting in trouble! That's about as low as it gets."

Her eyes were blazing as she glanced from one colleague to another.

"They can afford a lovely house and expensive vacations, but they won't pay their cleaning woman legally so that she could get insurance and retirement points and everything else that she's entitled to. They refuse to pay for that. They'll do everything to avoid paying taxes, without giving a thought to whether it's actually a crime. At the same time they expect free day-care centers to be provided for their children and a doctor to be available when they're sick, and they want the schools to offer good food. It's as if they can't see the connection between one thing and the other. It's so hopelessly stupid!"

Everyone at the table was looking at her in surprise. Even Kihlgård, who usually had some witty remark, didn't say a word. But maybe this was because his mouth was full of cinnamon roll, probably his third one.

"Take it easy, Karin," Knutas warned. "Spare us your diatribe."

"What do you mean? Don't you agree that it's damned wrong?"

Jacobsson glanced around the room, looking for sympathy.

"Do you have to turn everything into a political issue?" asked Knutas, sounding annoyed. "We're in the middle of a murder investigation here."

He deliberately turned away from her and looked at his other colleagues.

"So maybe we could go on now?"

Jacobsson didn't say another word, just sighed and shook her head.

"How did this couple get in touch with Dahlström?" asked Wittberg.

"Through friends of theirs who belong to the local folklore society. Apparently a number of people made use of his services."

"Maybe someone was unhappy with their garden shed," said Kihlgård with a snicker.

Knutas ignored his attempt at a joke and turned to Norrby.

"How's it going with the bank? Have you tracked down where the deposits came from?"

"Well, we've come to a dead end there. It's impossible to trace the money. Of course every bill has a serial number, but who keeps records of that? It's also impossible to find out who gave him the money since he made the deposit himself."

"Okay, then right now the important thing is to find out who hired Dahlström illegally. He could have been doing that kind of work for years. Strange that nobody he knew has said anything about it."

As Knutas left the meeting he had the distinct feeling that the issues associated with the murder were going to get much more complicated.

Johan's next meeting with Emma was about to occur much sooner than he had dared hope. The very next morning she called him at the hotel.

"I'm going to Stockholm tomorrow for a one-day conference, connected with my work."

"Are you kidding? Are we on the same flight?"

"No, I'm taking the boat. It was planned long ago."

"Does that mean that I can see you?"

"Yes. I wasn't thinking of staying overnight, but I can if I want to because there's a banquet in the evening. Teachers from all over the country are invited. I was planning to skip the banquet, but I can say that I've changed my mind and book a hotel room. That doesn't mean that I actually have to sleep there. . . ."

He couldn't believe his ears.

"Are you serious?"

She laughed.

"Would you like to have dinner together tomorrow night? Or are you busy?" she asked.

He thought for a moment.

"Let me see . . . Tomorrow night I was planning to stay home alone in front of the TV and eat chips, so I guess I won't be able to meet you. Unfortunately."

His heart was singing.

"But seriously—we could go to a fantastic new place in Söder. It's small and noisy, but the food is superb."

"That sounds great."

He put down the phone and clenched his hand in a fist, in a gesture of victory. Could it be that she had finally given in?

From the beginning Grenfors had doubted that *Regional News* should do a story about the murder of Henry Dahlström. In his view, it had just been a drunken fight. He was not alone. Many of his colleagues shared this opinion, and consequently they had settled for only a brief mention of the case so far.

If the editors decided not to report a story in the beginning, it was difficult to sell the idea later on. News stories were perishable goods. A story that was super-hot one day might seem musty the next. Four days had passed since Dahlström's body had been found, and that was an eternity in the news business. Grenfors didn't sound especially interested when Johan called him after lunch.

"So what's new about it?"

"Dahlström was doing odd jobs for people in their homes. Carpentry work and things like that. Getting paid under the table, of course."

"You don't say." Grenfors yawned audibly.

Johan could picture the editor checking the TT wire service on his computer screen as they talked.

"Someone deposited money into his bank account. Twice. Twenty-five thousand kronor each time."

"So they might have been payments that he was getting for work done illegally."

"Maybe. But there's a lot to report about the case, and we haven't done a single story on it yet," countered Johan. "Good Lord, a man literally had his head bashed in with a hammer in his darkroom. And this happened on little Gotland—don't forget that. All the other stations have reported it, but we've hardly said a word. Now it turns out that the victim was working illegally for people, and on top of that, mysterious deposits were made to his bank account. And we're the only ones who know about it. All indications are that this was not your ordinary drunken fight. It's in our territory, for God's sake, and we do such a shitty job of reporting on Gotland."

"Have the police confirmed the information?"

"Not the bank deposits," Johan admitted. "We found that out from a bank teller. The police refused to confirm whether it was true, but I'm convinced that it is. I know how Knutas reacts in this type of situation. But he did confirm the part about Dahlström working illegally."

"That might be enough. But today we're reporting on the gang rape prosecution in Botkyrka and the trial of the cop killer in Märsta. That's a hell of a lot of crime stories for one broadcast."

Johan lost his temper.

"I don't think we can wait on this. We've been dragging our feet on this story, and now we're the only ones who have the new information. The newspapers might have the story by tomorrow!"

"That's the chance we'll have to take. It's not really that interesting. Finish up your assignment today, and then I need you back here in the newsroom tomorrow. But we won't run the story tonight. It fits in better with the Friday broadcast. That's all the time I have right now. Bye."

Johan was fuming as he put down the phone. What a fucking attitude! Every other news program had the story about the trial and the gang rape, but they were the only ones with this news about the murder. Generally he respected Grenfors as an editor, in spite of his shortcomings. But sometimes it was impossible to understand the man. If only he were consistent in his journalistic approach, at least! But one day he could be so overzealous that he would hound the reporters relentlessly to get what he wanted for the broadcast. The next day he would be like this. And they would sit in endless meetings, discussing over and over how they could do a better job on their own news program.

Johan didn't mince words as he sat in the car on the way out to Gråbo, complaining about incompetent editors. His cameraman Peter was equally indignant. He was the one who had found out about the deposits to Dahlström's account. He had met a girl at a bar in Visby, and her sister was a teller in the bank where the deposits were made.

And now they ran the risk of being upstaged by the local press. Again.

Gråbo seemed dead and gloomy in the biting wind. The bleak weather didn't exactly invite outdoor activities. The cars in the parking lot bore witness to the fact that the people living there had limited incomes. Most of the Fords had at least ten years on them. An old Mazda hesitantly pulled out of its parking space and rattled off. At the recycling station, someone had toppled over a shopping cart from the ICA grocery store.

On their way to Dahlström's section of the building, they passed a low wooden structure that looked like a communal laundry room. One wall was plastered with wads of snuff, and the windows were covered with graffiti. The playground in front had a sandbox, swings, and worn-looking wooden benches. Not a kid was in sight.

They walked around to the back of the building, where Dahlström had lived. The blinds were closed, preventing any curiosity-seekers from looking inside. The surrounding property consisted mainly of an overgrown lawn, and the patio was nothing more than a piece of wooden fencing with worn patio furniture that had seen better days. There was a stack of used disposable grills. Leaning against a cinderblock wall was a rusty bicycle and an overflowing garbage bag that seemed to contain empty cans. A rickety fence with peeling paint faced the passageway that continued on toward the woods.

They decided to try talking to the neighbors.

At the fourth apartment they tried, someone finally answered the doorbell. A young guy wearing only boxer shorts peered at them, bleary-eyed with sleep. His hair was dyed black and stood straight up like a scrub brush. An earring gleamed from one ear.

"Hi, we're from Regional News in Stockholm. We'd like to know something about the man who lived downstairs, the one who was murdered."

"Come on in."

He showed them to the living room and motioned for them to have a seat on the couch, while he sat down on a Windsor chair.

"A horrible thing, that murder," he said.

"What was your opinion of Dahlström?" asked Johan.

"A decent old guy. Nothing wrong with him. It didn't bother me that he was an alcoholic, at least. Besides, he had periods when he didn't drink as much, and then he spent a lot of time working on his photos."

"Was that something everybody knew about? The fact that he took photographs?"

"Sure. He used that old bicycle storage room as his darkroom. He's had it for the six years that I've lived here."

The guy looked as if he had just graduated from high school. Johan asked him how old he was.

"Twenty-three," he replied. He had moved away from home when he turned seventeen.

"What kind of contact did you have with Dahlström?"

"We said hello to each other if we met, of course, and sometimes he'd knock and ask if I had anything to drink. That's about all."

"Have you noticed anyone new visiting Dahlström lately? Anyone who was different in some way?"

He gave them a wry smile.

"Are you kidding? Just about anyone who came to visit him was different. Recently I saw a chick peeing in the flower bed."

"Did any of the neighbors complain?"

"I don't think it ever got that bad. Most people probably thought he was a pretty decent guy. But in the summer some did complain when he had parties outside, in back of the building."

"What are people around here saying about the murder?"

"Everyone's saying that the killer must have been someone that Flash knew, someone who had a key to his apartment."

"Why is that?"

"Well, the old lady who lives above him heard a sound at his door one night, about a week before his body was found. Someone went inside without ringing the doorbell while Flash was downstairs in the basement."

"Couldn't it have been Dahlström?" asked Peter.

"No, she could tell that it wasn't him. She knows the sound of the slippers that Flash wore."

"Who do you think would have a key?"

"No idea. He had one buddy that he hung out with more than others. I think his name is Bengan."

"Do you know his last name?"

"No."

"It must be Bengt Johnsson. He was the one the police arrested, but then they let him go. Apparently he had an alibi. Is there anything else you can tell us about Dahlström?"

"There was one strange thing that happened this summer. Flash was talking to a guy down by the harbor. It was fucking early in the morning, not even five o'clock. I happened to notice because they were standing in an odd place, between two containers outside a warehouse. As if they were up to something."

"So they weren't just hanging out and drinking?"

"The other guy wasn't one of Dahlström's usual buddies. I could see that at once. He looked much too neat to be a wino."

"Really? In what way?"

"He was wearing clean slacks and a polo shirt, like an executive on summer vacation."

"What else can you tell us about his appearance?"

"I don't really remember. I think he was younger than Flash, and he was very dark."

"Dark-skinned?"

"No, just really suntanned."

"What were you doing there so early in the morning?"

The guy smiled, looking a bit embarrassed.

"I was with a girl. We'd been out partying at Skeppet. That's a pub down at the harbor. Do you know it?"

Johan grimaced. He had a bad memory from the summer when he had spent the miserably wet Midsummer's Eve at Skeppet, and he ended up bent over a toilet all night.

"She had to catch the seven o'clock boat in the morning, so I went with her down to the harbor. We were just messing around a little, as they say. Before she had to go home."

"I suppose the police know about this?" said Johan.

"Oh no, they don't."

"Why not?"

"I don't like the police. I wouldn't tell them squat."

"Would it be okay for us to do an on-camera interview with you?"

"Not on your life. Then the cops will show up. And you can't say a word to them about what I've told you, either. I know all about protected informants, because my sister is a journalist and she told me that you're not allowed to reveal your sources."

Johan raised his eyebrows in surprise. This was some guy.

"That's true. Of course we won't say anything about the fact that you're the one who told us this. What kind of work do you do, by the way?"

"I'm studying at the college. Archaeology."

Even though they didn't get to do an on-camera interview, Johan was more than satisfied with the encounter. He had to contact Knutas—of course without telling him about where he had obtained the information. Knutas was fully aware of the ethical rules under which journalists did their work, so he would understand.

They tried to talk to the rest of the neighbors, but no one answered the doorbell. Behind the building it was deserted. They took a walk along the pathway. Peter filmed the surrounding area and suddenly gave a shout.

A police car was parked on the public footpath that led to the next residential area. Three uniformed officers stood together, talking. Two others were holding on to the leashes of dogs that were tracking something with their noses to the ground. Police tape had been put up to cordon off a grove of trees and bushes.

To their surprise, they noticed Knutas a short distance away.

"Hi," said Johan in greeting. "It's been a while."

"Yes, it has."

Knutas was not happy, to say the least. These confounded journalists kept turning up at the most inopportune moments. So far the investigation had been mostly spared any media attention. Reporters from the local press had called him this morning to ask questions. He didn't like it, but unfortunately it had become a natural part of his workload lately. On the other hand, he was grateful that Johan had tipped him off about Dahlström's moonlighting. Journalists were good at digging up their own information, and they were also available to relay information to the public when the police occasionally needed help. An interdependent relationship existed between the police and the media. But that didn't mean that the relationship was always easy to handle.

"What's going on here?" asked Johan.

Peter had immediately started the camera rolling, as he always did. Knutas realized that he might as well tell them the truth.

"We've discovered what we think is Dahlström's camera."

"Where?"

Knutas pointed to the grove of trees.

"Someone tossed it over there, and a canine unit found it a short time ago."

"What makes you think that it was his?"

"It's the same type of camera that he always used."

Just as Knutas spoke, they heard a shout from some shrubbery outside the area that had been cordoned off.

"We've got something," called one of the dog handlers.

The German shepherd began barking nonstop. Peter instantly turned the camera in that direction and jogged over to the shrubbery. Johan was right behind him. On the ground lay a hammer with brown splotches on the handle, the head, and the claw. Johan held out the microphone, and Peter let the camera record the ensuing commotion. They recorded the comments of the police, the camera on the ground, the dogs, and the drama when everyone present realized that the murder weapon had probably been found.

Johan couldn't believe his luck. It was sheer coincidence that they happened to show up at the decisive moment in a murder investigation, and then managed to get pictures of the whole thing.

They got Knutas to agree to an interview in which he confirmed that a discovery had just been made that might prove to be of interest. He refused to comment further, but that didn't matter.

Johan did a stand-up at the site with all the activity going on around him and reported that it was most likely the murder weapon that had just been found.

Before he and Peter left, Johan told Knutas, without revealing his source, about Dahlström's meeting down at the harbor.

"Why didn't this person come to the police?" asked Knutas angrily.

"The individual doesn't like the police. Don't ask me why."

Back in the car and with a gleeful smile on his face, Johan called Grenfors's direct line at the newsroom in Stockholm.

Several Months Earlier

He had called her cell phone again and again, asking her to forgive him. He had sent sweet picture messages and even a real bouquet of flowers. Fortunately, her mother had left for work before the flowers arrived.

Fanny had decided never to meet him alone again, but now she was wavering. He called and kept saying that he needed to made amends with her. No dinner this time. Horseback riding. He knew that was something she liked. He had a friend who owned some horses in Gerum, and they could each borrow one and go riding for as long as they liked. The invitation was tempting. Her mother couldn't afford riding lessons, and it was rare that she was allowed to ride any of the horses at the stable.

He suggested going riding on Saturday. At first she declined, but he wouldn't take no for an answer. He said he would call again on Friday night, in case she changed her mind.

She had such mixed feelings. More than two weeks had passed since that evening, and it no longer seemed as dangerous as it had then. Deep inside he was probably a very nice man.

When she stepped through the stable door on Friday afternoon, the horses greeted her with a low whinny. She pulled on her rubber boots and started working. Got out the wheelbarrow, the shovel, and rake. She took Hector out first and fastened his halter to chains on either side of the passageway. He had to stand there while she mucked out his stall. The horses stood on a bed of sawdust and hay, so the piles of manure were easy to gather up with the rake. It was much harder to deal with the urine, which soaked into the sawdust and turned it into heavy piles. She took care of one stall after the other. Eight stalls and almost two hours later, she was completely worn out, and her back ached. Her cell phone was ringing. What if it was him? Instead she heard her mother's twittering voice.

"Sweetheart, it's Mamma. Something has come up. The thing is that I've been invited to Stockholm for the weekend. Berit was supposed to go to the theater with a girlfriend, but the friend got sick, so

Berit asked me to go with her instead. She won a whole theater package tour from the Bingo Lotto, you know, and we're going to see *Chess* and have dinner at the Operakällaran and stay at the Grand Hotel. Can you believe it! It's going to be great! The plane leaves at six, so I've really got to start packing. Is that okay with you?"

"Sure, that's fine. When are you coming home?"

"Sunday evening. The whole thing works out perfect because I don't have to go to work until Monday night. Oh, this is going to be so much fun. I'll leave you some money. But I don't have time to take Spot out, so you'd better come home soon. He's getting restless."

"I suppose I'll have to," Fanny said with a sigh.

She was supposed to ride Maxwell, but now she wouldn't have time. She would have to change her plans and head home.

When she got to their apartment she found her mother on her way out, with newly applied lipstick and blow-dried hair, her suitcase and purse in her hand.

After her mother finally left, and after walking Spot, Fanny lay down on her bed and stared at the ceiling.

Alone again. No one cared about her. Why did she even exist? She had an alcoholic mother who thought only about herself. As if that weren't enough, recently she had started giving some serious thought to her mother's extreme mood swings. One day she was as happy as a lark and full of energy, only to change the next day into a limp dishrag. Depressed, listless, and filled with dark thoughts. Unfortunately the bad days were getting more frequent, and that was when she would turn to the bottle. Fanny didn't dare criticize, because it always ended with her mother having a fit and threatening to kill herself.

Fanny had no one to talk to about her problems. She didn't know where to turn.

Sometimes she dreamt about her father, imagining that one day he would suddenly appear in the door, saying that he had come to stay. In her daydream she saw him embracing her and her mother. They celebrated Christmas together and went on vacations. Her mother was rosy-cheeked and happy and no longer drank. In certain dreams they would be walking along a beach in the West Indies, where her father was born. The sand was chalk white, and the sea was turquoise, just like in the colorful travel magazines she had seen. They watched the sunset together, with her sitting between her parents. That was the sort of dream that she never wanted to end.

She gave a start when Spot jumped up on the bed and licked away her tears. She hadn't even noticed that she was crying. Here she lay, all alone, with only a dog for company, when other families were having a cozy time at home. Maybe her classmates were visiting each other, watching a video or TV, listening to music or playing computer games. But what kind of life did she have?

Only one person had shown the slightest interest in her. She might as well see him again. To hell with everything. She would sleep with him, too, if that's what he really wanted. There had to be a first time, after all. He had said that he would call her tonight. The invitation to go horseback riding still stood, and she decided to say yes.

She got up and dried her tears. Heated up a meat pie in the microwave and ate it without much enthusiasm. Turned on the TV. The phone was silent. Wasn't he going to call after all? Now that she had made up her mind? The hours passed. She took a can of Coke out of the fridge, opened a bag of chips, and sat down on the sofa. It was nine o'clock, and he still hadn't called. She felt like crying again, but couldn't squeeze out more than a few dry sobs. He had probably given up on her, too. She started watching an old movie as she ate the whole bag of chips. Finally she fell asleep on the sofa with the dog beside her.

The sound of the phone ringing woke her. At first she thought it was the landline, but when she picked up the receiver she realized it was her cell phone ringing. She got to her feet and hurried out to the entryway to rummage through her jacket pockets. The phone stopped ringing. Then it started again. It was him.

"I have to see you . . . I have to. Listen here, honey. Couldn't we meet?"

"Sure," she said without hesitation. "You can come over here. I'm home alone."

"I'll be right over."

She regretted it the moment she saw him. He reeked of liquor. Spot started barking but soon gave up. The dog wasn't the menacing type.

She stood awkwardly in the center of the living room, unsure what to do, as he threw himself onto the sofa. Now that she had invited him over, she couldn't very well ask him to leave, could she?

"Would you like anything?" she asked uncertainly.

"Come here and sit down," he said, patting the sofa cushion next to him.

From the clock on the wall she saw that it was two in the morning. This whole thing was crazy, but she did as he said.

It took only a second before he was on top of her. He was rough and determined.

When he forced himself into her, she bit herself on the arm to keep from screaming.

FRIDAY, NOVEMBER 23

At the next day's morning meeting everyone was talking about the discovery of the murder weapon. It was a breakthrough in the investigation, of course. By all accounts, the blotches on the hammer were blood. The hammer had been sent to the Swedish Crime Lab for DNA analysis. But there were no fingerprints.

Most of them had seen on the evening news how the hammer was discovered. Naturally Kihlgård made jokes about the police officers' comments that were caught on tape, and he drew a good deal of laughter from the others. Knutas was only moderately amused. He was annoyed by the extent of the information presented in the news story. At the same time, he understood that the reporter was just doing his job. It was so typical that Johan should end up right in the thick of things. He had an incredible talent for showing up exactly when things were happening. Everything had gone so fast out there that no one had thought of reining him in before it was too late. Yet, once again Johan had provided new facts that would benefit the investigation, even though the police didn't know the source of his report about the witness at the harbor. After the case with the serial killer that past summer, Knutas had learned to trust the persistent TV reporter, although Johan could drive him crazy with all the information he managed to dig up. How he did it was a mystery. If he hadn't become a journalist, he would have made an excellent police detective.

The news program had started off with a long segment about the murder, the latest developments in the investigation, the payments Dahlström had received under the table, and the witness who had seen Dahlström with an unidentified man down at the harbor.

"Why don't we start with the unreported carpentry work?" said

Norrby. "We've interviewed four people who hired Dahlström in addition to Mr. and Mrs. Persson. Two of them are members of the same folklore society as the Perssons. They all said more or less the same thing. Dahlström did a number of minor jobs for them. They paid him for the work, and that was that. Evidently he conducted himself in an exemplary manner, showed up when he was supposed to, and so on. They knew, of course, that he was an alcoholic, but he had been referred to them by friends."

"So it was through a referral from others that they got in touch with him?" asked Wittberg.

"Yes, and none of them had any complaints about his work. We're going to keep questioning people."

"The murder weapon wasn't the only thing we found yesterday. We also found his camera. Sohlman?"

"It's a professional camera, a Hasselblad. Dahlström's fingerprints were found on it, so we're confident that it did in fact belong to him. There was no film in it, and the lens was broken, so someone had treated it rather roughly."

"Maybe the murderer took the film," Jacobsson put in. "The darkroom had been searched, which indicates that the murder possibly had something to do with Dahlström's photography."

"*Possibly.* At the same time, we've received reports from SCL on the samples that were taken from Dahlström's apartment and darkroom. SCL have really outdone themselves—we've never received such quick results before," Sohlman murmured to himself as he leafed through the documents. "All the prints from glasses, bottles, and other objects have been analyzed. Many are from Dahlström's buddies who visited his apartment. But there are also prints that can't be ascribed to any of them. They may be from the perpetrator."

"Okay," said Knutas. "At least we know that much. As if the information about Dahlström's unreported carpentry work wasn't enough, Johan Berg has also found a witness claiming to have seen Dahlström with a man down at the harbor last summer. Unfortunately, this witness does not want to talk to the police."

From his notes he rattled off the description of the man at the harbor.

"They were standing in a narrow passageway between two containers and talking, around five in the morning. The witness recognized Dahlström and knew that this was far away from the places where he usually hung out. What do you think?"

"If there's one witness, there could be more," said Wittberg. "When exactly did this happen?"

"We don't know. Only that it was supposedly in the middle of the summer."

"Why was the witness down at the harbor so early in the morning?" asked Kihlgård.

"He was there with a girl who was going to take the morning ferry to Nynäshamn."

"So we're talking about a younger man. It might be one of Dahlström's neighbors. Wasn't there a young guy living in the building?"

"You're right about that. I think he lives on the floor upstairs."

Knutas glanced down at his papers.

"His name is Niklas Appelqvist. A student."

"If the witness, whoever he is, could at least tell us the name of the girl, then we could find out what day she left by looking at the passenger lists of Destination Gotland," said Jacobsson. "I think they keep the lists for three months."

"But how are we going to proceed if the witness doesn't want to talk to the police?" asked Norrby.

"Maybe the reporter would have better luck getting the information out of him than we would," said Jacobsson. "I think we should first ask Johan Berg for help. Maybe the witness is one of those types who's extremely hostile toward the police. For some inexplicable reason, those sorts of people do exist," she added sarcastically.

She turned to Knutas, giving him a big smile.

"So we're going to have to suck up to the reporter," she said gleefully. "And you're so good at that kind of thing, Anders."

Jacobsson gave him a friendly poke in the side. Kihlgård looked equally amused.

Knutas was annoyed, but he had to admit that she was right. Legally, he couldn't investigate the young man, but there was nothing to prevent him from asking Johan to find out the name of the girl. So the police were at the mercy of the journalist's goodwill. And that was a pisser.

Just as Johan entered the editorial offices of Regional News, his cell phone rang. It was Knutas.

"I wonder if you'd be willing to help us with something."

"What is it?"

"Do you think the witness would remember the name of the girl he was with when he saw Dahlström and another man down at the harbor?"

"I don't know. It sounded as if she was someone he spent only that one evening with."

"Could you ask him?"

"Sure. But it'll have to wait awhile. I just arrived at the newsroom."

The police wanted his help. How nice. This was a switch from the normal situation when, as a journalist, he had to beg, plead, and cajole to get any information. He would keep Knutas waiting for just a bit.

A pleasantly drowsy Friday mood had settled over the newsroom. Fridays often had a slower pace than usual because half of the evening news program was devoted to a longer story.

Grenfors was sitting alone at the big table in the middle of the room, the so-called news desk. It was the workplace for editors, anchormen, and broadcast producers—all the key people whose job it was to put together the programs, make decisions, and assign the stories. At this time of day the anchormen and producers hadn't yet put in an appearance. Most of the reporters were sitting at their own desks with phones pressed to their ears. In the morning they did their research and made appointments for interviews. The day often started off at a leisurely pace, which then accelerated and finally reached a crescendo of stress right before the broadcast. That's when they had to deal with stories that weren't finished in time, something in a report that had to be changed at the last minute because the editor wasn't happy with it, computers that crashed, video-editing machines that broke so that certain images couldn't be transmitted, and all sorts of other problems. Time was short, and they always worked up until the very last second. Everyone was used to that; it was their normal work tempo.

"Hi, there," Grenfors greeted Johan. "That was a good report yesterday. Great that we've got the story now. It feels like it's going to get bigger. We'll have to wait and see how it develops. Meanwhile . . . something else has come up."

The editor shuffled through the documents and newspapers that were heaped in a big, messy pile on the table.

"The police seized a record amount of Rohypnol in Kapellskär this morning. Could you look into it?"

Oh, right, look into it, thought Johan. That sounded easy enough, but he knew what Grenfors expected. A substantial story that he could use at the top of the broadcast, containing information that was a Regional News exclusive. He had strong doubts that it was a record amount. He had lost count of all the drug busts that had been made over the past year.

"Isn't National News doing the story?" he asked wearily. He had been hoping to go home early.

"Sure, but you know how they are. They do their report and we do ours. Besides, you have better contacts than all their reporters put together."

"Okay."

Johan went back to his desk. Before he got started, he called Niklas Appelqvist in Gråbo.

He answered at once. Yes, he had kept in touch with the girl for a short time. He might still have her last name and phone number somewhere. He recalled only that her first name was Elin and she lived in Uppsala. He promised to call back as soon as possible. Before Johan could pick up the receiver to call the Customs Agency, the phone rang. He heard his mother's voice.

"Hi, my dear boy. How are you? How was it on Gotland?"

"It was fine."

"Did you see Emma?"

"Yes, as a matter of fact, I did."

He was close to his mother, and by this time she knew almost everything about his complicated relationship with Emma. She listened and offered advice without expecting that he would follow it. She never judged him, and he appreciated that.

Johan's relationship with his mother had deepened after his father died of cancer almost two years ago now. There were four brothers, but Johan was the oldest, and he was closest to his mother. They had a need for each other. During the past year his mother had needed him more, and they had spent a great deal of time together, talking about his father and how life had changed. Especially for her, of course. She now lived alone in the big house in the suburb of Bromma. He had tried to persuade her to move so that she wouldn't have to take care of all the practical matters by herself. Her sons did help out quite a bit, but they also had their own lives.

She had now recovered from the worst of her grief. She had even started seeing a man who belonged to the same bowling club. He was a widower, and she seemed to enjoy his company. Whether there was anything romantic going on between them she had never mentioned, and Johan didn't want to ask. The fact that his mother was seeing this man took a lot of the pressure off because he no longer had to worry as much about her being alone.

Fanny was sitting at the kitchen table, looking at the reflection of her face in the window. She was alone. Her mother was at work, as usual. The neighbors across the courtyard had hung up their Advent stars already. In another month it would be Christmas Eve. Yet another Christmas alone with her mother. Other people got together with family and friends to celebrate with Christmas trees and presents. The coziest thing of all must be to sit around a big table and eat Christmas dinner together. A warm apartment, candles, and good company. But she and her mother had only each other. And Spot, of course. They never went to visit relatives. Fanny had begun to realize why. The relatives were afraid that her mother would either get drunk or have one of her outbursts. She was so unpredictable that no one could ever relax when she was around. They never knew what might happen. If someone said or did something that her mother took as a criticism, the rest of the evening would be ruined. That's why she and her mother were always alone. Not even her maternal grandmother was around anymore; she was senile and lived in a retirement home.

They never bought a real tree for Christmas, either. They just set up a dreary-looking plastic tree on the table, as if they were a couple of old retired people. They usually ate Christmas dinner in front of the TV. Store-bought meatballs, beet salad, and ready-made Jansson's Temptation, the traditional casserole of herring, potatoes, and onions in a cream sauce. All they had to do was heat it up in the microwave. Her mother would drink aquavit and wine and get more and more tipsy as the evening wore on. There was always some movie on TV that she wanted to see, but before long she would fall asleep on the sofa. Fanny would have to take Spot out for his evening walk. She hated Christmas. The fact that it was also her birthday didn't make matters any better. She was going to turn fifteen—that meant she was practically grown up. She felt like a child in an adult's body. She didn't want to get any older; she had nothing to look forward to. She leaned her head on her hands, inhaling the scent of her newly washed hair. In some strange way she found that comforting. She looked down at the curve of her breasts. They had caused all the problems; her body had ruined everything. If she hadn't gotten older, this whole thing would never have happened. Her body was a weapon that could be used both against others and against herself.

And him. Now she mostly felt sick whenever she thought of him. His sweaty hands would paw at her, wanting to get under her clothes; he whimpered and whined like a baby. He wanted to do all sorts of strange things with her, and she didn't dare protest. She felt disgusted with herself, revolted. He told her that now they were both involved, and she had to keep quiet about what they did together. He talked as if they shared a secret agreement, a pact. But that's not how it was. Deep in her heart, she knew that. He said that he needed her, that she was important to him, and he gave her presents, which she had a hard time resisting. And that made her feel guilty. She was equally at fault, and she had only herself to blame. But now she didn't want to go on. She wanted to get away from him, but for the life of her she couldn't imagine how to do that. In her daydreams she wished that someone would come around the corner and rescue her from everything. But no one ever showed up. She wondered what her father would say if he knew.

She went into the bathroom and opened the medicine cabinet. Spot followed and looked up at her with his sweet eyes. She took out the green box of razor blades and sat down on the toilet seat. Carefully she took out a blade and held it between her fingers. Tears welled up, hot and salty, and rolled down her cheeks to land on her lap. She held out one hand and studied her fingers. What use was this hand? The blue veins ran from her wrist and into her palm filled with her blood, which pumped through her body. How meaningless. Why was she born? To take care of her mother? So that some disgusting old man could paw at her?

She looked at Spot, and that was enough to make him wag his tail hesitantly. *You're the only one who likes me,* she thought. *But I can't keep on living just for the sake of my dog.*

She took a firm grip on the razor blade and pressed it against her leg, almost level with her kneecap. She wanted to watch it pierce her skin. She pressed harder and harder. It hurt. At the same time, it felt good, almost liberating. All her fear and pain collected there, in her leg instead of in her whole body. In one place. Finally the blood began to flow, running down her leg and onto the floor.

He saw Emma at once, as soon as she came through the door. He watched her for several seconds while she looked around. The restaurant was small, intimate, and very crowded. He was sitting in a corner at the back, and it was hard to see him from the entrance. Then she noticed him, and her face lit up. To think it was possible to be so beautiful. She was wearing a moss green jacket, and her hair was wet from the rain. It was unusual to see her in a restaurant in Stockholm, and he liked it.

They kissed. Her lips tasted of salty licorice, and she laughed into his mouth.

"What a day! I couldn't concentrate on anything. I didn't hear a thing they said. All I wanted was to get out of there. The course I was taking had absolutely nothing to say to me."

"Were the speakers boring?"

He could feel that his whole face was smiling.

She threw out her hands. "I'm sure they were brilliant, inspiring, and super-charismatic. Everybody else was very pleased. But for me, none of that mattered. I just sat there thinking about you and longing to get away."

Their hands met across the table, and Johan couldn't get his fill of looking at her.

This is how it should always be, he thought. On the ring finger of her left hand her wedding band gleamed, a reminder that he only had her on loan. Just as their food arrived, her cell phone rang. Johan could tell at once that it was her husband, Olle, calling.

"It was good," she said. "Interesting speakers. Mmm. I'm sitting here having a glass of wine with Viveka. Mmm. We're leaving soon. The banquet doesn't start until eight."

She glanced at Johan. Then she got a worried look on her face.

"What? He does? That's too bad. When did it start? Hmm. How high is his temperature? Oh no. Try to get him to drink some fluids . . . Is he throwing up, too? How typical that he should get sick when I'm not home. Aren't you supposed to play a match early tomorrow morning? Uh-huh. Okay. You and Sara aren't sick, too, are you? If he keeps on like that, you should probably give him some fluid-replacement mixture. Do we have any in the house? Hmm. I hope you get some sleep tonight."

"That was Olle," she explained unnecessarily. "Filip has the stomach flu. He's been throwing up all afternoon."

She took a sip of her wine and looked out the window. Just a quick glance, but enough for Johan to realize that everything was much more complicated than he wanted to believe. She had children that she shared with her husband and she always would. He had watched her as she talked on the phone, and he understood how much of an outsider he was. What did he know about childhood illnesses? He didn't even know Emma's children. They had no relationship to him.

After dinner he wanted to show her around. It had stopped raining, and they strolled down to Hornstull beach, past Reimersholme, and out to Långholmen. Even though it was dark, they walked across the Bridge of Sighs, along the path past the old Mälarvarvet, and over to the other side. The lights from Gamla Stan, the city hall, and Norr Mälarstrand were reflected in the water.

They sat down on a bench.

"Stockholm is so damn beautiful," said Emma with a sigh. "The water makes it seem like it's not a big city, even though there are so many people. I could see myself living here."

"You could?"

"Yes. I'm always so jealous when you tell me about everything going on here. All the people, the theater, the cultural events. It makes me really think about what I'm missing when I'm on Gotland. It's nice there, but nothing ever happens. And just the idea that I could be anonymous. I could sit here in a café and no one would recognize me. Just blend in with everyone else. Watch people and be entertained. And I don't really think the traffic is so bad. It must be the water," she said, looking out across the dark mirror of Riddarfjärden.

"Yes, I love this city. I always will."

"And yet you would be willing to move to Gotland?" she said, looking at him.

"For your sake, I would do anything. Anything at all."

When they went back to his apartment and got into bed like an ordinary married couple, Johan was struck by a feeling of unreality mixed with joy. They should be able to go to bed like this every night.

SATURDAY, NOVEMBER 24

Saturday started out with snow mixed with rain, a strong wind, and the temperature hovering just above freezing. Knutas and his children had made breakfast and put a bouquet of flowers on the table next to Lina's place. Each of them was holding one of her birthday presents, and they had cleared their throats to make sure that their creaky morning voices would be able to handle the birthday song. On their way upstairs they started singing "Happy Birthday," each of them in a different key.

Lina sat up in bed, still dazed with sleep, her red hair in a cloud around her head. She gave them a big smile and looked with delight at the presents. She was childishly excited about receiving gifts and started with the ones from Petra and Nils: a book, nail polish, and a calendar with cute firefighters holding kittens. Lina had been in love once before, with a firefighter. The children liked to tease her about her weakness for men in uniforms. She saved the present from her husband for last. Knutas watched his wife with anticipation. He'd had trouble coming up with something, but then a brilliant idea had occurred to him. There was one thing that he knew she really wanted. In spite of countless diets and halfhearted attempts to start exercising, she hadn't managed to lose any weight. Consequently, he had filled a box with everything that might help her out: a year's membership to Gym 1 in Visby, a jump rope and weights for exercising at home, and an introductory package to Weight Watchers.

When Lina realized what his present was, her expression darkened and red blotches appeared on her throat. Slowly she raised her head and met her husband's eyes.

"What's all this supposed to mean?" Her eyes narrowed.

"What do you mean?" he stammered uncertainly and then began

listing all the advantages of his gift. "You wanted to slim down, so here's everything you need. If you don't have time to go to the gym, you can work out at home, and Weight Watchers has a meeting for new members on Tuesday at Säve School. Plus you get a personal trainer for the first five times at the gym, so you'll learn how to use the machines correctly."

Knutas pointed eagerly at the brochure that was attached to the gift card.

"So you think I'm fat? That I'm not attractive anymore? Is that why you're giving me all these things? Because you want me to be more buff?"

Lina sat bolt upright in bed, and her voice rose to a falsetto. Startled, the children looked from one parent to the other.

"But you're always talking about wanting to lose weight. I just wanted to help you out."

"And you think this is the sort of thing that I'd want for my birthday? To be reminded how fat I am? Can't you at least let me enjoy my day?"

Now she was shouting and she had tears in her eyes. The children decided to leave the room.

Knutas lost his temper.

"What the hell is this? First you go on and on about weighing too much, and then when I give you things to help you lose a few pounds, you get mad. What the hell is that all about?"

He stomped downstairs and started banging the breakfast dishes around. Then he shouted to Lina, "Just ignore the whole thing. I'll take everything back. Forget all about it!"

He called to the children, "Here's breakfast, for anyone who wants it!"

"And what about you? Have you ever taken a look at yourself?" Lina yelled from upstairs. "I could buy you an arm exerciser for Christmas. And maybe some Viagra—that wouldn't hurt!"

Knutas didn't bother to reply. He could hear Lina still muttering angrily to herself upstairs. Sometimes he got really fed up with her hot temper.

The children came downstairs and ate their cornflakes in silence. Knutas spilled coffee on the tablecloth, but he didn't care. He looked at Petra and Nils. All three of them shook their heads in agreement. None of them could understand Lina's reaction.

"Go upstairs and talk to Mamma," said Petra after a while. "This is her birthday, after all."

Knutas sighed but followed his daughter's advice. Fifteen minutes later he had persuaded his wife that she wasn't at all fat, that he loved her just the way she was, and that she wasn't the slightest bit overweight. No, she wasn't.

She was afraid of him. It started when he discovered the cuts.

They had done it again, in their secret place. The sexual act was a torment for her. Pain and disgust in a violent combination. It was as if she took pleasure in punishing herself. When he was done and lay next to her, gasping, he took hold of her wrist.

"What's this?" he said, sitting up on the sofa.

"Nothing."

She pulled her hand away.

He grabbed both of her hands and held them out.

"Were you trying to kill yourself?"

"No," she said, ashamed. "I just cut myself a little."

"What the hell for? Are you crazy?"

"No, it's nothing."

She tried to pull her hands away, but she couldn't.

"Did you cut yourself just for fun?"

"No, it's just something that I do. I've done it for years. I can't stop."

"Are you out of your mind!"

"Maybe I am."

She tried to laugh it off, but the laugh got caught in her throat. Fear was blocking the way.

"You can't keep doing this—you know that, don't you? What if someone finds out? Your mother or a teacher at school or someone else? Then they'll start asking a lot of questions. And you might not be able to keep quiet about us. They can manipulate you and coax you into talking. They might call in a bunch of psychologists and shit!"

His voice had gotten so loud that he was shouting. Saliva flew from his lips. He suddenly seemed dangerous, unpredictable. She drew the blanket tightly around her and watched him anxiously.

"No one is going to notice," she objected quietly.

"That's what you think. It's just a matter of time before someone sees those cuts. I forbid you to do it again. Do you hear me?"

He fixed his eyes on her. They were dark with anger.

"Okay, I promise. I'll stop."

He shook his head and went into the bathroom. She stayed on the sofa, unable to move as her panic grew. When he came back he had calmed down. He sat down next to her and stroked her arm.

"You can't keep doing this," he said in a gentle voice. "You might really hurt yourself. I'm worried about you. Don't you realize that?"

"Yes," she said. Tears were stinging her eyes.

"Now, now, honey," he consoled her. "I didn't mean to be so harsh. I was shocked when I saw those cuts, and I'm afraid of losing you. So I don't want to see any more of this, okay?"

He put his hand under her chin and looked her deep in the eyes.

"Promise me, my little princess."

She shuddered inside but nodded obediently.

In the car on the way back, she was convinced that she would never agree to see him again. In her mind she went over and over how she would phrase the words. She practiced the lines like a broken record.

He stopped a block away from her building, and turned off the engine. He wanted her to come and sit in the front seat for a last embrace before they parted. Lately he had made her sit in the back because he was afraid they might be seen.

When he had his nose pressed between her breasts, she gathered her courage.

"I think it's best if we don't see each other anymore."

Slowly he raised his head.

"What did you say?"

"I think it's best if we don't see each other anymore. We have to stop this."

His eyes grew dark and his voice turned icy.

"Why are you saying this?"

"Because I don't want to see you anymore," she stammered. "I just don't want to."

"What the hell are you saying?" he snarled. "Don't want to! What are you talking about? What do you mean by 'don't want to'? It's you and me!"

"But I don't want to meet anymore. I can't do this anymore."

Now she just wanted to get out of the car. His aggressive tone scared her. She tried to open the car door.

"You little bitch. Who the hell do you think you are?"

He threw himself at her and grabbed her hard by the arms. With his lips pressed close to her ear, he snarled, "Do you think you can just stop seeing me? You better be damn careful, because you're treading on thin ice. Don't think you can just start setting the terms. I'll fix things so that you never set foot in that stable again—do you understand? One word from me, and you won't be able to show your face there ever again. Is that what you want?"

She tried to pull herself out of his grip.

"Let me make one thing damn clear—our relationship is over when I say it's over. And not a word about this to a single person, or you can say good-bye to the stable forever. Just keep that in mind, you little slut!"

He pushed her away from him. Sobbing, she finally managed to open the door and stumble out of the car.

In the next instant he was gone. The last thing she heard was the tires screeching as he turned the corner.

Emma looked at her husband over the rim of her wineglass. They were still sitting at the table, talking after dinner as they usually did on the weekend. The children were watching *Little Stars* on TV, quite happy with bottles of Coke and a big bowl of popcorn. Olle seemed content. Was it really possible that he didn't suspect a thing?

He refilled her glass. *How absurd,* she thought. *Yesterday I was sitting just like this with Johan.*

"That was certainly delicious," he said.

She had served lamb burgers with yogurt sauce and homemade baba ghanoush. There was now a Lebanese restaurant in Visby, and they had tried it out on one of the rare occasions when they went out to dinner. The chef had given her the recipe when she asked him for it.

Yet another dinner in the long series of meals that they had shared. Olle asked her to tell him about the course she had taken in Stockholm, and so she did. They'd hardly had any time to talk since she had come home.

"How long did you stay at the banquet?"

"Oh, not very long," she replied evasively. "I don't know what time it was. Maybe one."

"Did you leave with Viveka?"

"Yes," she lied.

"Huh. I called your hotel this morning, but you weren't there. And your cell phone was off."

She felt a burning sensation shoot through her body. Now she was going to have to tell another lie.

"I must have been eating breakfast. What time did you call?"

"Eight thirty. I couldn't find Sara's sneakers."

He kept his eyes fixed on her. Emma took another sip of her wine to gain some time.

"That's when I was in the breakfast room. The battery on my cell had run out, so I left it in my room to recharge."

"Oh, so that's what happened," he said, sounding satisfied.

A perfectly natural explanation. Of course that was what happened. His trust in her had been built up over many years. Why should he doubt what she told him? She had never given him any cause to do that.

The lies burned inside her, and for her the relaxed mood was now gone. She started to clear the table.

"Hey, sit down," he objected. "That can wait."

Their conversation moved on to other topics, and her feeling of uneasiness soon disappeared. They put the children to bed and watched an exciting thriller on TV. She curled up on the sofa with Olle's arm around her, the same as always. And yet it wasn't.

SUNDAY, NOVEMBER 25

Things finally fell apart the following morning. Emma's cell rang while she was in the shower, and Olle checked to see what the message was.

It said: "How are you? Longing for you. Kisses, Johan."

When she came out of the shower, Olle was sitting at the kitchen table. His face was white with fury, and he was holding her cell phone in his hand.

The floor gave way beneath her. She realized at once that he knew. Through the window she saw the children playing outside in the rain.

"What is it?" she asked in a feeble voice.

"What the hell is going on?" he said, his voice thick with anger.

"What do you mean?"

She could feel her lower lip quivering.

"You got a message," he shouted. "On this!" He waved her cell in the air. "From some Johan who is longing for you and sending you kisses. *Who the hell is Johan?*"

"Just wait and I'll explain," she pleaded as she cautiously sat down on the very edge of a chair across from him.

At that moment she heard the front door open.

"Mamma, Mamma, my mittens are wet," cried Sara. "Can I have another pair?"

"I'm coming," she called. She went out to the entryway and found another pair. Her hands were shaking.

"Here, sweetheart. Now go back out and play with Filip. Mamma and Pappa need to be alone to talk. So why don't you and your brother stay outside for a while. I'll call you when we're done."

She gave her daughter a kiss on the cheek and then went back to her husband in the kitchen.

"I've wanted to tell you, but it's been so difficult," she said, giving him an entreating look. "I've been seeing somebody for a while, but I'm so confused. I don't really know what I feel."

"What the hell are you talking about?"

His words cut right through her. She could hear how Olle was trying to control his anger by clenching his teeth. She didn't dare look at him.

"It can't be true! This is too fucking unbelievable!" he said.

He got up from the table and came to stand in front of her, still holding her cell phone in his hand.

"What the hell is going on here? Who is he?"

"He's the journalist who interviewed me after Helena was killed. The journalist from TV. Johan Berg," she said quietly.

Olle flung the cell phone to the floor with all his might. With a bang it was transformed into a pile of plastic and metal splinters. Then he turned to her.

"Have you been seeing him ever since then? Behind my back? For all these months?"

His face contorted with anger as he leaned toward her.

"Yes," she said weakly. "But you have to let me explain. We haven't been seeing each other the whole time."

"Explain!" he shouted. "You can explain to your lawyer. Get out! I want you out of here!"

He grabbed her hard by the arm and yanked her out of the chair.

"Get out! You don't belong here anymore. Leave right now, so I don't have to look at you. Go to hell! I never want to see you again! Do you hear me? Never!"

The children had heard the ruckus, and they now appeared in the doorway. At first they looked bewildered, then they both started to cry. That didn't stop Olle. He shoved Emma out onto the porch in her stocking feet and threw her jacket and boots after her.

"Here!" he yelled. "But you're not taking the car!" And he snatched away her car keys.

Then he slammed the door shut.

Emma put on her jacket and boots. The door opened again and her purse came flying out.

She was out in the cold. The street was deserted.

A Sunday morning in November, and it was over. She stared at the closed door. Her purse had fallen open and the contents were scattered all over the porch and front steps. Mechanically she gathered up everything, too numb to cry. She walked down to the gate and opened it, then turned right, although she didn't know why. She didn't notice the neighbor family a couple of houses away who were talking and laughing as they climbed into their car and drove off. The mother waved to Emma but got no response.

She felt empty inside, as if stunned. Her face felt rigid. What on earth had she done? Where should she go now? She couldn't go back to her own house.

The sports field next to the school was deserted. The wind was blowing from the north. She looked over at the main road where a few cars were driving past.

When did the buses go into town on Sundays? She had never needed to ask that question before.

MONDAY, NOVEMBER 26

The temperature in the sauna was 176 degrees Fahrenheit. Knutas filled a wooden ladle and tossed more water on the glowing hot stones. The temperature rose even higher.

They had swum a mile and were more than satisfied. Once a week Anders Knutas and Leif Almlöv would go swimming together, at least in the wintertime. Knutas swam regularly at Solberga Baths during all seasons of the year. He actually preferred to swim alone. He always thought more clearly when he was in the water, swimming one lap after another. But this was a way for the two of them to meet. They had to put up with a good deal of joshing from their friends because they went to the swimming pool—something that was more typical for women. Men played tennis or golf together, or they went bowling.

In the sauna they would discuss all sorts of daily trivialities, or just sit in utter silence. That was the sign of a good friend, Knutas thought. He didn't care for loud people who insisted on jabbering incessantly, even when they had nothing sensible to say.

Knutas described Lina's birthday fiasco, which gave Almlöv a good laugh. They would never completely understand women—they could certainly agree on that.

They had sons the same age, and they talked about the problems of puberty that had started showing up. Their sons were classmates and friends. A week or so ago Almlöv had discovered them smoking in secret. It turned out that they had lit a couple of old cigarette butts. Almlöv's son, who wore his hair long—to the dismay of his parents—had managed to burn several locks on one side.

They talked about their surprise at getting older, about the anxiety of bulging stomachs and slack muscles, about getting gray hair on their chests. Knutas didn't think about old age and death very often, but sometimes he noticed how life seemed to be running away from him, and then he would wonder how much time he had left. He pictured himself getting older and older, with all the accompanying infirmities and immobility. How long would he be able to remain active? When he was thinking along those lines, he would start worrying about the fact that he smoked, although not much. Mostly he sucked on an unlit pipe, filling it and tending to it, but lighting it only a few times each day.

Almlöv was struggling with the same anxieties, even though he didn't smoke. He told Knutas that he had bought a home gym, and he was working out for an hour every morning. The results were quite evident, as Knutas noted with envy. He appreciated his friend's candor and the fact that he could confide in him. But when it came to Knutas's job, other rules applied. And Almlöv never asked him about his work. Even so, Knutas sometimes wished he could tell his friend about one thing or another. It was often good to talk to someone outside police headquarters, someone who had a different perspective. Lina was usually the one who served as his sounding board. She had helped him many times to think along new lines.

It was eleven o'clock by the time Knutas arrived at his office. On his desk was a handwritten note from Norrby along with the transcription of an interview from the Uppsala police. The young woman who was with the witness at the harbor had been tracked down to an address there. Only one passenger of the right age and from that city had taken the boat on the day in question. Her name was Elin Andersson. The Uppsala police had apparently agreed to assist the investigative team by interviewing her over the weekend. She had conceded that she knew Niklas Appelqvist and that they had been together at the harbor on the morning of July 20 before she left. But she had not noticed anyone in particular down at the harbor. So it was as they had guessed—Dahlström's young neighbor was the one who had provided Johan Berg with the information. Knutas was extremely annoyed that such an important witness refused to talk to the police. And it wasn't because he'd been in trouble with the police. A search of police records had come up negative.

When he entered the conference room half an hour later, Knutas noticed at once a sense of excitement in the air. Jacobsson and Kihlgård had gone through Dahlström's papers over the weekend, and from the look on their faces, it was clear that they had found something that they were dying to share with their colleagues. Kihlgård had two big cinnamon rolls on a plate in front of him next to a big mug of coffee. He ate as he fiddled with the papers. Crumbs fell on the table.

Knutas sighed. "Do the two of you have something to report?"

"You better believe it," said Kihlgård. "It turns out that Dahlström kept detailed records on his clients. We have a long list of names and dates, what he built, and how much he was paid."

"The work he did was much more extensive than we thought," added Jacobsson. "He had been doing carpentry jobs for over ten years. His first job was in 1990. Some of the people who made use of Dahlström's services are very well-known in Visby."

Everyone gave Jacobsson their full attention as she held up a list of names.

"Would you believe—wait till you hear this—city council chairman and Social Democrat Arne Magnusson?"

A gasp of surprise rippled through the room.

"Magnusson?" said Wittberg, laughing. "That can't be true! The guy who's always defending high taxes and talking about how great it is to pay them? That's too funny! He's the worst moralizer in all of Visby."

"Yes, he's always lobbying for the restaurants to close at one A.M. in the summertime and for smoking to be banned," snickered Sohlman.

"If this gets out . . . the journalists are going to have a field day." Norrby threw out his hands.

"A garden shed in 1997," read Jacobsson from the list. "Five thousand kronor, paid under the table, along with several bottles of liquor. Can you believe it?"

Knutas grew serious. "This is totally insane."

"Just wait. There are more surprises on the list," said Jacobsson. "Bernt Håkansson, chief surgeon at the hospital, and Leif Almlöv, restaurant owner and your good friend, Anders!"

"What the hell?" Knutas turned bright red in the face. "Is his name on there, too?"

"A sauna in the country for ten thousand—that was a tidy sum."

There was a glint of mischief in Jacobsson's eye. She was enjoying teasing him. Kihlgård looked equally pleased. They had certainly found something to entertain themselves. How nice for them.

"At least he's not alone. There are at least a dozen names."

"No one from here, I hope?" said Wittberg uneasily. "Don't tell me that, for God's sake."

"No, luckily there aren't any police officers on the list. On the other hand, there is someone with your last name. Roland Wittberg. Are you related to him?"

Wittberg shook his head.

"Let me see," said Knutas.

He recognized a number of the names.

"What are we going to do with this?"

"To start with, we'll check up on them and see if there are any other links to Dahlström," said Jacobsson, snatching the list back.

Knutas called Leif as soon as he was back in his office. He felt tremendously out of sorts.

"Why didn't you tell me that you had hired Dahlström?"

Silence.

"Are you there?"

"Yes."

Knutas heard a deep sigh on the phone.

"Why didn't you say anything about the sauna?" Knutas persisted.

"You know how it is with all the crooked dealings in the restaurant business. I thought that if it came out that I had hired an illegal worker for a private matter, then people would think I did the same thing at the restaurant. I would come under suspicion and the authorities would make life hell for me."

"Why didn't you think of that before you let him build that sauna?"

"I know it was really stupid. At the time things weren't going well with the restaurant, and Ingrid kept nagging me about the damn sauna. That's no excuse, but maybe it's an explanation of sorts. I hope that I haven't put you in an embarrassing situation."

"I'll manage. Besides, there are others who have reason to be uneasy. We have a list of plenty of people who did the same thing. You wouldn't believe your ears."

After hanging up the phone, Knutas leaned back in his chair and started filling his pipe. He was grateful that no police officers were on the list, and he accepted his friend's explanation. Good Lord, who hadn't done something stupid? Once, many years ago, he had actually swiped a package of underwear from a shop on Adelsgatan. He was standing in the store, holding the package, when he was suddenly seized with a wild impulse to find out what it felt like to steal something. He walked right out the door with the package under his arm. He was so nervous that he was shaking, but when he exited the store, a giddy feeling of joy came over him. A kind of invulnerability. It was as if the act made him untouchable. After he had gone far enough from the store to know that he had escaped undetected, he glanced at the package, only to find that he had taken the wrong size.

Knutas still felt ashamed every time he thought about what he had done. He turned his chair halfway around and looked out the window. Somewhere out there a murderer was walking around.

Nothing indicated that they would find him among Dahlström's circle of acquaintances. On the contrary. Dahlström was apparently mixed up in something, but they had no clue what it might be. Whatever it was, he had done a good job of hiding it. The question was how long it had been going on. Probably not much longer than the date of the first deposit in his bank account, Knutas guessed. July 20. The same day that Niklas Appelqvist saw Dahlström with an unidentified man down at the harbor. It seemed likely that on that occasion the man had handed the money over to Dahlström, who later in the day went to his bank to deposit it. Twenty-five thousand kronor. The next deposit was made in October, and for the same amount. Was it possible that the two deposits didn't actually have anything to do with each other? From the beginning Knutas had assumed that they were connected somehow, but now he was no longer certain. The explanation might be as simple as payments for various carpentry work. But why would someone who had hired Dahlström for something so trivial decide to meet him down at the harbor at five in the morning? It was obvious that the man didn't want to be recognized.

Fanny's muscles were pleasantly tired. Calypso had been wonderful. She had gone out riding, taking her favorite route through the woods even though it was a bit too long for the sensitive racehorse. But never mind. It was so seldom that she went out, and she just couldn't resist.

He was a gentle horse and responded to her prods without the least effort. He made her feel quite proficient. They galloped for long stretches along the soft forest path. Not a living creature as far as the eye could see. For the first time in a long while she had felt something that resembled joy. She felt a surge inside her chest as they raced forward. She stood up halfway in the saddle, urging the horse on. Tears rose in her eyes from the speed. Knowing that they were going faster than she could actually handle made the whole experience even more exhilarating. This was truly living: to see the horse's ears pointing forward, to hear his hooves pounding dully on the ground, to feel the animal's power and energy.

As they went back to the stable at a walk with the reins drooping, she felt so relaxed. She sensed a budding hope that everything was going to be all right. First and foremost, she had to break things off with him for good. He had called her cell about twenty times that day, but she had refused to answer it. He wanted to apologize. She had listened to his messages, and he sounded upset and remorseful. He tried to convince her that he didn't mean what he had said. This morning he had sent a picture message with hearts and flowers. None of that had any effect on her anymore.

It was over, no matter what he said. Nothing could make her change her mind. She had decided to ignore his threat about getting her thrown out of the stable. She had worked there for a year, and everyone knew her. They wouldn't pay any attention to him. And if he tried, she was thinking about revealing everything. By law it was a criminal offense for him to have sex with her; she was fully aware of that. She was no fool. And he was an old man. He might even end up in prison. It would serve him right. It would be so great to be rid of him, to have her body to herself, and to get out of doing all the shit he wanted her to do. She longed to have herself back. Her mother wasn't going to change, but Fanny would soon be fifteen, and she wouldn't have to live at home much longer. Maybe she could even move out next year when she started tenth grade. There were plenty of kids out in the country who did that. They lived in town during the week and went home on the weekends. Why couldn't she do that, too? All she had to do was tell the school counselor or nurse about her situation, and she was sure to get help.

When she gave Calypso a hug in his stall, she felt so grateful to the horse. It was as if he gave her strength and self-confidence. And the faith that everything was going to work out.

She had ridden her bike only three hundred yards when she saw the headlights. He came driving along the opposite side of the road, slowed down, and rolled down the window.

"Hi. Are you on your way home?"

"Yes," she responded, stopping.

"Wait there," he said. "I just have to drive a little farther and turn the car around. Wait right there."

"Okay."

Reluctantly she got off her bicycle and stood at the side of the road. She watched him drive off and had a strong urge to do the same. Just bike home as fast as she could to get away from him. The next second she changed her mind. She was going to tell him it was over. Once and for all.

When he returned, he wanted her to get in the car.

"But what should I do with my bike?" she asked, resigned.

"Leave it in the ditch. No one's going to take it. We can come back and get it later."

She didn't dare do anything but comply. Her legs were shaking as she got into the car.

"I have to go home. Mamma is at work, and I have to take Spot out for a walk."

"No problem. I just wanted to talk to you for a minute. Is that all right?"

He asked the question without looking at her.

"Okay," she said, glancing at him out of the corner of her eye.

His voice sounded strained, and he seemed tense. His jaw moved as if he were clenching his teeth.

She thought he was driving too fast but didn't dare object. It was dark out, with little traffic on the road. He headed south toward Klintehamn.

"Where are we going?"

"It's not far. You'll be home soon."

Fear began to creep into her veins. They were getting farther and farther away from town, and she now realized where they were going. She debated with herself and decided it wouldn't be a good idea to protest. The tense atmosphere in the car told her that it would be best not to.

When they reached the house he told her to take a shower.

"Why should I?" she asked.

"You reek of the stable."

She turned on the shower and the hot water struck her bare skin but she couldn't feel it. Mechanically she soaped up while thoughts zigzagged through her mind. Why was he acting so strange? She dried herself off with a bath towel, trying to rid herself of the uneasiness that crept over her. She told herself that he was just tense because of what had happened last time. For safety's sake she put all her clothes back on. In case she had to run away.

He was sitting in the kitchen reading a newspaper when she came downstairs. That made her feel calmer.

"You put your clothes back on?" he said, his voice stony. He gave her a distracted look—his glassy eyes were fixed on her, but it was as if he didn't really see her.

Her sense of relief vanished instantly. What was wrong with him? Was he on drugs? His question hung in the air.

"Yes," she said uncertainly. "I thought—"

"What exactly did you think, my dear?"

"I don't know. I have to go back. . . ."

"Back? So you thought that we drove all the way out here just so you could take a shower?"

"No. I don't know."

"You don't know. Well, there's plenty that you don't know, sweetheart. But maybe it's just as well that you put your clothes back on. That might make it more interesting. We're going to play a little game, you see. Doesn't that sound like fun? You're so young that you like to play games, don't you?"

What had gotten into him? She tried to hold back the fear that shot up inside her, and she made an effort to act normal. It didn't help much. He grabbed her by the hair and forced her down on her knees.

"We're going to play dog and master. You're so fond of dogs, aren't you? You can be Spot. Is Spot hungry? Does Spot want a treat?"

As he talked he used his free hand to unbutton his pants, keeping a good grip on her hair with the other. She turned ice cold when she realized what he wanted. He pressed her hard against him. She felt nauseated but couldn't get away.

After a while he seemed to lose his concentration for a moment. He loosened his grip and then she saw her opportunity. She tore herself away and managed to pull free. Quickly she got to her feet and staggered out to the hall. She yanked open the door and dashed out. A fierce wind struck her. It was pitch dark and icy cold. The sea was roaring in the dark. She ran toward the road but he came after her. He knocked her down and slapped her in the face. He hit her so hard that she almost passed out.

"You damn little whore," he snarled. "Now I'm going to really let you have it."

Again he took her by the hair and then dragged her across the yard. The ground was soaking wet, and the water seeped through her clothes as she was pulled after him on all fours. Holes were torn in her pants, her hands were scraped badly, and blood ran from her nose. The sound of her sobs was drowned out by the howling wind.

Fumbling, he pulled out the key to the little building. The door opened with a screech. Abruptly he shoved her into the dark.

TUESDAY, NOVEMBER 27

When Majvor Jansson came home to her apartment after working the night shift, she discovered that the dog had peed on the hall rug. He jumped up and whimpered when she opened the front door. His water bowl was empty. She could tell at once that something was wrong. The door to Fanny's room stood wide open, and her bed had not been slept in. It was close to seven o'clock on this Tuesday morning, and it was clear that Fanny had not been in the apartment all night.

Majvor sat down on the sofa in the living room to think. *Don't panic,* she told herself. What was it that Fanny was going to do yesterday? Probably go out to the stable after school. She was always over there lately. They hadn't planned to see each other at home because Majvor had to go to work at five. That meant that Spot had been alone for fourteen hours! Anger bubbled up inside of her, but just as quickly it vanished. As she tried to gather her thoughts, a sense of uneasiness overtook her.

Fanny would never forget to come home if she knew that Spot was alone. Not of her own free will. Had she gone to a friend's house to spend the night? The likelihood of that happening was minimal, but she started looking through the apartment to see if her daughter had left a note. What about a message on her cell phone? She hurried out to the hall and pulled her cell out of her coat pocket. Nothing there, either. Spot had finished eating and was now whining loudly. He needed to go out.

As she walked between the apartment buildings, Majvor wondered what other possibilities there might be. Was Fanny mad at her? No, she didn't think so. They hadn't had a fight in a long time. In her heart she was aware that she might not be the sort of mother that Fanny really needed, but she couldn't help it. This was just how she was, and she didn't have the energy to make changes. It wasn't easy being a single mother.

Was this a sign of some kind of rebellion? Had Fanny run away with some friend that she didn't know about? Or a boy? Majvor hurried home with the dog, who now seemed much happier. She started making phone calls.

An hour later she was still at a loss. None of their relatives or acquaintances could tell her where Fanny had gone. She called the school. She learned that Fanny wasn't there, either. Anxiety was making her throat dry. She got out a bottle of wine and a glass. Something must have happened. What about the stable? Did she even have the phone number? A note with the number was stuck to the refrigerator. Fanny was always so organized. Majvor clutched the receiver tightly as she waited for someone to answer the phone.

"Hello," said a gruff male voice after the tenth ring.

She introduced herself. "Yes, hi, this is Majvor Jansson, Fanny's mother. Is Fanny there?"

As she spoke she realized that she didn't know who she was talking to, or even what the place looked like. Fanny had been working at the stable for over a year, but Majvor had never set foot in the place. Why hadn't she ever gone to visit? Now she cursed herself as it suddenly became crystal clear to her how little interest she had shown in her daughter. When was the last time she had helped Fanny with her homework? She didn't dare even think about that.

"No, she's not here," replied the man, sounding friendly. "She was here yesterday afternoon. But shouldn't she be in school right now?"

"She's not there, and she didn't come home last night, either."

Now the man on the phone sounded uneasy. "That's odd. Wait a minute," he said, and she heard him put down the receiver, then the sound of voices in the background as he shouted to someone. After a moment he was back.

"No, unfortunately, no one has seen her. I'm sorry."

A call to the hospital proved equally fruitless.

What about her room? Normally Majvor didn't go in there, since she and Fanny had a mutual understanding that the room was her private space.

At first glance everything looked the same as usual. The bed was neatly made and a book lay on the nightstand, next to the alarm clock. On the desk was a jumble of pens, several schoolbooks, elastic bands for her hair, scraps of paper, and newspapers. Majvor rummaged among Fanny's things, pulled out all the dresser drawers, then searched the bookshelf and the closet. She turned everything in the room upside down without finding any note with a message, or an address book or a phone number that might give her a clue about where Fanny had gone.

But hidden under several decorative pillows at the head of the bed she found what were obviously spots of blood on the reverse side of the bedspread. She tore off all the bedclothes. No blood on the sheet or the blanket, but under the bed she found a towel with more traces of blood. She was shaking all over as she punched in the phone number for the police.

As soon as he stepped inside, Knutas felt weighted down. He was glad that Sohlman had come with him. The whole apartment was depressing, with its cramped rooms and dreary colors. It was in a four-story building on Mästergatan in the Höken district, in the northeastern section of Visby and about half a mile outside the ring wall.

Majvor Jansson's eyes were red from crying when she opened the door. Since Fanny was not with her father, either, the police were taking the report of her disappearance very seriously. The bloodstains on the bedspread meant that there was reason to suspect an assault or a rape. That's why the police had decided to do a proper crime scene investigation of the girl's room. Sohlman immediately got to work.

Knutas noticed a faint smell of liquor on Majvor Jansson's breath.

"When did you last see Fanny?" he asked when they were sitting at the kitchen table.

"Yesterday morning. We had breakfast together before she left for school. I didn't have to go to work until five, but she usually goes to the stable after school, so we rarely see each other in the afternoon."

"How did she seem?"

"Tired. She's always tired, especially lately. That's probably because she doesn't eat properly. She's awfully thin."

"What did you talk about?"

"Nothing special. There's not much to talk about in the morning. She ate toast for breakfast, as usual. Then she left."

"What was the mood like between the two of you?"

"Same as always," replied Majvor flatly. At the same time she cast a pleading glance at Knutas, as if he might be able to tell her where her daughter was.

"What did she say when she left?"

"She just said bye."

"Is anything missing from the apartment? Clothes, a toiletry case, money?"

"I don't think so."

"And Fanny didn't leave a message? You're sure about that?"

"Yes, I've looked high and low."

"Tell me about Fanny. What's she like?"

"Well, what can I tell you? What are most kids like at that age? She doesn't say much, but I don't think she likes school. She's started cutting classes a lot. Maybe she's lonely. I don't know. She never brings any friends home."

"Why is that?"

"I have no idea. Maybe she's shy."

"Do you ever talk about these problems with your daughter?"

Majvor Jansson seemed disconcerted, as if it had never occurred to her that she was the one responsible for her daughter, and not the other way around.

"It's not easy to talk about things when you're a single mother and have to work all the time. I don't have a husband to support me. I have to do everything myself."

"I can understand that," said Knutas sympathetically.

Suddenly she fell apart and buried her face in her hands.

"Shall we take a break?" asked Knutas tactfully.

"No, we might as well get this over with so that you can start looking for her."

"Have you talked to anyone at her school about why she's been cutting classes?"

"Yes, a teacher called me. That was just a few days ago. He said that she hadn't been to his class for several weeks. We talked about the problem, but he seemed to think that she was just tired of school. I told Fanny that she had to go to school, and she promised to do better."

"Has Fanny mentioned anything new in her life? Someone new that she met?"

"No," replied Majvor, after giving it some thought. "I don't think so."

"Is there anyone in particular that she spends a lot of time with?"

"No, we don't have a big circle of friends, as they say."

"What about relatives?"

"My old mother lives at the Eken retirement home, but she's so out of it that it's almost impossible to talk to her. And I have a sister who lives in Vibble."

"Does your sister live alone?"

"No, she's married and has two children. Well, the son is her husband's, from a previous marriage."

"So they're the only cousins that Fanny has? How old are they?"

"Lena lives in Stockholm. I think she's thirty-two, and Stefan is forty. He lives here on Gotland, in Gerum. I was hoping that Fanny might have gone to stay with my sister."

Majvor started sobbing again. Knutas patted her arm.

"Now, now," he comforted her. "We're going to do everything we can to find her. I'm sure she'll turn up soon. Just you wait and see."

The message on his answering machine was a long one. Emma reported in a cracked, monotone voice that Olle now knew about everything. For the time being she was staying with her friend Viveka. She asked him not to try to contact her, and she promised to call when she could. Johan immediately tracked down Viveka's phone number, only to be told by Emma's friend that he needed to respect her wish to be left alone.

It was a form of psychological terror, and he had a hard time coping with it. He played a game of floorball but couldn't stop thinking about Emma. He went to a movie but left the theater without knowing what the film was about.

On Tuesday evening she called.

"Why won't you talk to me?" he asked.

"My whole life has fallen apart. Isn't that a good enough reason?" she said angrily.

"But I want to help you. I realize that this must be terribly hard for you. And I get so worried if we don't have any contact."

"Right now I can't be responsible for whether you're worried or not. I have enough to think about."

"How did he find out?"

"Your text message. You sent it while I was in the shower, and he checked my cell phone."

"I'm sorry, Emma. I'm really sorry. I shouldn't have texted you on a Sunday. That was stupid."

"The worst thing is that I still haven't had a chance to talk to the children. He won't answer the phone, and he's turned off the answering machine. I've gone over there, but nobody was home. And he took my keys, so I can't even get into the house." Her voice broke.

"Take it easy," he consoled her. "I assume he just has to let off some steam. He's had a shock. Isn't there anyone who could talk to him? What about your parents?"

"My parents! Not a chance. Do you know what he did? He called all of our friends and family and told them that I'd found someone else. He even called my grandmother in Lycksele! My parents are really upset with me. I've tried to talk to them, but they're siding with Olle. They can't understand how I could treat him so badly. And what about the children—why didn't I think about Sara and Filip? Everybody is against me. I don't know how I'm going to deal with this."

"Can't you come here? So you can get away from things?"

"No, I can't."

"Should I come over there?" he asked. "I could take some time off."

"What good would that do? Right now the most important thing is for me to have contact with my children. Do you have any idea what it's like not to be able to talk to your own children? I told you that I needed two months to think things through, but you refused to respect my wishes. You just couldn't let me have some time in peace and quiet. You kept calling and pressuring me, even though I told you not to. And now look what's happened! And it's all thanks to you, for God's sake!"

"So this is all my fault? What about you? Don't you think that you share some of the blame? I didn't force you into this, did I? You wanted to meet, too."

"All you can think about is yourself because you don't have to take anyone else into consideration. But I do. So leave me alone," she said, and slammed down the phone.

He noted that this was the second time she had done that recently.

That afternoon the real job got started of mapping out Fanny Jansson's activities during the past few days before she disappeared. The search was carried out on a wide front. The police interviewed everyone who worked at the stable, as well as the few relatives that she had. They visited her school to talk to her classmates and teachers. Their image of Fanny became clearer.

She appeared to be a solitary girl who would turn fifteen on Christmas Eve. Her classmates didn't think she was interested in being friends with any of them. When they started school together, some of them had tried to get her to join in various activities, but she always declined, and finally they gave up. She always seemed to be in a hurry to get home after school, until she started going to the stable, and then she was in a hurry to go there. No one really had much to say about her. They thought she was probably nice enough, but she never took the initiative to make contact with any of them, and that's why she had ended up alone. She only had herself to blame. She didn't seem to care, and that was also a bit irksome. Nothing seemed to bother her.

The teachers described her as quiet but smart—although lately something had changed. She seemed distracted for no obvious reason, and she had become even more withdrawn. At the same time, it wasn't easy to figure out kids her age. There were so many emotions at play; new patterns emerged, they started talking back, made friends and then dropped them; the boys started using snuff, the girls began wearing makeup and padding their bras, and the hormones practically gushed out of the kids. Irritability and aggression were common, and it wasn't always easy to keep up with all the mood swings or how a particular student was developing.

Her relatives didn't have much to say, either. They seldom saw Fanny. Her mother drank and had an unpredictable temperament, which prevented any sort of normal socializing. Of course they realized that it must be a difficult situation for Fanny, but that didn't mean that they wanted to get involved. They had enough problems of their own, they said dismissively.

Adult responsibility, thought Knutas. *There is something called normal, decent adult responsibility. Isn't there any sort of collective feeling among people anymore? Nobody is prepared to deal with a child who goes astray, not even within their own family.*

The neighbors all had the same impression of Fanny: a solitary, modest girl who seemed to carry a heavy responsibility at home. It was commonly known that her mother had a drinking problem.

The last person to see Fanny before she disappeared was a man at the stable. His name was Jan Olsson. According to him, she arrived at the stable around four, as usual, and worked with the horses. She was given permission to take one of them out for a ride. She was gone for about an hour and was elated when she returned. She didn't get to go out riding very often, so she was thrilled whenever she had the opportunity. Both she and the horse were sweaty, and Jan Olsson said that he suspected she had galloped harder than she really should have. But he didn't say anything because he felt sorry for the girl and thought she deserved to have a little fun.

When he was taking a cigarette break outside on the stable hill, he saw her pedaling off in the dark, heading toward home. After that there was no trace of the girl.

Knutas decided to go out to the racetrack to meet in person both the trainer who owned the stable and Jan Olsson. By now it was past seven o'clock, and when Knutas called the stable, everyone had left. He tried their home numbers, but no one answered. He would have to wait until first thing in the morning.

WEDNESDAY, NOVEMBER 28

The trotting track was located about half a mile from the center of town. When Knutas and Jacobsson drove up the stable hill, they came within a hair's breadth of colliding with a sulky. The huge gelding snorted and swerved to the side. The driver's admonishing words calmed the horse. Knutas got out of the car and inhaled the smell of horse and manure. He looked toward the racetrack, which was partially hidden in the cold and damp haze. The grandstands were barely visible through the mist.

On both sides of the stable hill stood rows of stables. A solitary horse was jogging around in an enclosure. A steel contraption of some kind was keeping the horse on the path and regulating its pace.

"It's called a horsewalker," said Jacobsson when she saw Knutas's look of puzzlement. "Horses that aren't going to be taken out riding can still get exercise. They may have an injury or be suffering from a cold or something else that means they shouldn't be ridden as hard as usual. Ingenious, isn't it?"

She led the way into the stable.

The horses had just been given their lunch feed, and the only sound was a pleasant munching along with an occasional stomping. Everything seemed very orderly. The floor was scrubbed clean, and the green-painted stalls were properly closed with locks. Halters hung on hooks outside each door. Shelves were filled with neat rows of supplies: bottles of liniment and baby oil, scissors, rolls of tape, hoof scrapers. Shin guards were stacked in baskets, along with rolls of binding tape, brushes, and other grooming tools. A barrel of sawdust stood in one corner. A black kitten lay on top of a feed box, sound asleep. In one window a radio was playing music at low volume.

They had made an appointment to meet with Sven Ekholm, who was both the trainer and the owner of the stable, but he was nowhere in sight. A stable girl appeared and took them over to a closed door that led to a coffee room.

Ekholm was sitting with his legs propped up on a round coffee table, talking on the phone. He motioned for them to sit down. Daylight was doing its best to penetrate through the dusty windowpanes. Spots of dried coffee marred the red plastic tablecloth. The table was covered with papers, stacks of racing newspapers, vitamin bottles, mugs, glasses, filthy riding shoes, rubber boots, and some three-ring binders. The ceiling was coated with spiderwebs. In one corner there was a kitchenette with a couple of hot plates, a dirty microwave, and a dusty coffeemaker. The walls were covered with finish-line photos of various horses, and a pile of dried roses lay on top of a cabinet. It wasn't hard to see what took priority in the world of these people.

Ekholm took his feet off the table and finished his phone conversation.

"Hello, and welcome. Would you like some coffee?"

They both said yes. Ekholm was a handsome man in his forties. He was muscular and moved with grace. His dark hair was tousled. He was wearing black pants and a gray turtleneck sweater. With some difficulty he managed to find clean cups, and after a moment they each had a cup of coffee; a plastic box of gingersnaps sat in front of them on the table.

"Can you tell us about Fanny Jansson?" Jacobsson began. "We understand that she spends a great deal of her free time here at the stable."

Sven Ekholm leaned back in his chair.

"She's a smart girl who works hard. Not very talkative, but she has a good way with the horses."

"How often is she here?" asked Knutas.

"How often is she here at the stable, you mean?" asked the trainer and then went on without waiting for a reply. "Probably four or five times a week, I would guess."

"When was she last here?"

"Yes, when was she last here?" Ekholm repeated. "I think the last time I saw her was a week ago, maybe on Thursday or Friday."

"How did she seem?"

"How did she seem?" Ekholm rubbed his chin. "I was busy driving, so I just said a quick hello. It might be better if you talked to the others in the stable—they spend more time with her than I do."

"Is Fanny paid for her work here?"

"Is she paid? No, that's how it is with stable girls, you know. They come here because they think it's fun to be around horses. To groom them and take care of them. That's how girls are at that age."

Sven Ekholm took a quick sip of coffee.

"How long has Fanny been coming to the stable?"

"How long has she been coming here? Hmm, maybe a year or so."

"Does she have a particularly good relationship with any of the employees?" asked Knutas, who was starting to get annoyed by the man's tendency to repeat every question.

"Any of the employees that she has a particularly good relationship with? Well, yes, that would be Janne. They seem to get along well. Otherwise she's quite shy, as I said."

"And how often are you here?" asked Jacobsson.

"Hm, what should I say? Twenty-five hours a day," he said with a grin. "Well, practically every day. I've been trying to take at least one day off every other weekend. I do have a wife and kids, too—I can't just live at the stable."

"How well do you know Fanny?"

"Not very well. She doesn't exactly welcome contact. I always have so much to do that I can't just sit around chatting with all the young girls who come here."

Why didn't Ekholm repeat the questions when Jacobsson asked them? Knutas found it enormously annoying.

"Where do you live?" Jacobsson went on.

"Right nearby. We've taken over my father's farm. Well, my father still lives there, in the guesthouse."

"Does your wife work at the stable, too?"

"Yes, she does. We have six full-time employees, and she's one of them."

"How is the work divided up?"

"We all help each other, training the horses and taking care of them, and lending a hand around the stable. It's a full-time job all year-round, even when the racing season is over."

"We'd like to talk to everyone. Can you arrange that?"

"Sure, no problem. Right now it's just me and Jan, I'm afraid. But later in the day, or tomorrow."

Knutas realized that he would have to ask one more question, just to see if the trainer had decided to stop repeating them.

"How many others work at the stable? Girls who work for free after school, and so on?"

"Girls who work for free after school, and so on? Well, we have quite a few of them. We used to have more, but it doesn't seem to be as popular as it once was. Or else maybe they have too much home-work lately," said the trainer, giving Knutas a smile.

As they left the coffee room, Jacobsson noticed that her colleague's expression was as dark as a thundercloud.

The interview with the stable hand, Jan Olsson, went better.

The man was slightly older than the trainer, maybe forty-five, Knu-tas guessed. He was darker than most Swedes. Brown eyes that were almost black, distinct eyebrows that grew together, and a stubble that looked to be several days old. Wiry and muscular from years of work-ing with horses. Not an ounce of fat on his body—that was evident from the shirt and dirty pants that he had on. He was not wearing a wedding ring. Knutas wondered if he lived with anyone but decided to wait to ask that question. Instead, he asked him to tell them once again what happened when Fanny left the stable. Olsson gave the same account as had been recorded in the previous report.

"Try to recall any details you can," said Knutas. "Anything that might seem insignificant could actually be important."

Jan Olsson ran his hand over the stubble on his face. He made a very frank and sympathetic impression.

"No, I really can't think of anything. She takes care of the horses and doesn't usually talk much. When she came back from her ride, she was happier than I've seen her in a long time. Her eyes were actu-ally shining. After grooming Calypso and taking care of the harness, she said good-bye and left on her bike."

"What do you think might have happened to her?"

"I don't think she committed suicide, at any rate. She was much too happy and upbeat when she left here. I have a hard time imagining her going off to kill herself."

"How well do you know her?"

"Quite well, I think. She seems to like being here, but I understand that she doesn't have an easy home life. She's always in a hurry to rush home because she has to take the dog out. As I understand it, her mother is rather difficult, but I've never met her."

"Has Fanny ever talked about any friends or anyone she hung out with?"

"She doesn't seem to have any friends, since she spends all her time over here. Those of us who work in the stable are much older. Although she sometimes talks to Tom, who works in the next stable."

"Is that right?"

"I've seen them talking to each other on the stable hill once in a while. They seem to get along. Fanny isn't exactly the most open person, so I notice when she talks to anyone."

"Are they the same age?"

"God, no. He must be thirty, at least. He's American but I think he's lived in Sweden for a long time. You can tell because of the way he speaks Swedish."

"What's his last name?"

"Kingsley."

"And how long has he worked here?"

"At least a year, maybe more."

Tom Kingsley was busy wrapping the hind leg of a horse when they entered the adjoining stable. Knutas and Jacobsson kept back a safe distance.

"We've heard that you know Fanny Jansson, the girl who has disappeared. Is that right?" Knutas began.

"Well, I can't say that I really know her. I've talked to her once in a while."

He didn't look up, just went on with his work.

"We need to ask you a couple of questions."

"Sure, I just need to finish this. I'm working on the last leg right now."

In spite of a distinctly American accent, his Swedish was fluent. When he was done, he stood up with a grimace and stretched out his back.

"What do you want to know?"

"How well do you know Fanny Jansson?"

"Not very well. We talk occasionally."

"How did you happen to meet each other?"

"Good Lord, we both work here. Of course we would see each other around the stables. We're always running into each other."

"What do you talk about?"

"Mostly about the horses, of course. But other things, too. How she's doing in school and about her home, and things like that."

"How do you think she's doing?"

"Not great, actually."

"What do you mean by that?"

"She complains about her mother, says that things are tough at home."

"In what way?"

"She told me that her mother drinks too much."

"So she has actually confided in you a great deal?"

"I don't know about that."

"Have you seen each other outside the stable?"

"No, no. Just here."

"Do you know whether she has met anyone new lately? A boyfriend, maybe?"

"I have no idea."

"When did you last see her?"

"It was on Saturday."

"Where?"

"Here, outside." He nodded toward the stables.

"How did she seem?"

"The same as usual."

"Do you have any idea where she might be?"

"Not a clue."

There was no one else at the stable to question. They left Tom Kingsley and went back to their car.

"What do you think happened?" asked Knutas as they drove back to police headquarters.

"It's possible that she might have killed herself."

"I have a hard time imagining that. She's too young. Fourteen-year-old girls who commit suicide are rare. They're usually at least a couple of years older. Besides, she didn't seem particularly depressed, even though things might have been worse than they seemed on the outside. I think all three men at the stable seem credible, although the trainer was damned irritating."

"I agree," said Jacobsson. "I didn't get any weird vibes from any of them."

By the afternoon Fanny had still not turned up. Her mother called Knutas to hear how the search was going. She was distraught. Her sister in Vibble, south of Visby, had stepped in to look after her. Knutas decided to begin searching the areas surrounding Fanny's apartment, her school, and the stable. A bulletin was broadcast on the local radio station and immediately attracted the interest of the media. Radio Gotland and both of the local newspapers, *Gotlands Tidningar* and *Gotlands Allehanda,* wanted to interview him.

Knutas tried to be generous with the press and agreed to brief interviews.

He dealt with one journalist after the other, and they all asked basically the same questions. He kept the interviews short, telling them only when Fanny had disappeared, where she was last seen, and what she looked like. He asked the reporters to say that the police were appealing to the public for help.

The search brought results. Fanny's bicycle was found by a passerby. It had been tossed into a ditch less than a kilometer from the stable. It was immediately taken in so that the techs could examine it.

Johan Berg also called.

"Hi. Am I disturbing you?"

"I'm very busy at the moment."

"I'm calling about the girl who disappeared. It just came over the wire service. What happened?"

Knutas gave him the same information that he had given to the other journalists, but he also told Johan about the bicycle. He thought he owed him that much.

"Do you suspect foul play?"

"Not at the moment."

"Do you think she might have committed suicide?"

"We can't rule out that possibility, of course."

"What's her home life like?"

"She and her mother live alone in an apartment here in Visby."

"Is she an only child?"

"Yes."

"The description says that she has a dark complexion. Was she adopted, or is her mother from some other country?"

"Her father is from the West Indies."

"Where does he live?"

"In Stockholm, with his wife and kids. They don't have any contact with each other."

"Could she have gone there?"

"We've talked to the father, of course. And she's not there."

"She could still have gone to Stockholm," said Johan.

"Sure."

"Did she take along any money, or her passport?"

"There's nothing to indicate that. All her belongings are still at home," replied Knutas impatiently. Why couldn't Johan Berg ever be satisfied with the same information he gave to all the other journalists? He never gave up asking more questions.

"The fact that her bike was found tossed aside could mean that she got into a car. Was it found near a road?"

"That's right. I have to go now."

"I realize that you've got your hands full, what with the murder investigation, too. Is there anything to indicate she might have fallen into the hands of the same perpetrator as Dahlström?"

"Not at the moment."

Knutas shook his head as he put down the phone. What a stubborn man that journalist was.

The next second the phone rang again. The switchboard told him that a woman from the youth clinic in Visby wanted to talk to him. He told the operator to put her through.

"Hi, my name is Gunvor Andersson, and I'm a midwife. The girl that I think you're looking for was here recently."

"Is that right? How do you know it was her?"

"I recognized her from the description on the radio. She was here several months ago, asking for birth control pills."

"Did she say why?"

"She said that she had a steady boyfriend. I asked her whether she really felt old enough to have intercourse. I said that we usually don't recommend the Pill for such young girls. She said that they had already done it. I told her that since she's under fifteen, it's a crime to have sexual intercourse with her. On the other hand, we can't very well refuse to give the Pill to a girl who wants to protect herself. We usually require a parent's consent in the case of such young girls, but when I said that I would have to call her mother, she didn't want anything more to do with us. She just got up and left. I tried to stop her, to say that we could talk about it, but before I knew it, she had walked right out the door."

"Did you find out who her boyfriend was?"

"No, unfortunately. She refused to say anything about him."

After Knutas finished talking to the woman, he called Majvor Jansson.

"Did you know that Fanny has a boyfriend?"

"No, I'm sure she doesn't."

"She went to the youth clinic to ask for birth control pills."

"What?"

"Yes, I've just talked to someone over there. She went there several months ago to get a prescription for the Pill, but when they told her that they would have to contact you, she left. I need you to think about this some more. Was there anything to indicate that she had a boyfriend? Was she spending time with anyone?"

There was a long silence on the other end of the line.

"She never said anything about it. But it's hard to keep tabs on her, because I work nights and I'm a single mother. She could always meet someone in the evening, since that's when I'm at work."

Majvor Jansson was clearly about to start crying again.

"I was thinking of trying to get a different shift, now that she's getting older. But I didn't think there was any danger yet. She's only fourteen, after all."

In the meantime, the search continued. A hundred volunteers offered to help the search-and-rescue groups that had been organized at various sites. The sense of alarm about what had happened to Fanny was growing with every hour that passed.

At 8:00 P.M. the investigative team gathered for a meeting at police headquarters. The mood was tense. Knutas told them about his phone conversation with the woman from the youth clinic and Fanny's failed attempt to obtain birth control pills. Sohlman, who looked worn out, told them about the results of searching Fanny's room.

"We've found three packets of morning-after pills hidden among the clothes in Fanny's closet. Two were empty; one still had both pills. That proves that she has had intercourse with someone."

"It doesn't take much detective work to come to that conclusion," Jacobsson interjected acidly. "But morning-after pills? Aren't they supposed to be used in extreme emergencies? Surely they're not meant to be used for birth control?"

She glanced around the room. When she saw the blank expressions on the faces of her colleagues, she realized that she worked with a bunch of middle-aged men who had all been cast from the same mold and who probably knew nothing about how that sort of pill worked.

"How many pills did she take?" asked Jacobsson, turning to Sohlman.

"There are two in each package, and from what I understand, that counts as one dose. So she took four pills, or two doses."

"Where do you get them? In a drugstore? Can a fourteen-year-old go out and buy them? Don't you have to be at least fifteen?"

No one at the table could answer Jacobsson's questions.

"All right," she said with a sigh. "I'll call the youth clinic."

Her colleagues looked relieved to get out of hearing any more embarrassing questions that they couldn't answer.

Sohlman went on. "Bloodstains and hairs that are not hers were found on the bedspread. They are short, dark, coarse hairs. In her bed we also found sperm and pubic hair, but we can't say yet who they're from. Everything has been sent to SCL. We also sent over some things that her mother didn't recognize and couldn't explain where Fanny had gotten them."

He read from a list: "One bottle of perfume, one necklace, several rings, one sweater, one dress, and two pairs of underwear. Quite sophisticated underwear, I might add," he said, clearing his throat. "We haven't found anything of interest on her bike."

When Sohlman fell silent, a heavy mood settled over the room. Their apprehension that Fanny was in trouble had been significantly reinforced by his report.

Wittberg broke the silence. "What the hell should we do?" he said with a resigned sigh. "What do we have to go on?"

"There's plenty we can do," Knutas objected. "While we wait for the lab results, we need to expand the search area. Tips have been coming in from the public, and they have to be processed."

"How should we divide up the work between the Dahlström investigation and this case?" asked Norrby.

"We'll work on them in tandem. We've done that before. Don't forget that we don't know what's happened to Fanny Jansson. She might turn up tomorrow."

When Johan came home from work on Wednesday evening, he found to his surprise that Emma was sitting on the steps. She looked pale and hollow-eyed, wearing her yellow quilted jacket.

"Emma, what are you doing here?" he exclaimed.

"I'm sorry that I was so mad yesterday, Johan. I just don't know what to do."

"Come inside."

She followed him in and without a word sank down on the sofa.

"I'm about to lose my footing altogether. Olle still won't let me talk to the children. I was thinking of going over to their school yesterday, but the school counselor advised me not to. She thinks that I should wait. I've talked to their teachers, and the children seem to be doing all right. The only thing they seem to know is that we're going through a crisis, and that I've taken a leave of absence from my job."

She pushed back her bangs. "Is it okay if I smoke?"

"Sure, go ahead and smoke. Do you want something to drink?"

"Yes, please. A glass of wine or a beer, if you have any."

Johan took two beers out of the fridge and sat down next to her.

"What are you thinking of doing?"

"That's exactly what I don't know," she said, sounding annoyed.

He touched her cheek.

"Have you quit your job?"

"I called in sick. Without giving any explanation. My job feels like the least important thing at the moment."

"Olle will calm down. You'll see. Don't worry about that. After a while you'll be able to talk to each other again."

"I just don't understand why he reacted so strongly. He's shown so little interest in me and our relationship during the past few years. He really shouldn't be surprised. But to hell with him. The only thing I can think about is Sara and Filip. You have no idea how tough this is."

He reached out his hand and caressed her cheek.

She grabbed his hand, kissed it, and put it on her breast. When he kissed her, the response was fierce. It was as if she were hungering for him, for physical contact, for solace. He wanted to transmit his own strength to her, to give her the energy she obviously needed. There was something disconsolate and desperate about the way she made love to him that night.

Afterward she fell asleep, curled up in his arms like a child. For a long time Johan lay in the dark, looking at her profile and listening to her breathing.

THURSDAY, NOVEMBER 29

The media's interest in the disappearance of Fanny Jansson continued to grow as the hours passed. More and more people became involved in the search groups, and the police were using helicopters and infrared cameras in the woods around Visby as they intensified their search. On Thursday morning both evening papers ran big articles about the missing girl. Her picture dominated the front pages.

When Johan came into the Regional News editorial offices, he was met by Grenfors waving several newspapers in his hand.

"What the hell is this?" he shouted. His face was bright red. "Both *Aftonbladet* and *Expressen* have big spreads about the missing girl. Weren't you supposed to keep on top of this story?"

"Could you let me take off my jacket first?" Johan snapped back. He had waited at the Hornstull subway station for twenty minutes for a train that never came. The red line was having problems again. And then Stockholm Local Traffic had the nerve to raise the price of a monthly pass.

Grenfors stubbornly followed him as he went to his desk.

"How come we didn't have anything to report?" he continued, standing behind Johan.

Since Johan was painfully aware that he had been concentrating too much on Emma and too little on his job lately, he had no good answer. She had flown home this morning, and it would probably be a while before they saw each other again.

"I'll make some calls and check things out," he said.

"Maybe there's a connection to the murder of that alcoholic. The killer is still on the loose, after all."

"Do you think I should go over there?" asked Johan hopefully.

"That depends on what you find out."

He got out the local papers from the stack of dailies and listened to the Radio Gotland morning news on the Internet. It was true that they were reporting that Fanny Jansson was still missing, but the police also seemed to be working with a number of new clues. It was the same story as in the newspapers, which had reported how the search was being conducted and the fact that the girl's bicycle had been found.

It was damn stupid that he had been so lax at keeping tabs on the investigation. Regional News was now way behind in reporting the story. It was a big disadvantage that he wasn't on site in Gotland and able to follow developments. The evening papers were both speculating, of course, whether the same person who had murdered the alcoholic might have struck again.

With a sigh he picked up the phone and punched in Knutas's number. No answer, and his cell was turned off. Damn it. He tried Karin Jacobsson. He had dealt with her quite a bit during the summer. She sounded stressed.

"Jacobsson here."

"Hi, this is Johan Berg from Regional News. I wonder how it's going with the search for Fanny Jansson."

The voice on the other end of the line softened. Johan realized that he was still in the good graces of the Visby police, at least for the moment.

"We're working on a wide front. The search is now under way in the area around her school, her apartment building, and the racetrack, which is where she was last seen. But so far the results have been meager. We've found her bicycle, but I'm sure you already know that."

"Yes. Are there any prints on it?"

"You'll have to take that up with Anders Knutas. He's the only one who can decide what we tell the media."

"I've been trying to reach him, but he doesn't answer his phone."

"No, he's in a meeting with the new officers from the National Criminal Police right now. It will probably go on for another hour."

"Have you brought in more personnel from the NCP? Why is that?"

"As I said, you'll have to talk to Knutas."

"Okay. Thank you anyway. Bye."

He leaned back in his chair. The fact that the police were receiving more help from the NCP meant that they were taking a serious view of the case. Something else must have come to light, indicating that a crime was involved. He got up and went over to the desk where Grenfors was sitting with a phone pressed to his ear, as usual.

Sometimes Johan wondered how much time he wasted waiting for people to finish talking on the phone. He noticed that Grenfors had dyed his hair again. The editor had recently turned fifty, and he was meticulous about his appearance. He was always dressed in a sporty and youthful manner. On principle, he never ate lunch with his colleagues; instead, he preferred to make use of his pass to the gym in the television building. He was tall, slim, and trim. He looked good for his age. Max Grenfors was married to an attractive woman who was fifteen years younger and an aerobics instructor.

When the editor finally put down the phone, Johan told him what Jacobsson had said.

"Let's wait and see what Knutas has to say. It's too late for you to go over there today, unless they have something really significant to report. From here you can put together some text for the anchorman, so that we can at least keep the pot boiling. You and Peter can fly over tomorrow if it seems worthwhile."

That evening Johan went out with his friend Andreas. They started at the Vampire Lounge on Östgötagatan, where the drinks were cheap and the atmosphere relaxed. The female bartender had short cropped hair and was dressed all in black and wore big earrings. When she turned around to rinse some glasses, a tattoo was visible at the small of her back. She mixed each of them a frozen margarita in a glass with a spiral stem. The bar was filled with a relatively young crowd, most of them with a pack of Marlboro Lights in front of them on the bar. In the restaurants at lunchtime hardly anyone ever smoked, but in the evenings nearly everyone had a cigarette hanging from their lips.

"You seem a little out of sorts," said Andreas after they had run through the usual chitchat about their work and various sports events.

"Not really, just a little tired," said Johan as he lit a cigarette, like everyone else in the place.

"How are things going with your Gotland girlfriend, Emma?"

"Good, but it's tough, too, you know. With her husband and kids and everything."

Andreas shook his head. "Why are you getting mixed up with a married woman who has little kids? And who lives on Gotland! Could you make your life any more complicated?"

"I know," said Johan with a sigh. "But you don't understand because you've never really been in love with anyone."

"What the hell to you mean? Of course I have. I was with Ellen for five years," Andreas protested.

"Sure, but what do you really know about love? You had your doubts the whole time. You were always grumbling about one thing or another. The fact that she was a vegetarian, that she was always late, that she was messy, and that she didn't seem to have any plan for her life. And the fact that she kept studying and studying, but it never led anywhere and she never had any money. Have you forgotten about all that?"

Andreas let out a roar of laughter.

"Of course not, but do you know what she ended up doing? I ran into her downtown a month ago. Newly married with a baby on the way. She lives in Saltsjöbaden and is head of a big advertising agency. And on top of that, she's damn cute!"

"You see? You never can tell about anyone!" said Johan, laughing.

They started talking to three cheerful girls from Västberga, and then they all continued on to Kvarnen, the legendary Södermalm pub. Johan ran into some of his journalist colleagues and got into such an intense discussion about worldwide current events that both Andreas and the girls got bored and left.

When Johan caught a cab home around three in the morning, Emma was once more on his mind. What was she doing right now? He wanted to send her a text message but restrained himself. They had agreed that it would be her turn to call next.

SATURDAY, DECEMBER 1

Olle had suddenly called and invited her home for dinner. Finally she would be able to see the children. It was not even a week since she had last seen them, but it felt like a month—at least. She had called the night before and had a chance to talk to them for the first time since she was thrown out of the house. Both Sara and Filip sounded happy and strangely unaffected, in spite of everything that had happened. She wondered what was going on inside their young heads.

During the week various scenarios had fluttered through her mind. One moment it seemed right to get a divorce; the next she wanted nothing more than to be a family again, and she wished that she had never met Johan.

In the middle of everything she became very aware of the fragility of life. She was surrounded by stage sets that were ostensibly solid, but they could crumble at any moment and completely change everything.

At the same time, she was struck by her own stupidity. What was she thinking? That she could have an affair on the side, just to satisfy her own need for validation? She hadn't realized that she was playing with fire.

Was she prepared to sacrifice everything for Johan? She should have asked herself that question after the first kiss.

Her husband had given her his love, he had taken responsibility, he had kept the promise he had made when they got married. But what about her?

When he had reacted by throwing her out, the ground opened up beneath her.

Right now she had no idea what to think. Except that she was eager for the meeting with Olle to go well. She was deathly afraid that he was going to do something final, such as handing her divorce papers. There was something in Olle's voice when he called, a different tone that indicated something had changed. And it made her nervous.

She felt like a stranger on the evening of her visit—a guest in her own house. Olle looked happy when he opened the door. He took her coat and hung it up as if this were the first time she had ever come to the house. The situation was absurd. Irritation was just seconds from becoming visible on her face. But then the children came running out to the hall.

She was showered with soft kisses and fierce hugs. She loved holding their warm bodies close and breathing in their scent. Both children were eager to show her the gingerbread house that they had made with Pappa.

"Oh, how lovely," she told the children as they pointed to the towers and pinnacles. "It looks like a real castle!"

"It's a gingerbread castle, Mamma," said Filip.

Olle stood in the doorway. He was wearing an apron, his hair was disheveled, and he looked like a marvelous father. She felt an instinctive urge to give him a hug, but she controlled herself.

"Dinner is ready. Come on, let's eat."

When they had finished eating and the children were sent out to watch cartoons on TV, Olle refilled their wineglasses.

"Well, I've been wanting to have a proper discussion with you. That's why I asked you to come here tonight. I didn't want to talk on the phone."

"Okay," she said cautiously.

"I've been thinking and thinking. At first I was so mad. I never thought you would do something like this to me. When I found that text message, it made me see red. I really felt as if I hated you, and I wanted to tell the whole world about what you had done. It was as if I'd been living a lie. How could I have been so fucking stupid and not suspected anything? It was all so damn crazy. Not to mention how I felt about that jerk from TV. So many times I've been on the verge of going to Stockholm to rip him to shreds."

He took a sip of wine.

"But in spite of everything I realized that there was nothing to gain by punching him in the mouth. Maybe an assault charge, but that would undoubtedly make him happier than it would me."

Emma couldn't help smiling.

"My anger faded after a couple of days, and then I started to think more clearly. I thought about us, how we are together. I've replayed our whole life in here."

He tapped two fingers against his temple.

"Everything we've done together and all my feelings for you. I've come to the conclusion that I don't want to. Get a divorce, that is. Even though you've hurt me terribly, because you really have. But no matter how bad it is, I realize that I'm also partly to blame for the whole thing. I haven't paid much attention to you, I haven't listened when you wanted to talk. Not that I'm excusing what you did, but that might have contributed to it. It will take a while before I can trust you again, but I'm prepared to try."

Emma was totally confused. This was not what she had expected.

"Olle, I don't know. It's all so sudden. I don't know what to say."

"You don't have to say anything. But at least now you know what I want," he said and got up to make coffee.

They drank their coffee in front of the TV with the children and then put them to bed. She left the house without voicing any decision, either to Olle or to herself.

SUNDAY, DECEMBER 2

Five days had passed since Fanny Jansson had disappeared, and there had been no progress. The girl was still missing. With each day that passed, the police became more and more convinced that there had been foul play. Knutas's frustration grew. Not only did his mood get worse, his sleep was also affected. It was Sunday and the first day of Advent, but he was already awake by six o'clock. He had slept badly, with a hodgepodge of dreams. The dream images had merged into one another: Henry Dahlström with his head bashed in, Fanny Jansson wandering through the Botanical Gardens, Martin Kihlgård from the NCP chewing on pork chops served by Prosecutor Birger Smittenberg. Everything became jumbled together in his groggy mind, and he awoke exhausted, not knowing where he was or what time it was. He found himself staring at his wife's ear and realized that the whole thing had been a dream. Maybe it was the wind that had made him uneasy. It was roaring and howling over the roof, whistling through the rain gutters.

The weather had turned in the night. The wind was now coming from the north, and the temperature had dropped several degrees. Outside it was pitch dark, and snow was whirling in the gusty wind. Lina stretched out in bed next to him.

"Are you awake?" she asked, sounding sleepy.

"Yes. I was having such strange dreams."

"About what?"

"I can't really remember. It was just a mishmash."

"My poor boy," she murmured, nuzzling the back of his neck. "It must be your work that's getting to you. And look at this weather. Are you hungry?"

She was mixing Danish words with Swedish. He liked to tease her by saying that she still sounded as if she had oatmeal stuck in her throat when she talked. But he had adopted quite a few Danish words and expressions himself, and the children spoke an odd blend of Gotland Swedish and Danish.

When they sat down at the breakfast table he clearly noticed the pain. An aching, throbbing pain on the insides of his elbows, around his wrists, and at the backs of his knees, which confirmed the change in weather. It was a pain that he had lived with for as far back as he could remember. After the new weather conditions had gone on for a few days, the pain would vanish as quickly as it had appeared. There was no explanation for it, and no one in his family had experienced anything similar. By now Knutas was so used to it that he didn't think much about it. It was worse when the weather changed from warm to cold, like today.

He poured himself another cup of coffee. The uncertainty about Fanny Jansson was still gnawing at him.

Some of his colleagues were guessing it was suicide. He didn't believe in that theory, but as a matter of routine he had checked out several commonly used spots. One of them was Högklint outside of Visby, a steep precipice with a sharp drop to the sea below. But their search had turned up nothing.

As for the murder of Dahlström, they had made no further progress. The investigation had come to a standstill, and the only positive thing was that the media's interest in the case had begun to wane.

The impasse meant that Knutas could afford to take a day off and spend it with his family. Christmas was right around the corner. It was Shop Window Sunday, and they had made plans to meet Leif and Ingrid Almlöv to take a stroll downtown.

Knutas had been looking forward to forgetting all about the investigation, but the Almlövs immediately started talking about it.

"It's so horrible, the story about that girl who's missing," Ingrid began as soon as they had said hello. "She works at the stable where my father has his horse, Big Boy. Actually, we own half the horse."

"We own it together, but your father is the only one who's really interested. He was the one who wanted to buy it," said Leif.

"Well, it's terrible, at any rate. What do you think has happened to her?" asked Ingrid, turning to Knutas.

"It could be anything. Maybe she was in an accident, maybe she killed herself, or maybe she ran away from home. It doesn't have to involve any sort of crime."

"But you think that it does?"

Knutas didn't reply. Lina jumped in and started talking about the Christmas decorations that had been put up all over town.

The stores had made a real effort to create a holiday atmosphere. The wind had now subsided and the falling snow made everything look magical. Garlands of evergreen boughs were hung overhead between the buildings, and lights attached to the branches cast a warm glow over the streets. At Stora Torget, booths had been specially set up for the day, selling Christmas candy and handicrafts. Hot glögg and gingersnaps were available. The loudspeakers were blaring Christmas carols, and later in the afternoon people would gather to dance around the big Christmas tree in the middle of the marketplace. A fat Santa was handing out sparklers to the children. Even the smallest shops were open on this Sunday, and they hadn't seen so many people crowding onto the biggest shopping street, Adelsgatan, since high season last summer.

No matter where they turned, they saw familiar faces. They stopped to talk with people on every street corner. All four of them were well-known in Visby—Knutas in his capacity as detective superintendent, Lina as a midwife, and the Almlövs as restaurant owners. They went into a café to have hot cocoa with whipped cream and saffron rolls.

Knutas's cell phone rang. It was Karin Jacobsson.

"We've heard from Agneta Stenberg. She's the girl who works at the same stable as Fanny Jansson, but she's been away on vacation. She came home today, and she says that Fanny has a relationship with that man Tom Kingsley."

"What sort of proof does she have?"

"I've asked her to come in and talk to us. I thought you might want to be here."

"Of course. I'll be there in ten minutes."

Agneta Stenberg sat down on the sofa in Knutas's office, across from
Knutas and Jacobsson. Her dark suntan was accentuated by her white
turtleneck sweater. *How on earth has she managed to get such a tan in
only one week?* thought Jacobsson.

Agneta got right to the point.

"I think that they're more than friends. I've seen them hugging and
carrying on several times."

"Are you sure?"

"Of course I am."

"What do you mean by 'carrying on'?" asked Jacobsson.

Agneta squirmed nervously. She looked embarrassed.

"It's the kind of things that you notice. They stood very close together. You could see him stroking her arm. Intimate gestures that
only happen between people if something is going on. Do you know
what I mean?"

"Yes, we do," said Knutas. "When did this start?"

"They met on the stable hill and they've been talking to each other
for a long time. It might have been in October that I noticed them
hugging for the first time. It was near one of the outdoor stalls, a short
distance away from the stable. It made me really uncomfortable, to tell
you the truth. I mean, he's at least twice her age."

"What makes you think that there was anything strange about it?
They could just be friends, giving each other a hug."

"I don't think so. When they caught sight of me, they let go of each
other. And after that I've seen them hugging at other times."

"Did they do anything else?"

"No, not that I saw."

"Have any of you talked about this at the stable?"

"I mentioned it to a couple of people, but they thought it was probably just friendly hugging, that they were just friends."

"Why do you think they thought that?"

"It's because she's so young. No one could imagine that a nice guy
like Tom would be seeing her. Everybody thinks he's so great."

"But you don't?"

"Oh sure, there's nothing wrong with him, but that doesn't mean that he might not be taking advantage of Fanny. She looks older than she is."

"Have you ever asked Fanny about her relationship with Tom?"

"No."

"What about Tom?"

"No. But maybe I should have." She gave them a solemn look. "What do you think has happened to her?"

Knutas's expression was worried as he replied. "We don't know," he said. "We really don't know."

Knutas called Tom Kingsley and asked him to come down to the station. He seemed reluctant but promised to be there within the hour.

"Maybe Kingsley is the secret boyfriend," said Knutas to Jacobsson as they had coffee and sandwiches while waiting for him to show up.

"It's possible," said Jacobsson between bites. "But why didn't he say anything about being close to her when we talked to him at the stable?"

"Maybe he was ashamed. I would be if I was seeing a fourteen-year-old girl."

"If it's true that they have a relationship, that alone would make him a suspect. If you're thirty years old and you start having an affair with a fourteen-year-old, there's something seriously wrong. That much is clear."

Tom Kingsley seemed nervous and tense when he at last showed up almost two hours later. He was wearing his stable clothes, and Knutas was bothered by the horse smell.

"I'm sorry about my clothes, but I've come straight from work," said Kingsley, as if he had read their minds.

"That's okay," lied Knutas. "When we met you at the stable the other day, you described your relationship with Fanny as superficial. You said that you don't know each other very well. Do you stick by what you said?"

Kingsley hesitated.

"Yes . . . you might say that."

"But you don't seem quite so certain anymore."

"That depends on what you mean."

Knutas felt a growing irritation. He found people who lied to his face tremendously annoying.

"In what way?"

"What does it mean to know someone well? I'm not sure."

"You said that you usually just chat a little."

"That's right."

"So you don't have any sort of closer relationship?"

"Not really."

"We've been given information that indicates otherwise. We've been told that you've been seeing each other. That you have a romantic relationship."

Tom Kingsley's expression darkened.

"Who the hell has been spreading lies like that?"

"We can't tell you that. But is it true?"

"Who the hell would say such a thing? They're out of their minds!"

"Just answer the question. Do you or do you not have a relationship with Fanny Jansson?"

"That's sick." Kingsley shook his head. "She's just a child, for God's sake."

Knutas was about to lose his patience.

"Yes, that's exactly what we want to know, and we have our reasons," he snapped. "Answer the question."

"Of course I don't. Fanny and I are just good friends. Nothing more. Nobody should be spreading lies that we're seeing each other."

"Why didn't you say anything about this before, when we talked to you the first time? Why didn't you say that you're in the habit of hugging each other?"

"We're not in the habit of hugging each other, damn it."

"But have you ever hugged?"

"I may have given her a little hug, but it was just a way of comforting her. She needs support. The girl has a terrible home life. Her mother drinks, and she doesn't have a father or any brothers or sisters. She has no friends. She's all alone. Can you understand that? She's all alone!"

Tom Kingsley had grown very angry.

"So you deny having a relationship with Fanny. Is that correct?" asked Knutas.

Kingsley merely shook his head in reply.

"How do you explain that people think the two of you have been seeing each other?"

"It must be their sick imaginations. Can't a guy even show a girl a little kindness and concern? This is crazy, damn it! Is Agneta the one who told you this? Agneta Stenberg?"

Knutas and Jacobsson looked at each other in surprise.

"Why would you think that?" they said in unison.

"Because she's jealous, of course. She's been following me around for months, but I told her that I wasn't interested. We had a party for the stable employees a while back, and that's when she really put the moves on me. I finally had to tell her to get lost."

Knutas was amazed at Kingsley's verbal prowess. He spoke perfect colloquial Swedish. If it weren't for a slight accent, anyone would take him for a native speaker.

When the interview was over, Knutas felt disappointed. He had been counting on catching Kingsley off guard so that he would be at a loss to come up with an answer. But that hadn't happened.

MONDAY, DECEMBER 3

There was no new trip to Gotland for Johan. *It's just as well,* he thought grimly. He hadn't heard a word from Emma all weekend. And yet they had just had such a cozy time together. He couldn't figure her out. If only she hadn't started to waver again.

At the moment Gotland seemed far away, also in terms of his work. Just as Grenfors finally seemed to be paying attention to the Gotland murder case, the police had reached an impasse. And besides, an act of madness had occurred at Stockholm's Medborgarplatsen in Södermalm at the very same time. Late on Monday afternoon, the newsroom learned that a madman had gone berserk with a crowbar, killing at least one person. Five others were injured, including an infant. Regional News was tipped off about the event practically as it was happening. Johan immediately took off with a camerawoman. In the car on the way there, he sat with his cell phone pressed to his ear, alternating between talking to the duty officer, emergency services, and the newsroom.

The camerawoman drove swiftly and expertly through the traffic, constantly changing lanes to gain time and occasionally making an illegal move, which was necessary for anyone who wanted to make good time. At Medborgarplatsen she brazenly parked the car right on the open square and instantly pulled out her camera.

Ambulances and police cars were on the scene. The police were starting to cordon off the area, and crowds of people watched in dismay as medics tended to the wounded.

Johan interviewed both the police and witnesses, who said that the man, without any sort of provocation, had started attacking anyone who happened to cross his path. Finally he threw down the iron bar and disappeared down the stairs to the subway station at Björn's Garden. All traffic had been halted, and the police were searching the subway cars and platforms, using dogs.

The newsroom was seething with activity when Johan returned. Grenfors was talking on two phones at once, the program producer was running between video-editing machines to make sure the reports were all ready on time while he also kept in contact with the national news program, which of course was also working intently on the drama in Södermalm.

The idea was for the news programs to collaborate; interviews were divided up among the reporters, clips were exchanged back and forth. The Regional News footage was much in demand, since their camerawoman had been first on the scene. The producer was busy lining up appropriate individuals to interview live in the studio. The county police commissioner was called in, along with the head of the homeless shelter, since many people had gotten the impression that the man who had gone amok was homeless. In the meantime, he was still at large.

Regional News sent a direct feed from Medborgarplatsen. People had started arriving there to light candles and torches and to leave flowers. The casualty count was now at two, since the infant had died from his injuries.

On his way home in the subway, Johan was again struck by the unusual working conditions of journalists. When the most horrible events occurred, they had to set aside their own feelings because their first priority was to report the story. Their professional role took over, but it had nothing to do with a hyena mentality, as some people scornfully implied when they poured out their venom at the media. Johan thought that, like himself, most journalists were driven by a desire to get the story—it was that simple. It was all a matter of reporting, as quickly and accurately as possible, what had happened. It was each reporter's responsibility to gather as much material as he could in order to present the best possible report.

Back in the newsroom, they went through all the material, discussing it with the editors. What was relevant to include in the broadcast and what was not? All close-ups of the wounded were omitted, interviews with people who were clearly in shock were rejected, and anything that was considered an invasion of privacy was cut.

Each day was a new day with more ethical discussions. And behind each news story there was careful deliberation, especially in the case of stories of a sensitive nature, such as this one. Of course there were occasional oversights when a name or a photo was broadcast that should not have been made public; the editors didn't always see the story before it was shown, since time was often tight. Yet for the most part, things went smoothly with regard to the ethical rules that applied to all journalists. Of course, there was always the occasional rotten egg who crossed the prescribed boundaries. Some TV stations and newspapers had stretched those boundaries rather far, but still, this applied to only a handful of reporters.

TUESDAY, DECEMBER 4

The perpetrator from the Medborgarplatsen attack was caught the next day as he lay sleeping in the corner of a garage in Skärholmen. That gave the media reports about the incident a new impetus.

That's the way the newsroom operated—the hottest story came first, and everything else had to wait. Something that was of intense interest one day could be completely forgotten the next. The list of priorities was constantly being revised at the morning meetings, during the day, and at the onset of each new event. The content of the workday was continuously being changed, renewed, and reversed to take in new points of view. One thing was certain—the job was seldom monotonous.

For that reason, the entire day had passed before Johan could think about Emma. But when he reached home, she once again dominated his thoughts. He called her even though he wasn't supposed to. She sounded tired.

"How are things going?"

"Better. I picked up the kids from school today."

"That's great."

"Yes."

Silence. Johan felt uneasiness settling in his stomach.

"Have you talked to Olle?"

"I'm at the house right now. He's reading a story to the children."

"What are you doing there? Have you moved back in?"

"No, but we have to be able to spend time together. You do understand that, don't you?"

She sounded annoyed, and she was speaking in a low voice, as if afraid that someone might hear.

"So he's not mad anymore?"

"Of course he's mad, but he has calmed down enough that we can talk, which means a lot to me. But I don't want to risk causing any more trouble by talking to you right now. Bye!"

Johan stared at the phone in bewilderment. At the same time the freezing temperature outdoors swiftly moved inside and took up lodging in his guts. All of a sudden she was giving priority to Olle again. She sounded as if he didn't mean shit to her, and that threat sapped him of all energy. He couldn't bear to lose her again.

WEDNESDAY, DECEMBER 5

Emma stared at the indicator in her hand. It just couldn't be true. Did two intersecting blue stripes forming a plus sign really mean that she was pregnant? It had been so long since she'd done this sort of test. With a pounding heart she got out the package. The directions couldn't be clearer. A blue line in the window meant not pregnant. Two blue lines intersecting meant pregnant. How could this be possible? She and Johan had slept together only once recently, two weeks ago. And she could hardly remember the last time she had slept with her husband. Frantically she searched her memory. When was the last time with Olle? It must have been last summer. She counted the months since then: August, September, October, November, December. Good Lord, that would make her five months pregnant, and she ought to be showing more than she was. But her period was only three weeks late, and she'd had regular periods all fall. She felt suddenly faint when she realized what that meant. It had to be Johan. That Friday in October. His work had brought him to Gotland, and he had called her up. She was feeling weak and had agreed to meet him at the newsroom before he went back home. They had made love on the sofa. Damn it. How could she have such incredible bad luck? The one time they had given in when they were supposed to be taking a break from each other, and she ended up pregnant. That kind of thing could only happen to her.

She felt tears filling her eyes. This was more than she could take.

She just about jumped out of her skin when someone knocked on the bathroom door. She heard Olle's voice saying, "Emma, are you almost ready?"

"Yes, just a minute."

She tossed the indicator and the empty package in the wastebasket. She couldn't say anything about this right now. She needed time to think. Quickly she washed her hands and opened the door.

"What's wrong? Why are you so pale?" Olle gave her a worried look. "Are you sick?"

"You might call it that. I'm pregnant."

THURSDAY, DECEMBER 13

Every seat was taken in Visby Cathedral on this morning to celebrate the Saint Lucia holiday. Knutas was sitting with Lina and Nils on the third pew to the right of the center aisle. The cross vaulting in the church ceiling high overhead and the magnificent arches cast long shadows, in contrast to the glow of hundreds of burning candles. The churchgoers were whispering quietly to each other as they waited with anticipation. Only an occasional cough or shuffling of feet from the pews broke the gentle murmuring.

The Lucia procession in the cathedral was one of the high points of the year. Petra was one of the bridesmaids. She sang in the youth choir, which was now participating in this year's Lucia procession, just as all the other choirs had done for as far back as anyone could remember. Knutas glanced through the brochure about the church as they waited for the event to begin. Construction of the St. Maria Cathedral was started in the twelfth century with funds collected from the German ships that docked at Visby. In the beginning it was meant to serve only German merchants, but later it became the church of the entire German congregation. After the Reformation, it was opened to everyone. No extensive changes to the church had been made since the Middle Ages, and that seemed to Knutas quite evident as he sat there admiring the high ceiling, the beautifully painted windows, and the pulpit, which had probably been imported from the German city of Lübeck in the seventeenth century.

Suddenly a faint singing could be heard in the church, and everyone turned their heads to look back toward the entrance. The tones of the traditional Lucia song grew louder, and the white-clad figure of Lucia appeared in the doorway. Slowly she walked forward, wearing a long white dress. On her head was a wreath with candles. Behind her walked the bridesmaids, two by two, with tinsel wrapped around their waists. They each held a lit candle. Behind them came the star boys, wearing paper cones on their heads.

The glow of the candles made it a magical spectacle, as the young people dressed in white walked forward, singing in their clear voices. A star boy who couldn't have been more than ten or eleven sang so beautifully in a loud and lovely voice that Knutas felt tears fill his eyes. In the middle of the solo, his cell phone began vibrating in the inside pocket of his jacket. Cautiously he pulled out the phone and held it up to his ear. It was hard to make out what Karin Jacobsson was saying on the other end. He managed to squeeze past the other people sitting on the pew and went out to the entryway.

"This better be important. I'm here watching my daughter in the Lucia celebration at the cathedral," he said.

"Fanny Jansson was found dead out on Lojsta Heath."

It took almost an hour to reach the site. Jacobsson and Knutas took the 142 down to Hejde and then headed out to Lojsta Heath. Old limestone farm buildings stood at the turnoff into the woods. A flock of black sheep with shaggy winter coats was crowded together at the fence, staring at them as they drove past.

A police car was waiting to show them the way. They bumped over the unpaved forest road, which was normally used only by tractors. The snow on the ground between the trees was untouched, and there was no wind. The low mixed forest had dense undergrowth, with withered ferns, heather, and lingonberry bushes. Here and there a few remaining berries shone bright red among the snow-covered hillocks. At the end of the road the forest opened into a clearing where another police car was parked. A short distance away, near an embankment, crime scene tape had been put up. The air was cold and fresh.

Fanny's body lay in a hollow beneath several thick spruce trees covered with heavy green moss.

The site was relatively protected. The girl was fully dressed in dark riding pants, a short quilted jacket that was unbuttoned, and a brown woolen sweater that was torn at the neck. Her face was dark against the snow. Her beautiful long hair, which was spread out on the ground, seemed strangely alive. Her eyes were wide open, staring up at the sky. When Knutas took a closer look, he noticed that there were red specks in the whites of her eyes. Dark bruises covered her throat.

Her body had been found by a woman who was out riding. She had fallen off her horse when it was startled by a fox. The horse had wandered off and led her to the clearing. The woman had hurt her back in the fall, and she was also in such a state of shock that she had been taken to the hospital in Visby.

On their way back to the city, Knutas's cell phone started ringing. The third call was from Johan.

"What happened?" said the familiar voice on the phone.

"Fanny Jansson has been found dead," said Knutas wearily.

Jacobsson was driving the car so he could devote all his attention to answering the journalist's questions.

"Where?"

"In a wooded area out on Lojsta Heath."

"When?"

"At eight thirty this morning."

"Who found her?"

"A woman who was out horseback riding."

"Was she murdered?"

"All indications are that she was, yes."

"How?"

"I can't go into that right now."

"How long has she been there?"

"That's something the ME will have to determine. I can't answer any more questions. We're going to hold a press conference later today."

"When?"

"Sometime this afternoon. You'll have time to get here."

Johan and Peter landed right after lunchtime at Visby airport. The cab ride into town didn't take long.

Police headquarters in Visby had changed radically since they were last there. The ice blue metallic facade had been replaced with a soft beige stucco. The rooms were now bright and airy, and they had been decorated in a typically Nordic style that was very tranquil, with natural materials and muted shades of white and blue.

The old and rather shabby room in which they had previously held press conferences was nothing but a memory. The journalists were now shown into a spacious room on the ground floor with rows of stainless steel chairs facing a podium. Thin curtains hung in front of the windows that faced the drab wall of another building. The press had already started setting up their microphones at the podium. Johan counted four reporters from competing TV networks.

He was grateful that he had been entrusted with the task of reporting for all the news programs on Swedish TV. There hadn't even been any discussion about it. After Johan's highly praised reporting on the homicides last summer, the national editors had no doubts: Johan Berg was the man for the job. He was pleased that his report would be aired on all the news programs that evening. He felt a great satisfaction knowing that he would be reaching so many viewers and have such an impact.

He took a seat in the front row while Peter set up his camera. His colleagues from the local media greeted him. He recognized some of them from press conferences that summer.

A moment later Anders Knutas, Karin Jacobsson, Martin Kihlgård, and Lars Norrby all took seats on the podium.

"Welcome," Knutas began. "For those of you who don't know me, I'm Detective Superintendent Anders Knutas, and I'm in charge of this investigation."

He introduced the others and then went on.

"As you already know, the body of Fanny Jansson was found in a remote wooded area on Lojsta Heath. Her body was found around eight thirty this morning by an individual who was out horseback riding. Fanny Jansson was murdered. The injuries that she sustained could not have been self-inflicted, so there is no question of suicide, as we had previously speculated."

"What were her injuries?" asked Johan.

"I'm not at liberty to discuss that," replied Knutas curtly.

He sighed a bit. In spite of the fact that he had barely started on what he had intended to say, the questions had already begun. A number of hands were waving in the air. He had a hard time dealing with the eternal impatience of journalists.

"We'll answer your questions in a moment," he said, "but first I want to present some of the facts."

He had no intention of allowing them to run the show. The reporters lowered their hands.

"The body had been lying at the site for some time. We don't yet know how long. Fanny Jansson was fully dressed when she was found, and there are no signs of sexual assault. The crime scene has been cordoned off, and the area is being searched by our technicians. An ME will be here tomorrow to examine the body. The area will be kept under guard until the body can be moved and the technical investigation has been completed. That is all I have to say at the moment. Do any of you want to add anything?"

He gave his colleagues an inquiring look, but they shook their heads.

"Then we'll take questions."

"How long has the body been there?"

"It could be a matter of weeks, meaning the entire time that Fanny has been missing. But we're not at all sure about that. We'll have to wait for the ME's report."

"Was any sort of weapon found?"

"I have no comment."

"Can you say anything about how she was killed?"

"No, I can't."

"Did the perpetrator leave any clues?"

"I can't divulge that, out of consideration for the ongoing investigation."

"Does Fanny Jansson have any connection to the place where she was found?" asked Johan.

"Not as far as we know."

"Was she murdered at the site, or was she moved there?"

"We have reason to believe that she was killed somewhere else and that her body was later moved to the wooded area."

"What makes you think that?"

"As I said earlier, I can't divulge anything about any evidence or other information found at the crime scene," said Knutas with forced composure.

"Who found the body?"

"A local woman. I don't want to give her name."

"Are there any witnesses?"

"It's possible. We haven't yet started interviewing anyone who lives in the area. But we're going to appeal to the public for information. We want to talk to anyone who may have seen or heard anything suspicious, especially during the last few weeks, in connection with the place where the body was found. No information will be considered too insignificant. Everything is of interest."

Knutas gave them the number for the police hotline and the press conference was over.

That evening Johan presented live reports on all the news broadcasts, giving the television viewers the latest update. He and Peter had a late supper at their hotel and then went to bed.

Again Emma didn't answer her phone when Johan tried to call her. It had now been more than a week since they had last talked to each other. Her friend Viveka had explained to him that Emma was ill and wanted to be left alone. He would just have to wait until she decided to call.

The ME was expected on Gotland the following day, but that evening Sohlman was able to present to the investigative team a preliminary report along with some visual images.

"It's difficult to say how long she has been lying there, but her body is quite well preserved, as you can see, as a result of the cold weather. The perpetrator also covered the body with moss, so no animal got to her. Fanny was fully dressed when she was found, but her sweater was torn at the neck. Her clothing will be examined more closely when the ME arrives, but we're leaving her body where it is until he gets here tomorrow. I can make an educated guess and say that she died from lack of oxygen. Do you see the red specks in the whites of her eyes and the bruises on her neck? Without going out on a limb, we can assume that she was strangled.

"She apparently offered some resistance, since her sweater was torn. I'm hoping that the perpetrator has left some evidence on her clothing—skin particles or saliva, for instance. The body was protected by the woods and the moss. It was also lying in a hollow, so we hope we can find some traces from the killer. We've taken scrapings from under her fingernails. There are skin particles that most likely came from him. Everything is being sent to SCL, as usual.

"When it comes to the location of the body, we can conclude that she was probably killed elsewhere and was then dumped in the woods. There are no traces of blood or anything else that might indicate the murder was committed at the site. We haven't yet been able to examine the body, but we did discover one thing. She has cuts on her wrists."

Sohlman clicked through the photographs until he found the pictures of Fanny Jansson's hands. Cuts were clearly visible on both of her wrists.

"Someone has cut her here. She probably did it herself."

"So she did try to kill herself, after all," exclaimed Norrby.

"Well, I'm not so sure about that," Sohlman objected. "I think it's more likely that she was one of those girls who cut themselves. It's not all that uncommon among teenage girls who are depressed. She had cut herself in other places as well, for instance behind her ears. The cuts are superficial, so there's no question of a real suicide attempt. It's possible that there are more cuts hidden under her clothing."

"Why would she do that?" asked Wittberg.

"Girls who cut themselves do it because they don't know how to handle their fears," Jacobsson explained. "When they cut themselves, all their anxiety collects in that one spot. It's also possible that they experience the pain and the blood as liberating. It's something concrete and controllable. The moment they cut themselves, all their other anxieties disappear; their fear becomes concentrated in the part of their body that is being subjected to pain."

"But why would she cut herself in such odd places?"

"Probably so that it wouldn't be visible."

Knutas switched on the lights and looked at his colleagues with a serious expression on his face.

"We now have two murders to investigate. The question is whether there is any connection between them. What does a fourteen-year-old schoolgirl have in common with an alcoholic man in his sixties?"

"As I see it, there are two obvious connections," said Kihlgård. "First, alcoholism. Fanny's mother drinks, and Dahlström was an alcoholic. Second is the racetrack. Dahlström bet on the horses, and Fanny worked at a stable at the trotting track."

"Those are two reasonable connections," said Knutas. "Is there anything else that might not be as obvious? Anyone?"

No one replied.

"All right," he said. "That's all for now. Both lines of inquiry need to be explored without bias."

FRIDAY, DECEMBER 14

It felt as if the dawn would never come on that cold December morning. Knutas was having oatmeal with his wife and children in the kitchen. They had lit candles, which made their shared breakfast a bit more pleasant. Lina and the kids had baked saffron rolls while he was out at the site where Fanny was found. He was going to need them. Today he had to pick up the ME at the airport and then drive back out to the forest clearing. He put on a wool sweater and got out his warmest winter jacket. The frost of the past few weeks was holding on.

The children were upset and worried, and they wanted to talk about Fanny's murder. They had been greatly affected by the death, since Fanny wasn't much older than they were and they knew her by sight. Knutas ran the palm of his hand over their cheeks as they stood at the front door on their way to school.

In the car on his way to the airport, he felt a cold sweat come over him, and he was overcome by such nausea that he had to pull over and stop for a moment. Everything swam before his eyes, and he felt a tight pressure in his chest. Occasionally he suffered from panic attacks, a form of anxiety, but it had been a long time since the last one. He opened the car door and tried to calm his ragged breathing. The images of Fanny's body, combined with his worries about his own children, had apparently brought on this attack. With his type of work, it was impossible to protect his kids from all the shit he was forced to deal with: drunkenness, drugs, and violence. As his children were growing up, society seemed to be getting more and more brutal. It was probably worse in the big cities, but even here on Gotland the change was noticeable.

He tried not to say too many negative things about his job. At the same time, he could seldom come home and tell them that he'd had an uplifting sort of day. Of course he was always relieved when a case was solved, but it was hardly a matter of feeling elated. When an investigation was successfully completed, he just felt tired afterward. There was no sense of catharsis, as some people might think. Instead, he mostly had a feeling of emptiness, as if he were utterly deflated. Then all he wanted to do was go home and sleep.

After a few minutes he felt better. He rolled down the window and slowly continued driving to the airport.

The ME was waiting for him outside the terminal. His plane had landed earlier than anticipated. It was the same doctor that Knutas had worked with last summer, a lean man with thinning hair and a horselike face. His extensive experience lent him an air of gravity and authority. On their way out to the site where the body was found, Knutas told the doctor about everything they knew so far.

By the time they arrived, it was ten fifteen in the morning, and Fanny Jansson's eyes were still staring up at the gray December sky. Knutas grimaced with dread as he thought about what the beautiful girl lying on the ground might have gone through. Her body looked so small and thin under her clothing. Her cheeks were brown and smooth, her chin softly childish. Knutas was annoyed to feel tears welling up in his eyes.

He turned his back and gazed at the woods, which were dense and inaccessible. Over near the tractor road he could see that the forest thinned out a bit. Since he had previously studied the map of the area, he knew that some distance away there were open fields and pastures. A crow cawed from far off, otherwise everything was silent except for a quiet rustling from the dark green branches of the trees. The ME was now fully involved in his examination, and would be for the next several hours. Erik Sohlman and a couple of the other techs were assisting him with his work.

Knutas realized that his presence wasn't needed. Just as he got into the car to drive back to police headquarters, Karin Jacobsson called him.

"There's one person who has ties to both Dahlström and Fanny Jansson."

"Really? Who is it?"

"His name is Stefan Eriksson, and he's the stepson of Fanny's aunt in Vibble. She has a daughter of her own, but she divorced the father early on and married someone else, a man who had a son from a previous marriage. Fanny and this Stefan have seen each other for years at various family gatherings and the like. He's forty years old, married with two children, and he also happens to own a horse at the stable."

"I know that. We've been down the whole list," said Knutas impatiently. "What about him?"

"He was an intern under Dahlström when he was in high school. He worked at the newspaper for two weeks. After that he was a temp for *Gotlands Tidningar* and later he also worked for Dahlström when he started his own business. This Eriksson owns a café in town, the Café Cortado on Hästgatan, but his hobby is photography."

"Is that right?" exclaimed Knutas in surprise. This was new information to him.

"He and Dahlström may have kept in contact over all these years, even though Eriksson denied it when Wittberg and I interviewed him. A most unpleasant type of person. I could easily imagine him—"

"All right, but let's not jump to any conclusions," Knutas interrupted her. "What else?"

"I asked him if he spends any time at the stable, and he said that he's there now and then. The staff at the stable confirm this. He would also occasionally drive Fanny home."

"Does he have a police record?"

"No. On the other hand, there have been a number of complaints filed against him for suspected neglect. His family used to raise sheep, and the animals were evidently treated badly, according to the person who complained. Eriksson no longer has any sheep."

"I want to talk to him myself. Where is he?"

"I think he's at home. He lives in . . . oh my God!"

Jacobsson abruptly fell silent.

"What is it?"

"Stefan Eriksson lives in Gerum, which is only a couple of miles from the place where Fanny Jansson's body was found."

"I'm ten minutes from there. I'm on my way."

Gerum is not a real town. It's just a church with a few scattered farms right next to the large and inaccessible Lojsta Heath. The landscape is flat, but Stefan Eriksson's farm and surrounding property were the exception. It stood on a hill with a panoramic view of the area. The farm consisted of a stone farmhouse with two wings and a large barn. A late-model Jeep was parked outside along with a BMW.

When Knutas rang the bell, he heard dogs barking inside. No one came to the door.

He took a stroll around the farm and looked in the windows of the separate wings. One was apparently used as an artist's studio, and there were paintings leaning against the walls. A painting of a woman's face was set on an easel in the middle of the room. Crowded onto a table splotched with paint were cans and tubes of paint along with paintbrushes.

As he peered in the windows, Knutas was interrupted by the sound of someone clearing his throat behind him. The detective was so startled that he jumped and dropped his pipe on the ground. A man was standing right behind him.

"Can I help you with something?"

Stefan Eriksson was almost six foot six inches tall, by Knutas's estimate. He had on a blue down jacket and a black knit cap.

Knutas introduced himself. "Could we go inside to talk? It's starting to get cold."

"Of course, come with me."

The man led the way inside. Knutas was practically knocked down by two Dobermans, who seemed beside themselves with joy.

"So you're not afraid of dogs?" asked Eriksson without making any attempt to calm the animals.

They sat down in what must have been the good parlor. *To think that people still have rooms like this*, thought Knutas. *A remnant of bygone times.*

Stefan Eriksson was clearly fond of antiques. A mirror in an elaborate gold frame hung on the wall. Next to it stood a bureau with curved legs and lion's claw feet; along one wall stood a grand cabinet with rounded feet. The room smelled stuffy and dusty. Knutas felt as if he were sitting inside a museum.

He declined the offer of coffee. His stomach growled, reminding him that lunchtime was long past.

"Well, I don't really understand what you want. I've already talked to the police," said the tall man, who had sat down on a plush armchair. The dogs had settled at his feet, with their eyes fixed on their master.

"I need to ask you a few additional questions, but first I would like to express my condolences."

The man sitting across from him did not change expression.

"It's true that Fanny was my cousin, but we hardly knew each other. And we're not real cousins, anyway. My father—"

"I know about the family ties," Knutas interrupted him. "How often did you see each other?"

"Very rarely. Sometimes at someone's birthday celebration. There were problems with her mother, so they didn't always come. Majvor can't keep away from the bottle."

"How well did you know Fanny?"

"There was a big age difference between us, so we didn't really have anything in common. She was a little girl who sometimes came to visit with her mother. She never said anything. You'd be hard-pressed to find a more silent girl."

"You own a horse at the stable where Fanny worked. Didn't you ever see each other there?"

"That old nag is practically useless. It costs a lot more to keep her than she ever brings in from racing. But of course I do stop by the stable once in a while. Occasionally Fanny was there at the same time."

"Did you sometimes give her a lift home?"

"Not very often."

"Which car did you drive?"

Stefan Eriksson shifted uneasily in his chair. A frown appeared on his face.

"What are you getting at? Am I under suspicion?"

"Not at all," said Knutas dismissively. "I'm sorry if I seem pushy, but we have to talk to everyone who knew Fanny."

"I understand."

"So which car did you drive?"

"The BMW that's parked outside."

"You knew Henry Dahlström, too, didn't you?"

"Yes, I was an apprentice for him eons ago when I was still in school. After I graduated I sometimes filled in for him at *GT,* and I also worked as a temp at Master's. I mean, Master Pictures, his company."

"How did you happen to meet him?"

"I'm interested in photography, and he was teaching a course that I attended when I was in high school. And then, as I mentioned, I was an apprentice for him."

"Did you keep in contact over the years?"

"No. When the business folded, he went completely downhill."

"Do you still take photographs?"

"When I can. I'm married and have children and we moved out here. The café that I own in town also takes up a lot of my time. It's Café Cortado, on Hästgatan," he added.

Knutas detected a note of pride in the man's voice. Café Cortado was one of the most popular cafés in town.

Suddenly the dogs rushed for the door and began barking. Knutas gave a start. Eriksson's face lit up.

"That's my wife and kids. Just a minute."

He got up and went out to the entryway. The dogs were barking wildly and jumping around.

"Hi, sweetheart. Hi, kids. How are you?"

Eriksson's voice took on an entirely different tone. It was suddenly filled with love and warmth.

His wife and children had clearly been out celebrating Lucia. Maja Eriksson came in to say hello. She was dark and sweet and soft-spoken. Knutas noticed the tender way in which Eriksson looked at his wife.

No, he thought. *It can't possibly be him.*

He thanked the man for his time and left.

The discovery of Fanny's body caused a big stir in the media. The evening papers devoted a great deal of attention to the news, as did Regional News and the local media on Gotland. There was much heated debate about what could have happened to the girl. The newspapers printed maps that allowed their readers to locate exactly where Fanny was found. The farms that were closest to the site received visits from reporters and photographers. The newspapers were filled with speculations and hunches about what the motive behind the murder might be, and the TV and radio stations broadcast interviews with the stable staff as well as with the girl's neighbors and classmates.

Without talking to Johan, Max Grenfors had called Majvor Jansson and persuaded her to agree to an interview. Grenfors was very pleased with his success in getting the mother to tell her story as an exclusive on Regional News. But he encountered quite a different reaction from Johan, who refused to interview her, which prompted Grenfors to give him a real tongue-lashing.

"I've managed to get her to agree to an exclusive interview, so of course we're going to talk to her!"

Johan was standing out in a field near the place where the body had been found. He was with Peter and a farmer who thought he had seen car headlights in the area late one night a couple of weeks earlier.

"I'm not interviewing someone who's in a state of shock," said Johan firmly. "The woman doesn't know what she's doing. She can't see the consequences at the moment."

"But she wants to do it. I talked to her myself!"

"Exactly what do you want me to ask her, one day after her daughter was found murdered? *How does it feel?*"

"Damn it, Johan. She wants to talk. Maybe it's a way for her to work through the whole thing. It's her own decision. She's unhappy with the police work and wants to say something about it. She also wants to appeal to the public for help in finding the murderer."

"Fanny was found yesterday. That's less than twenty-four hours ago. I can think of better ways to work through things than by talking on TV. In all good conscience, I don't think we can do it."

"For God's sake, Johan. I told her that you'd be at her sister's house in Vibble at two o'clock."

"Max, you can't trample on my journalistic integrity. I won't do it. I simply won't have this on my conscience. The woman is in shock and should be in a hospital. She's extremely vulnerable right now, and I think it's rotten if we try to take advantage of her weakness. She doesn't realize the impact of TV. We have to make certain decisions for people if they're not capable of doing it for themselves."

Johan glanced at Peter, who was standing next to him and rolling his eyes. He told Johan to give Grenfors his greetings and say that he refused to film an interview with the girl's mother. At the same time Johan could hear Grenfors breathing harder on the other end of the line.

"Just do the interview and we'll make the ethical decisions back here in the newsroom," shouted Grenfors. "See to it that you go out there to meet her. I want it on tonight's program. I've already promised the interview to *Aktuellt, Rapport,* and *24.*"

"And all of them want it?" asked Johan dubiously.

"You bet they do. So get going. Otherwise she might change her mind and talk to somebody else!"

"Fine. Let TV3 interview her, or the newspapers if they want to. But I won't do it."

"So you refuse?" Grenfors went on.

"What do you mean by 'refuse'?"

"You won't carry out the assignment that I've asked you to do. That's a dereliction of duty, damn it!"

"Call it whatever you like. I'm not going to do it."

Johan closed his phone, bright red in the face. His breath was visible in big billowing puffs all around him. He turned to Peter and the farmer.

"What a fucking pig."

"To hell with him," said Peter, in an attempt to console him. "Let's get back to work. I'm freezing to death."

The farmer, who had listened in astonishment to the phone argument while he waited to be filmed, was now interviewed. He told them about the car that he had seen driving along the tractor path one evening two weeks earlier when he was out in the barn tending to the evening milking. As he was crossing the barnyard, he saw lights from the road. No one ever drove out here so late at night. He couldn't say what type of car it was. He had stopped and waited for a while, but when the car didn't reappear, he gave up and went inside his house.

Johan and Peter headed back to town. They were planning two reports, one that dealt with the police work and another that focused on the feeling of shock the day after among the schoolkids, the stable staff, the neighbors, and the ordinary citizens of Visby.

Many had still been hoping that Fanny would be found alive, even though hope had dwindled with each day that passed. Now there was a great sense of sorrow.

Back at the hotel that evening, Johan tried to get hold of Grenfors, but the editor refused to talk to him. He had found a trainee to do the interview with Fanny's mother, but after discussions with the producer and editors, the piece was never aired. No one else seemed to be interested in it, either. *It's just a matter of prestige,* thought Johan when a colleague later recounted on the phone the wrangling going on in the newsroom. Good Lord, sometimes his job was like kindergarten.

The important thing was never to forget your purpose and to keep asking yourself why you were doing a particular story and whether it had general interest. And then you had to weigh that against the harm that you might cause people. He was sure that he had made the right decision when he refused to contact Majvor Jansson. No one could make him interview people who were in shock.

That was one lesson he had learned after all his years working in TV. On a few occasions he had done what some overzealous editor wanted and interviewed people who had just lost a loved one or who had been involved in an accident. Just in order to be accommodating. Afterward he had realized that it was wrong. Even though at the time of the interviews the individuals had wanted to talk in order to share their grief or to draw attention to a problem, they were confused and unable to think clearly. To dump the responsibility on them was indefensible. Besides, they didn't comprehend the scope of their participation. The impact of TV was enormous. Images and interviews could be repeated in all kinds of contexts, without allowing the person involved any opportunity to stop them. And each time his or her grief would be torn wide open.

She felt as if she were in a soundproof glass bubble, cut off from the rest of the world. Someone had pulled the cord, stopped the noise, brought the merry-go-round to a halt.

Emma was lying on her back on the floor of Viveka's small living room. Her friend was away for the weekend, so she had plenty of peace and quiet to think things through.

It was very tranquil in the living room. She didn't want any disturbing sounds—no radio, no TV, no music. She wished she could sink deep into an undemanding darkness that would simply embrace her.

Another body was growing inside of her body. A tiny human being that was part of her and Johan. Half him and half her. She closed her eyes and ran her hand over her smooth abdomen. Nothing was visible on the outside yet, but her body was sending her signals. Her breasts were tender, she had started suffering from morning sickness, and her craving for oranges was just as strong as during her previous pregnancies. She wondered what kind of person was inside her. A girl or a boy? A little sister or a little brother?

She let the tips of her fingers move in circles under her shirt, sliding down to her crotch and then back up to her sore nipples. The baby was telling her that he or she was inside, already taking nourishment through the umbilical cord, and growing bigger every day. She had figured out that she was in her eighth week. How far had the fetus developed? She and Olle had followed closely the various stages of development when she was pregnant with Sara and Filip. He had read aloud to her from a book about what was happening each week. They had been so filled with anticipation.

Now everything was different. This weekend she would have to make a decision. To have the baby or not. She had made a promise to Olle. He had reacted with surprising composure to the news that she was pregnant, even though it was quite clear that he was not the father. With icy determination he had told her that if she decided to have the child, their divorce would be inevitable. He had no intention of taking care of Johan's kid and being saddled with her lover for the rest of his life. If they were going to continue as a family, there was only one choice—to get rid of it, as he said. Get rid of it. The words sounded absurd to her ears. As if it were merely a matter of picking off a scab. Just scrape it off and flush it down the toilet.

She wished that someone else could make this decision for her. No matter which option she chose, it was going to be trouble.

MONDAY, DECEMBER 17

On Monday morning the phone began ringing the minute Knutas stepped through the doors of police headquarters.

"Hi, this is Ove Andersson, the building superintendent at Jungmansgatan. We met in connection with the murder of Henry Dahlström."

"Yes, of course."

"Well, the thing is that we're cleaning out the darkroom that Dahlström was using here. It's going to be a storage room for bicycles again. I'm standing in the room right now."

"Yes?"

"We've found something odd, behind a vent. It's a plastic bag with a package inside. It's taped up and I didn't want to open it because I thought I might destroy some evidence."

"What does it look like?"

"It's a brown paper package with ordinary tape around it, very lightweight, about the same size as a stack of postcards."

Under Knutas's intense supervision, Sohlman opened the carefully wrapped package, which had been delivered to the crime tech division. It turned out to contain photographs. Rather blurry, but there was no doubt about the subject matter. Almost identical, they all seemed to have been taken from the same angle. In the pictures they could distinguish a man who was having intercourse with a young woman, or rather a girl. She seemed to be half the size of the man. Her face was hidden, partly by him and partly by her long black hair. Her arms were stretched up in an unnatural position, as if she had been tied to something. The man was bending over her, almost covering the girl's body with his, but one of her legs was visible. She had dark skin.

Sohlman and Knutas looked at each other.

"It must be Fanny Jansson," Knutas said at last. "But who's the man?"

"God only knows."

Sohlman ran a hand over his forehead. He took out a magnifying glass and began scrutinizing the photos.

"Look at this. There's a painting hanging on the wall behind them. You can see a bit of red and a . . . What's that? Maybe a dog?"

He handed the magnifying glass to Knutas. One corner of the painting was visible.

"It looks like a dog lying on something red. It could be a cushion or a sofa."

Sohlman eagerly looked through the other pictures, but none of them revealed anything more.

Both men sank down on their chairs. Knutas dug his pipe out of his pocket.

"Well, we now have the connection," muttered Knutas. "Dahlström took pictures of someone who had a sexual relationship with Fanny Jansson. He must have photographed them on the sly and then blackmailed the man for money. That's where the twenty-five thousand came from. That would explain everything: the man at the harbor, the money, Fanny . . ."

"That means that the man we're looking at in these pictures is the perpetrator," said Sohlman, tapping his gloved index finger on the man's pale back.

"Presumably. It's easy to figure out why he killed Dahlström. But why Fanny? If it is her, that is. We can't be completely positive."

Knutas picked up one of the photographs and held it out.

"Who the hell is he?"

Knutas summoned the investigative team to a meeting to discuss the surprising discovery. The mood was one of nervous elation—rumors about the contents of the package had quickly spread through the corridors. Sohlman had scanned the photos so that he could project them on the screen at the front of the room. Wittberg was the first to speak.

"Are we positive that the girl in the photos is Fanny Jansson?"

"Her mother was just here, and she identified her. You can see the girl's watch on her left wrist. Fanny got that watch as a birthday present last year."

"How did the mother react?" asked Jacobsson.

"She fell apart," said Knutas with a sigh. "And who wouldn't, seeing their child in that sort of situation?"

"What kind of damn pervert is this guy?" growled Norrby.

"The only thing we've been able to determine so far is that we're dealing with a grown man—definitely not a boy her own age."

"It looks like she's tied up," Kihlgård interjected. "Her arms are stretched above her head. She's tied to something."

"Look at this," said Sohlman, putting up the most detailed of the photos. "There seems to be a painting in the background. The only thing we can really make out is the image of a dog lying on a red sofa or something similar. Yellow-patterned wallpaper with a faint border is visible in the background, as well as a glimpse of the back of a chair. It looks like an antique chair with a high back and carved decorations. The photographer took all the pictures from the same angle. The fact that they're so blurry could be because they were taken from outside, through a window. The question is: Where were the photos taken? It has to be somewhere in town or nearby, at some easily accessible place. Otherwise how would Dahlström have discovered Fanny and the unidentified man?"

"Maybe it's a storeroom," suggested Norrby. "Or a meeting room. Or it could be in the home of somebody that Dahlström knew."

"The room looks brightly lit. Can you see how the daylight is coming through the window? I have the impression that it's a big room," Jacobsson said.

"I really wonder how the man met Fanny," said Wittberg. "Could he be a friend of her mother?"

"How disgusting, if that's the case. That would be horrible." Jacobsson grimaced.

"I think the pictures look pornographic," said Kihlgård, holding one up. "It might very well be a sex ring. Maybe there was a whole gang of guys who were exploiting Fanny, and this is just one of them. Maybe she got drawn into prostitution and was forced to sell her body to the neighborhood men."

"Up until now we've been lucky to be spared that type of activity here on Gotland. At least as far as we know," said Knutas with a sigh.

"Or pedophiles," murmured Jacobsson. "Fanny might have been one of many children being exploited. We might have a pedophile ring right around the corner, and we don't have the faintest idea about it."

"The Internet. We have to check the Internet. I have a friend who's working on a big pedophile investigation in Huddinge. I'll ask her whether there might be anyone in that ring who has connections to Gotland."

"Good idea," said Knutas approvingly. "This could be about almost anything at all."

He was interrupted by his cell phone ringing. The others listened in silence to his murmuring. When he was finished, he looked at his colleagues alertly.

"That was Nilsson at SCL. The samples taken from Fanny Jansson's bedroom have been examined. No match was found in the police records, but the blood and hairs that were taken from her bed have been compared with the evidence from Dahlström's place. There's no doubt whatsoever—they match."

Late that evening Knutas went back home and found his entire family gathered in front of the TV. They answered his greeting by saying, "Shh—this is so exciting!"

He sighed and went out to the kitchen, opened the refrigerator, and took out a plate of leftovers, which he heated up in the microwave. The only one who wanted to keep him company was the cat, who rubbed against his leg and then hopped onto his lap and curled up. The cat seemed completely unaware of the problem she caused him. It wasn't easy to lean forward to eat with a cat curled up on his lap.

The idea that a murderer and sexual predator was on the loose on

Gotland gave him goose bumps. At first the perpetrator had given in to Dahlström's demands and made two payments, but after that it clearly got to be too much. But actually deciding to murder the man who was blackmailing him was a big step. Maybe the killer thought he could get away with it if he made it look like a drunken brawl. And then there was the money from the racetrack. Most likely he knew about it and made use of the fact. He probably stole the money to mislead the police. The fact that Dahlström's apartment had been searched must mean that he was looking for the photos. The same with the darkroom. But his search had been in vain. The package was hidden inside a vent, and no one had bothered to look there, neither the killer nor the police.

After the murder the perpetrator left the scene. He tossed the murder weapon and the camera into a grove of trees some distance away. He presumably had a car parked farther away, near the next apartment complex.

Knutas poked at his food: meatballs with reheated pasta. He poured on some more ketchup and aimlessly stirred it into his food. He took a gulp of milk. Not a sound from the living room. The movie must be very exciting.

And then Fanny was killed. Although maybe that's where they really ought to start, since it was where the whole thing began. The story of the fourteen-year-old girl. How had the man met her in the first place? He must somehow be part of her world.

Knutas put that question aside for the time being and continued his train of thought. The man was using her sexually; there was no doubt about that. It was anyone's guess how long it had been going on. No one seemed to know that she was seeing anybody. He doubted that this was a love relationship in the usual sense. The man might have threatened her, or else she was dependent on him in some way. But what had prompted him to kill her? He had already gotten rid of Dahlström, so he wasn't being blackmailed anymore.

He was taking a big risk by committing another murder. It might not have been planned, of course. Maybe it happened as a result of some sex game. Fanny appeared to be tied up in the photos. Maybe the killer had strangled her by mistake and then dumped her body in the woods.

There was another alternative. Maybe Fanny had become so difficult that he found it necessary to kill her. Maybe she was threatening to expose him, or simply wanted to end the relationship.

The strange thing was that no one had noticed anything—not a single person.

His heart lurched when he thought about the body in the woods. The faces of various people flashed through his mind. Fanny's mother. How was she responsible for what had happened? Why hadn't she paid more attention to her daughter? Fanny had been all alone with this problem. She had felt so bad that she had even tried to harm herself. She was only fourteen and still a child. Yet no grown-up had cared about her, not even her mother.

It was the same situation at school. Even though the teachers had noticed that something was wrong with Fanny, they did nothing. She was there, right in front of everyone's eyes, but no one saw her.

THURSDAY, DECEMBER 20

As Knutas sat in his office drinking coffee, someone knocked on the door. Karin Jacobsson stuck her head in.

"Good morning! It sure is interesting how people can forget all about something and then suddenly remember the most important details."

She dropped onto a chair across from him and rolled her eyes.

"That guy Jan Olsson from the stable called to say that Fanny had gone out to visit Tom Kingsley."

"Is that right?"

"One time last fall Jan Olsson had to go over to Tom's place to drop something off."

"What did he drop off?" queried Knutas.

"He didn't say," Jacobsson went on impatiently. "But listen to this. Fanny's bicycle was outside Kingsley's house, and Olsson noticed that her jacket was hanging in the hallway."

"Did he see her?"

"No. Tom didn't invite him in."

"Okay, that's enough to bring Kingsley in. I'll call Birger so we can get a search warrant for his house."

Knutas reached for the phone to call the prosecutor.

"Sure, but there's just one problem," said Jacobsson dryly.

"What's that?"

"Tom Kingsley has left. He's on vacation in the States."

"For how long?"

"He has to be back at work on Monday, according to the stable owner. But he booked an open-ended round-trip ticket and hasn't yet made his return reservation. So we don't know when he'll be flying home."

"We're going in anyway."

Tom Kingsley's house stood in a wooded glade, not far from the race-track. It was actually a summer cottage that he had been renting ever since he came to Gotland.

The road up to the house was not much wider than a tractor path. The police cars jolted their way forward. Knutas and Jacobsson were in the first car, with Kihlgård and Wittberg following behind. Prosecutor Smittenberg had immediately given the go-ahead to search the premises. Ordinarily, Tom Kingsley should have been notified, but no one knew where he was.

All the windows were dark. When they got out of the cars, it looked as if no one had been to the house in a while. The snow cover was untouched.

They had obtained keys from the landlord, whom Jacobsson had managed to locate during the course of the morning.

The ground floor of the house consisted of a small entryway and a living room on the right, with access to a cramped kitchen. The house was furnished simply but nicely: a dining table next to the window, a fireplace, and against one wall an old-fashioned wooden sofa with seat cushions covered with striped fabric. Between the kitchen and the living room was a woodstove. The kitchen, with windows facing the woods, was sparsely furnished: low kitchen benches, a pantry, an old electric stove, and a small refrigerator.

A narrow staircase curved up to the second floor, which had two small bedrooms and a hallway. It was neat and clean. Knutas lifted up the bedspreads. The bed linen had been removed and the mattresses underneath were worn. The police officers began methodically going through all the drawers and cupboards. Kihlgård and Jacobsson took the second floor, Knutas and Wittberg the first floor.

It wasn't long before Wittberg shouted, "Come and look at this!"

With tweezers he was holding a piece of paper that looked like instructions of some kind.

"Do you know what this is?"

The others shook their heads.

"It's instructions for taking morning-after pills."

FRIDAY, DECEMBER 21

The discovery of the pill instructions in the home of Tom Kingsley, combined with the fact that he had definitely denied having any sort of close relationship with Fanny, made the prosecutor decide to issue a warrant for Kingsley's arrest in absentia. The fact that Fanny's fingerprints were found on the instructions made the police even more convinced that Kingsley was the man they were looking for. After checking with the airlines, they determined that a week earlier he had flown to Chicago on SAS. The Stockholm police were informed, and employees at the SAS ticket offices were told to keep a lookout for Kingsley and to sound the alarm when he booked his return flight.

Knutas felt relieved, even though he didn't know where Kingsley was. Now it was just a matter of waiting for his return.

In the meantime, he could take a much-deserved weekend to relax. Away from any kind of police work. He and Leif were going out to the Almlöv family summer house in Gnisvärd, on the coast about fifteen miles south of Visby, as they always did right before Christmas. He hadn't been sure that he could actually get away this time because of the investigation. But a warrant had been issued for Kingsley's arrest, and they couldn't do anything else until he returned home. So Knutas had decided that it would be possible, after all. It was only a twenty-minute drive from Visby, and he could be reached by cell phone if anything happened.

As for preparing for Christmas, he had done everything that was expected of him—the traditional buying of the Christmas tree with the children, and all the grocery shopping and cleaning that he had done together with Lina. Late one evening he had made his own pickled herring in a sherry sauce, as he always did for the Christmas and

Midsummer holidays. During his lunch hour he had run out to buy Christmas presents and had actually managed to buy everything, wrap all the gifts, and compose the traditional rhymes to go with them.

Now he was ready for his reward. Two days of solitude eating good food and doing some fishing—interests that he shared with Leif.

He hurried home after work on Friday afternoon and packed a bag with clothes and his fishing gear. It had been snowing all day. The snowplows had been working nonstop to make the roads passable. Knutas couldn't remember the last time it had snowed so much on Gotland. If only it would stick around until Christmas.

In the car on their way south he felt himself relaxing more with every mile they put behind them. They were playing Simon and Garfunkel full blast. The wintry landscape slid past outside the windows, with expanses of white fields and an occasional farm.

A beautiful layer of snow covered the yard when they arrived.

It's actually silly to call this place a summer cabin, thought Knutas. *It's more like a manor house.* The typical Gotland-style limestone house from the mid-nineteenth century was impressive with its whitewashed walls, pitched roof, and smooth gables. During that era bigger houses were being built on Gotland to keep pace with the increasing prosperity in the countryside. This house had no less than seven rooms and a kitchen, divided into two wings. The farm also had a boathouse that was used as a storeroom and food cellar. Next to the house stood a sauna, only a few yards from the dock where Leif's fishing boat bobbed up and down all year-round.

The place was rather isolated. The nearest neighbor lived a couple of hundred yards away.

"I can just imagine how cold it is in the house," Leif warned his friend when he opened the heavy, creaking front door.

"It doesn't feel so bad," said Knutas as they stepped inside. He carried the bags of food out to the kitchen and started putting away the provisions. "But I suppose it will seem worse if we sit still."

"I'll turn on the electric heat and make a fire in the fireplace, but it will take a while to get rid of the dampness."

Several hours later they sat at the table with plates of roast beef and potatoes au gratin that smelled of garlic, along with a bottle of a robust Rioja wine. It had been a long time since Anders Knutas had felt so good.

"How many times have we done this? Is this the fifth or the sixth year? This year it seems even more necessary than usual."

"Yes, I think we both needed to get away," Leif agreed. "There's been a hell of a lot to do at the restaurant. The worst is when there are problems with the staff. One of my best waitresses had a miscarriage and had to go to the hospital. Then another waitress had to go to Stockholm because her mother died. And to top it off, I caught one of the bartenders stealing from the till. All within a couple of weeks. And as usual, these kinds of situations always happen at the least convenient time. Right now we're up to our necks in Christmas reservations. It's lucky I have such a superb chef, otherwise I'd never be able to handle all this. He can fix pretty much anything. I actually offered to stay home this weekend, but he persuaded me to go. I was thinking we could postpone this to some later date," he added apologetically.

"I'm glad we didn't. Tell him thanks from me." Anders took a sip of his wine. "At least you should be happy that the restaurant is doing so well. It's always full of people, and it's been like that ever since you opened. I don't know how you do it."

"So what about you? How's it going with the investigation?"

"Good. We finally seem to be on the right track."

"What a nasty business."

"It's been damn tough. When we know that a murderer is on the loose and we're blindly fumbling around, not being able to make sense of things . . . it's frustrating."

"So you're not doing that anymore? Blindly fumbling around, I mean?"

"No, I'm convinced that we're close to solving the case. You know that I can't discuss any investigations with you, but this much I can tell you: I think we're very close now."

"Is it someone you've suspected for a long time?"

"No. Actually, someone completely unexpected has turned up."

"So why haven't you caught him?"

"Enough questions, Leif. You know I can't answer them."

Leif held up his hands. "Of course. Would you like some more wine?"

They spent the rest of the evening playing chess in front of the fireplace. And they opened another bottle of Rioja.

It turned out to be a late night. They didn't get to bed until after midnight. Anders was given one of the upstairs bedrooms. The room was simply but beautifully furnished. The limestone walls were rough and bare. The slate roof was supported by heavy timbers. A wide wooden bed with a white flowered bedspread stood along one wall, and next to it were three country chairs painted blue. A little window with a deep recess faced the sea. The rhythmic sound of the waves lapping against the shore lulled him to sleep.

When he awoke, he had no idea how long he had slept. It was pitch dark in the room. He couldn't understand what had awakened him. He lay still with his eyes open and unseeing in the night, listening for sounds that weren't there.

He reached out his hand and turned on the lamp on the nightstand next to the bed. It was three ten in the morning.

His mouth was dry, and he needed to go to the bathroom.

Afterward he paused next to the window. He could hear the sea, but it seemed very calm. There was a light on in the boathouse. Strange. Was Leif out there at this hour? Maybe he had forgotten to turn off the light.

The snow gleamed white in the darkness, and the glow from the outdoor lights cast long shadows. Nothing was going on, so he went back to bed.

It took a long time before he fell asleep.

The days had passed and Johan hadn't heard a word from Emma. He had been back in Stockholm almost a week, since nothing new had occurred on Gotland that would warrant a trip to the island. At least nothing that he knew about. The police were being very tight-lipped. He had tried to put the pressure on Knutas several times, but he hadn't gotten anything useful out of him. Experience told him that they were close to catching the perpetrator. The police always reacted the same way when an investigation entered a sensitive stage. They all just clammed up.

He was longing for Emma terribly, but she refused to talk to him. Maybe a solution was near on more than one front. Oh, just let it happen, he felt at the same time. Bring on the shit, so we can get this over with once and for all. He was tired of all the worrying and all the planning for a future with Emma. Wondering how he would manage on Gotland, as a stepfather, as a man with responsibilities. Cooking pasta and reading good night stories and blowing noses and balancing things among Emma, her ex-husband, the kids, the in-laws; birthday parties, deciding where to spend Christmas Eve, and feeling torn between Stockholm and Gotland. And, to be honest, how much fun would it be to take over a family that already existed? He was a romantic who dreamed of getting married and eventually becoming a father. For Emma, none of it would be for the first time.

Marrying again, having children again. Did she even want to have children with him? They had never talked about that. Why hadn't they?

It was probably just as well that they put an end to things, once and for all. He might meet some girl in Stockholm who didn't have a broken marriage and kids as baggage. Then it could be a magical experience for both of them. Everything would be so much simpler—just the fact that they could live in Stockholm, close to their families, their work, and their friends. The conditions for having a successful and good life together would be so much better. Why make life more difficult than necessary? It was hard enough to make a relationship work. Did he also have to hassle with other people's children and ex-husbands? No thanks.

But there was just one hitch. Emma was the one he wanted.

SATURDAY, DECEMBER 22

On Saturday morning Anders woke up when Leif knocked on the door and barged into the room.

"Wake up, sleepy-head! It's eight o'clock and breakfast is ready!"

Groggy with sleep, he sat up in bed. Leif was looking shamelessly frisky.

"I've already been out to chop wood. It's glorious weather. Just have a look outside," he said, nodding toward the window.

Anders turned his head. To his great surprise, he saw the sun gleaming over the expanse of the sea, which was blue and relatively calm.

He had almost forgotten how beautiful the view was. When they arrived the day before it was already dark.

"Incredible! I'll be right down."

He took a quick hot shower. *What a luxurious summer house this is,* he thought as he admired the lovely tiled wall.

Breakfast was on the table when he came downstairs to the kitchen: a real Gotland loaf of rye bread, butter, cheese, liver sausage, ham, salami, and vegetables. The aroma of strong coffee was spreading through the kitchen. A fire was crackling in the fireplace.

Anders appreciated Leif's sense for food, and he dug in with a good appetite.

"What service," he said, grinning at his friend, who was sitting on the other side of the table, studying a nautical chart.

"Tomorrow it's your turn to make breakfast. I was thinking that we should take the boat out, since it's such good weather. A light wind and forty-one degrees."

"It's great to see sunshine in the middle of December. That's a real treat."

"Did you sleep well?"

Anders hesitated for a second. "Like a rock. How about you?"

"Same here. I always sleep well in the country."

Anders cleared the breakfast dishes and packed up his gear. He was looking forward to the fishing trip.

Two days left before Christmas. Anticipation was shining in the children's eyes. At the same time, she found herself as far away from the idyllic family scene and the serenity of Christmas as she could get. She woke up in Viveka's guest room, feeling sick. The pregnancy probably wasn't the only reason. It had been a late night. She and Viveka had consumed a lot of wine and stayed up talking half the night.

She might as well go ahead and drink wine. She no longer needed to think about the well-being of the baby. She had made up her mind, but she wasn't able to get an appointment for an abortion until after Christmas. She was going to have to spend the entire holiday noticing the clear signs of her pregnancy. A constant reminder of the child growing inside of her.

She still hadn't dared talk to Johan. She didn't want him to influence her decision. Of course it was selfish, but she didn't see any other option. She had chosen to lock him out. She had distanced herself from him completely and refused to speak to him on the phone. She defended her actions by telling herself that it was sheer self-preservation. It was lucky that he had gone back to Stockholm. That made things a little easier. To see him now would be disastrous. And she had to think about the children she already had.

They had decided to celebrate a completely normal Christmas, with the whole family together. To visit relatives and friends and do everything they usually did. She would just have to suffer through the nausea as best she could. She had only herself to blame, and Olle didn't seem to be the least bit sorry for her. There wasn't a trace of the sympathy he had exhibited when she was pregnant with his own children.

When she saw Sara and Filip she was filled with tenderness. They had no inkling of the chaos that was raging inside their mother.

The doorbell rang. With a sigh she got out of bed and fumbled for her bathrobe. It wasn't even ten o'clock.

When she opened the door she found herself looking at the faces of her husband and children.

"Good morning!" they cried in unison.

"You have to get dressed," Sara told her eagerly. "Hurry up!"

"What's going on?"

Emma cast an inquiring glance at Olle, who was looking sly.

"You'll see. Go and get ready. We'll wait."

Viveka was now up, and she came out to the entryway.

"Hi. Has something happened?"

"No. We're just here to pick up Emma," said Olle cheerfully.

"Come into the kitchen and wait." She turned to the children. "Would you like some juice?"

"Yes!"

Fifteen minutes later Emma was ready, and they set off. Olle drove south, heading away from Visby. In Vibble he turned onto a road leading through the woods.

"Where are we going?" she asked.

"You'll see soon enough."

They parked outside a solitary house and rang the bell. Dogs could be heard barking inside. The children were jumping up and down with excitement.

"That's Lovis," shouted Filip. "She's so cute!"

A young woman of about twenty-five opened the door, holding a baby in her arms, and with a golden retriever circling her legs. The dog was overjoyed to see the visitors.

Emma had to wait in the hall while the others hurried out to the kitchen. She could hear them whispering. Then they came out to join her, first Olle with an adorable golden puppy in his arms, followed closely by the children.

"Merry Christmas!" said Olle, handing her the puppy, who wagged her tail and stretched out her snout to lick Emma's hands. "You've always wanted to have a dog. She's yours, if you want her."

Emma felt herself beaming as she took the puppy in her arms. The dog was small, soft, and plump, and she eagerly licked Emma's face.

The children were looking up at her happily. A ribbon was tied around the puppy's neck with a card attached: "To Emma with all my love—your Olle."

She sank down onto the bench in the hall, with the puppy climbing all over her.

"See how much she likes you?" Sara chattered.

"She just wants to keep licking and licking," said Filip with delight as he tried to pet the puppy.

"Do you want to keep her?" asked Olle. "You don't have to. We can leave her here."

Emma looked up at him without saying a word. Everything that had happened flashed through her mind. His coldness had scared her, but it probably was because he felt hurt. And with good reason. Of course she understood. She saw hope in the faces of her children. For their sake she would have to try.

"Yes," she said. "I want to keep her."

The call came into police headquarters as Jacobsson and Kihlgård were sitting in the pizzeria on the corner. The Stockholm police reported that Tom Kingsley had booked his return flight for the following day. He was due to land at Arlanda Airport at 2:45 P.M. They assumed that he planned to continue on to Visby the same day. The next flight for Visby was scheduled to depart at 5:10 P.M. The police at Arlanda would apprehend him at the airport and then escort him to Visby. Wittberg called to convey the information, and Jacobsson sent a text message to Knutas to update him.

"That's great," said Jacobsson, breathing a sigh of relief. "Maybe we can finally put an end to this whole story so we can have some time off during Christmas."

"I certainly hope so. If he really is the killer."

"And why wouldn't he be?"

"You just never know. Surely he should realize that he's going to come under suspicion sooner or later. There's nothing keeping him here. If Kingsley really is the perpetrator, we have to ask ourselves why he doesn't stay in the States. Why would he come back here and risk getting caught?"

"Maybe he's convinced that he's not a suspect."

"Sure. But it wouldn't surprise me at all if the guy turns out to be innocent and we have to start from scratch."

Kihlgård stuffed the last bite of the aromatic calzone into his mouth and wiped his lips with the back of his hand.

Jacobsson gave him a dubious look. "Optimist," she muttered.

"I think it's strange that Knutas seems so certain that Kingsley is the perp. Just because the investigation has come to a dead end, that doesn't mean he has to grasp at straws."

"Then how do you explain the morning-after pill?" Jacobsson objected.

Kihlgård leaned back and lowered his voice. "It could be that Fanny trusted Kingsley enough that she asked his advice about those blasted pills, and then she left the instructions at his place. That's not inconceivable, is it?"

Jacobsson looked at him skeptically. "Is that what you really believe?"

"Why not? We shouldn't lock ourselves into Kingsley. That's crazy." Kihlgård ran his hand through his thick mane, which was sprinkled with gray.

"So what should we do?" asked Jacobsson.

"How about having some dessert?"

Anders steered the little fishing boat out to sea. It was always so peaceful standing at the helm. Leif was preparing the nets on deck. He came from a family of fishermen and was quite experienced. When he was ready, he came to stand next to Anders in the wheelhouse.

"There's not much salmon on this side of the island, so we'll have to fish for cod instead."

"That's too bad. It would have been great to have fresh salmon for dinner."

"We can always try, by trolling. I'll toss out the lines behind the boat and let them trail in our wake. Now that it's so cold, the fish are right below the surface. If we're in luck, we'll catch a salmon or a steelhead."

They passed Tofta Beach, and Anders was amazed at how deserted it looked. The emptiness of the rippling sand dunes was a huge change from the hordes of swimmers in the summertime. Tofta was by far the most popular beach on the island, especially among young people. In the summer the beach towels were spread out so close together that you could hardly see the sand.

Leif gazed across the sea.

"Can you see the two Karlsö islands over there? It's incredible how clear they are."

Both islands stuck up from the water, the big one behind the little one. Anders had been out there so many times. His whole family went out to Big Karlsö every May to see the colonies of guillemets. That's when the unusual auks hatched their young.

Glints of sunlight kept coming through the clouds, and even though the wind was picking up, they decided to stay out at sea while the nets were in the water. Leif unpacked some sandwiches and a thermos of hot chocolate, which they enjoyed on deck. It was hard to believe that Christmas Eve was just a couple of days away.

Anders was tired, so he went into the cabin to lie down for a while. He fell asleep to the sound of the waves lapping against the hull. After an hour he woke up to find Leif nudging him.

"We have to pull up the nets. It's getting windy."

Anders was surprised to see how quickly the weather had changed. Gusts of wind met them as they came up on deck, and the sky was now dark. The boat was pitching back and forth as they pulled up the nets. It was a nice haul—they counted nine cod. The trolling lines brought in two salmon. Not exactly spectacular specimens, but still not bad.

"Now we'd better see about getting back home as fast as possible," said Leif. "I was listening to the marine report while you slept. There's a storm on the way."

It would take them an hour to get back to Gnisvärd. Darkness fell, and as they passed Tofta, the first squall set in. The boat listed abruptly. Anders, who was on his way up the companionway to the wheelhouse, fell headlong through the door.

"Damn it!" he shouted as he hit his head on the table.

It wasn't far now to land, but the boat was being tossed right and left. The fish were in buckets on deck, and when the first wave struck, Leif yelled, "We need to bring in the fish or they'll all end up back in the sea. Be careful when you open the door."

Leif kept his eyes fixed on the black water, battling the swells as best he could. Anders reached for the door handle and pushed open the door. One bucket had turned over, and the fish lay scattered on deck. The next wave crashed over the gunwale and washed some of the catch overboard.

Anders gathered up the remaining fish and threw them back into the bucket. *God, this is nuts,* he thought. *Here I am practically risking my life just to save a few lousy fish.* He could see Leif's tense face through the window.

Anders stumbled his way into the wheelhouse. His clothes were soaked through.

"Fucking hell. How's it going?" he asked Leif.

"Okay. We're close to shore, so it's going to be all right. But this weather is damn awful."

Suddenly the lights of the Gnisvärd dock appeared in the dark. Anders breathed a sigh of relief. They were only a hundred yards away.

When they once again had solid ground under their feet, Knutas realized how scared he had actually been. His legs could barely hold him up. They secured the boat and hurried back to the house.

"What an ordeal," Anders gasped. "Right now all I want is to get out of these clothes and take a hot shower."

"You do that," said Leif. "I'll make a fire in the meantime."

Up in his room, Anders discovered that his cell phone was gone. Damn, it must have been washed overboard when he was out on deck. Now Jacobsson wouldn't be able to reach him. He would have to ask Leif if he could borrow his cell. He also wanted to call Lina and tell her about their dramatic adventure. There was no phone in the house, in spite of all the other modern conveniences.

They warmed themselves up with some Irish coffee as they made dinner.

Leif prepared the salmon with an expert hand. He started by slitting open the fish with a sharp knife. Then he removed the guts and pulled the backbone away from the filets. Anders felt his mouth watering as he watched Leif brush the filets with oil, sprinkle them with herbs, and place them on a bed of coarse salt. Then he put the fish in the oven to bake.

When it was ready they hungrily launched into the salmon, washing it down with strongbeer. They talked about the day's drama. What an adventure. It could just as easily have ended in disaster. Outside the window the wind was blowing harder, and more snow was on the way.

After a number of shots of whiskey with their coffee, they were both feeling fairly intoxicated. They listened to some music and talked about trivial things, and by the time Anders went upstairs to bed, it was two in the morning. Leif had passed out on the sofa.

Anders fell into bed and should have fallen asleep instantly. Instead he was wide awake, thinking about the investigation, about Kingsley. According to Jacobsson's text message, the suspect was supposed to return home later today. The case that had consumed all his thoughts, day and night, for the past month would most likely be solved just in time for Christmas Eve. He was looking forward to enjoying Christmas dinner with his family and relatives without having to think about the murder. He suddenly felt a great longing for Lina and the kids. He had an urge to get in the car and drive straight home.

He realized that he wasn't going to be able to sleep. It was fruitless to try, so he got dressed and tiptoed down the stairs. The sofa in the living room was empty, so Leif must have gone to bed even though he hadn't heard him.

Anders sat down on one of the leather armchairs and started to fill his pipe. He lit it and inhaled deeply. He liked smoking when he was alone. He seemed to enjoy it more.

A painting caught his attention. It was of a woman with a dog resting on her lap. The woman was young and slender and wore a sleeveless red dress. Her eyes were closed, and her head was tilted toward one shoulder, as if she were asleep. Her lips were the same color red as her dress. The dog was looking out at the viewer. It was a beautiful painting.

Knutas leaned forward to see who the artist was. He got up from the armchair and ran his finger along the gilded frame. Moved his eyes to the wallpaper, which was a pale yellow with a slightly brighter border. Next to the painting stood a chair with a high back, richly decorated, and two turned posts with knobs. The details were merging into a puzzle, and slowly he realized where he had seen this chair before. It was without a doubt the distinctive chair back that was visible in Dahlström's photographs. Norrby, who was interested in antiques, had explained that it was an English Baroque chair.

At first he was overcome with utter confusion. How could Dahlström have taken pictures of Fanny in Leif's house? Had he and some companion exploited her in the summer house without Leif's knowledge? Did it happen while Dahlström was building the sauna?

His thoughts moved on and in his mind everything began coalescing to create an appalling pattern. Leif owned a horse at the stable and he had hired Dahlström. His appearance matched the description. It could just as well have been Leif in the photos. His friend of twenty years. An electric shock wave of ice-cold instinct shot through his body, making its way into every nook and cranny. He lost his grip on his pipe, which fell to the floor, scattering bits of tobacco over the rug.

He took another look at the painting to make sure that he was right. No, no. He couldn't believe it, refused to believe it. The thought passed through his mind that he should just go to bed and pretend that he hadn't noticed anything. He should bury his head in the sand and go on as usual. Part of him wished that he'd never seen that painting.

He tried to convince himself that there must be some other answer. Suddenly it occurred to him that Leif had been out in the boathouse the night before. What was he doing out there?

He had to go and take a look. Quickly he put on his shoes and jacket and then opened the front door as quietly as he could. He crossed the dark yard as his thoughts whirled. A jumble of irreconcilable images appeared in his mind: Leif in the sauna, on the ski slope, as Santa Claus at their house, playing soccer on the beach, standing in Dahlström's darkroom with a hammer in his hand and acting with cold-blooded brutality, bending over Fanny Jansson's young body in the photographs. He went around the corner of the house, and it took a few seconds before he noticed the figure in front of him. Suddenly he was standing face-to-face with Leif, who was holding his hands at a strange angle behind his back, as if he were hiding something. But Knutas never managed to see what it was.

SUNDAY, DECEMBER 23

Lina sounded worried when she called Karin Jacobsson early in the morning.

"I haven't heard from Anders since yesterday morning. Have you?"

"No, his cell is turned off. I've tried to call him several times."

"Leif doesn't answer, either. I just talked to Ingrid. I'm starting to worry. They were going out in the boat yesterday, and since then a real storm has blown in. I hope nothing has happened."

"I'm sure they're fine," Karin reassured her. "Anders said that he'd be here this afternoon. His cell battery probably ran out. Don't they have a phone at the summer house?"

"No. I'm thinking of driving out there to see if everything's all right. This is making me nervous. It's so unlike Anders not to call."

Jacobsson checked her watch. Ten fifteen. Kingsley wasn't supposed to land until that afternoon.

"Listen, I'll go out there myself. I can get away at the moment."

"Are you sure?"

"Yes. I'll be there in half an hour. We'll call you as soon as I get there."

"Thank you."

Jacobsson had tried to call Knutas on his cell many times without getting through, and she had started feeling uneasy herself. On her way out to Gnisvärd, she called the Marine Rescue Service. No, nothing had happened, as far as they knew. She got the same answer from the Coast Guard.

The road was slick. The temperature had dropped overnight and the slush had frozen, transforming the road into a sheet of ice. Jacobsson kept a safe distance from the other cars and was grateful that there was very little traffic.

When she came to the sign for Gnisvärd, she turned off and continued along a smaller road toward the old fishing village. The Almlöv summer house was half a mile away, in a secluded spot near the water. She had been there once before, for a crayfish party. The house had a marvelous location with its own dock.

The car was parked in the yard, and the boat was tied up at the dock. So they had to be close by.

It was almost eleven thirty. The house seemed deserted. No smoke from the chimney, and the lights were turned off. Of course it was daylight, but the clouds made it seem quite dark outside.

She knocked on the door. No answer. Pounded harder. Still no reaction.

She saw no sign of human activity anywhere, except for the footprints in the snow leading back and forth between the house and the dock. Maybe they were out taking a walk.

Imagine having a place like this, she thought enviously. *Such peace.* She looked out at the sea and the boathouse made of limestone. Farther down toward the water, right next to the dock, stood the sauna. That was the one that Dahlström had built. He had been paid under the table for it. She started walking across the yard. She didn't notice the person who appeared right behind her.

She heard only a brief rushing sound before she fell to the ground.

On the day before Christmas Eve the call that he had been dreading came through. Her words were like a battle tank that mowed him down. Powerful and inexorable.

"It's not going to work anymore. I can't keep doing this. I have to make up my mind, once and for all. I really care a lot for you, Johan, but I'm not ready to split up my family."

"I see," he said tonelessly.

"You have to understand. I just can't," she said, sounding more insistent. "It's for the sake of my children, too. They're still so young.

And Olle and I get along fine, actually. It's not exactly a passionate sort of love, but it works."

"How nice for you."

"No, don't do that, Johan. I realize you're upset. This is really hard for me, too. Don't make things worse than they already are."

"Right."

"Don't be like that," she cried, sounding annoyed. "Don't make me feel even more guilty than I already do!"

"So that's how it is. You just call me up and tell me it's over, after you've said a hundred times that you love me, and that you've 'never felt this way about anyone else,'" he said, doing a terrible impression of her by raising his voice to a falsetto.

"Then in less than a minute you tell me that *I* have to understand, that *I* shouldn't make things worse than they already are, and that *I* shouldn't make you feel guilty. Thanks a fucking lot. How considerate of you. But you think you can just crush me underfoot like a cockroach. No problem at all. First you throw yourself into my arms and tell me that I'm the best thing that's ever happened to you—well, except for your kids that you're always talking about—and then you think it's perfectly all right to just call me up and say it's over!"

"It's good that you brought up the part about my children," she said, her voice icy cold. "That just confirms what I've suspected all along! You think it's a nuisance that I have kids! Unfortunately, they're part of the package, you know."

"Don't go saying that Sara and Filip have been some sort of obstacle, damn it. As you know, I've been fully prepared to take care of both you and the children. I've been daydreaming about moving to Gotland and maybe getting a job at the radio station or at one of the newspapers. The children would live with us, and I've thought about what my relationship would be with them. I wouldn't force things. I'd take it easy. I would just be there for them and do the best I could. That's what I've been thinking. And that maybe they would eventually get to know me and want to be with me, that we would play soccer and build tree houses and things like that. I love you—don't you understand that? Maybe you don't realize what that means. It's so damn easy for you to bring up the whole issue with the children.

You're using Sara and Filip as some kind of fucking shield so that you won't have to change your life!"

"Great," she said sarcastically. "You said their names. I think that's the first time I've ever heard you do that! So now you seem to think it's time to show some interest in them. Well, it's a little late for that."

Johan sighed in resignation.

"Think whatever you like," he said. "But I'm sure that's exactly how things stand. You simply don't dare break things off with Olle. You're too scared. You should at least acknowledge this to yourself and stop putting the blame on anything else."

"You think you know everything," she snapped, now sounding on the verge of tears. "Maybe a lot of things have been happening over here that you don't know anything about. Everything is so easy for you, but life can be very complicated. I hope you'll learn that someday. You don't know shit about what I've been going through."

"Well, tell me! You've shut me out for weeks now. I've called and called, and the closest I can get to you is by talking to Viveka. How can I do anything if I don't know what's going on? Tell me what it is, and I'll help you. I love you, Emma. Can't you get that into your head?"

"No, I can't. I can't tell you what it is," she said in a stifled voice.

"What do you mean? What can't you tell me?"

"Nothing, Johan. I have to go now. Merry Christmas, have a nice holiday, Happy New Year, and have a great life!"

She hung up.

Karin Jacobsson woke to find herself tied to a bed. A rope had been wound around her body, and she was completely immobilized, as if she were in a vise. Her arms and legs were numb, and her head hurt. She tried to get her bearings in the room as best she could from her immovable position. She was in a child's bedroom that she recognized from her previous visit. On the table was an old-fashioned Parcheesi game with different-colored wooden cones as markers. There were chairs with homemade cushions covered with a tiny flower pattern and a Strindberg lamp. A polished hardwood floor, white cotton curtains at the window. How idyllic and homey it all was.

The house was quiet. Who had hit her?

What had happened to Knutas and Leif?

She listened for any sounds but couldn't hear a thing.

How long had she been lying here? She had arrived at about eleven thirty. Through the window she saw that it was still overcast and impossible to figure out how high the sun was in the sky.

She tried to move her hands, which were tied to the sides of the bed. The rope cut into her wrists.

It wasn't any better with her legs. With an effort she managed to lift her head and look around. Her jacket was lying on a chair. She arched her body, straining against the rope the way she had seen escape artists do. Tense and release, tense and release. Stubbornly she kept on, varying it by twisting and turning her wrists as she tried to loosen the rope.

At the same time her concern about Anders and Leif grew.

It bothered her that it was so quiet in the house. If someone had tied her up like this, shouldn't that person be close by? Karin felt her anger growing. She had no intention of lying here like some sacrificial lamb, waiting for someone to take her to slaughter. She tensed her muscles and arched her body up toward the ceiling as hard as she could.

The rope loosened enough to give her new hope. She repeated the movement. Suddenly she felt the rope release. The next instant she was able to free one hand and her left arm.

In a matter of minutes she was free and off the bed. She stretched her body, waved her arms, and shook out her legs to get the blood circulating. She crept over to the window and looked out. She could see the water, which was motionless and gray, the boathouse and the sauna down by the shore. Not a soul in sight. She put on her jacket and put her hand in her pocket for her cell phone and car keys. They were gone.

The plane landed on schedule at Arlanda Airport. After Tom Kingsley came through passport control, the police were waiting for him.

The arrest was undramatic. Kingsley mostly looked surprised. The police explained to him that he was under arrest. Then he was cuffed and escorted by two plainclothes officers to the domestic terminal to wait for the plane to Gotland later that afternoon.

The news that he had been arrested was received with relief and joy at police headquarters in Visby. Kihlgård called Knutas but got no answer. He tried Jacobsson's cell, but again with negative results.

"Why the hell can't we get hold of the two top officers when something is finally happening?" he roared.

"Karin was driving out to Gnisvärd this morning," said Wittberg. "Anders has apparently not answered his cell phone all weekend. She was worried that something might have happened. Hell, I forgot all about that."

"What do you mean by 'something might have happened'?" growled Kihlgård.

"He and Leif were going out in the boat, and there were nearly gale force winds."

Kihlgård looked at his watch.

"Let's drive out there. We've got time."

A dull thudding sound was audible as Jacobsson came out into the yard. It sounded like pounding and it was coming from inside the boathouse.

She peered through the window but couldn't see anything unusual. Not a sound. She stood still and waited. She pressed her body against the locked door to hear better. Then the thudding resumed, at a slower beat. It sounded almost halfhearted now.

She needed something to break the window. Her car stood where she had left it, next to Leif's. In the trunk she found a tire iron. It was now or never. With a crash the glass shattered and fell in like confetti. Jacobsson whispered through the broken window, "Anders, are you there?"

The whimper that came in response indicated that he had been gagged. She leaned down and looked inside. There in the dark she could make out her boss lying on the floor, his hands and feet bound, a rag stuffed in his mouth.

She turned around and looked up at the house. Not a sign of life. She reached inside for the latch and opened the window, cutting her hand on the broken glass. Damn it. She was bleeding, but that didn't matter. She climbed in.

When she looked into Knutas's eyes, she had never seen him so helpless. Quickly she started untying the rope that held the gag in place. He gasped when at last he was free.

"Thanks. I'd almost given up hope. I thought I was going to rot in this damn place."

"Where's Leif?" asked Jacobsson as she wrestled with the knots that held Knutas's wrists behind his back.

"I don't know. How did you happen to come out here?"

"We started getting worried when we didn't hear from you. But when I got here someone hit me over the head and tied me to a bed inside the house. I managed to get free and came out here looking for you. I heard you thumping."

"It was Leif."

Jacobsson paused. "What?"

"I think it was Leif who murdered both Dahlström and Fanny."

"Are you out of your mind!"

"No, I mean it. I'll explain later."

Something in his voice made her realize that it was true.

"Is the car still here?" he asked.

"Yes, it's parked outside."

"What about the boat?"

"It's at the dock."

"We have to get out of here. We have to get help."

The door was locked from the outside, so they climbed out the window and ran across the yard to the road.

After they had gone a hundred yards from the house, they heard a deafening boom. They turned around to a sea of fire. The sauna down by the water had exploded into an inferno of flames, building materials, and smoke. They watched the macabre spectacle in silence.

"He blew the whole thing up," gasped Knutas.

They approached the burning building and saw the flames reflected in the water.

The only thing Knutas could think about was whether Leif was inside.

Neighbors who had heard the explosion came driving up. They had alerted both the police and the fire department. Knutas and Jacobsson were tended to by their colleagues. Knutas managed to convince the medics that he didn't need to go to the hospital. He at least needed to stay at the scene long enough to see how things developed. Jacobsson felt the same. Finally they agreed to sit inside an ambulance to watch everything going on around them. Uniformed and armed police officers went into the house while others searched the area with dogs. The firefighters fought the blaze down at the dock, and several officers crept inside the boathouse with their guns drawn. *The whole scene is right out of a movie,* thought Knutas.

Gradually the police offices regrouped in the front yard. The firefighters had the fire under control, and now it was just a matter of putting it out completely. They had not yet found Leif Almlöv.

WEDNESDAY, DECEMBER 26

The residential street was quiet and deserted, but inside the houses the Christmas dinner celebrations were fully under way. In some driveways sparklers were burning in the winter darkness, and cars were parked outside the gates.

He paused outside the fence to look at the house. There were lights in all the windows. Advent stars made of straw and wood gave off a gentle glow. In the living room a tall Advent candle in a cast-iron holder was visible along with two big amaryllis plants. The red flowers bore witness to much careful tending. He saw the family moving about inside. Back and forth between the living room and the kitchen. He knew that they had a dining table in the living room.

He caught a glimpse of Filip playing with a puppy. Did they have a new dog? Not a good sign. Not at all.

He opened the gate. The gravel crunched under his feet. The snow had vanished again, melting away on Christmas Eve. Now a gray haze had settled over the idyllic residential neighborhood in Roma.

He went up to the front porch and saw through the window that Olle had noticed him. Now there was no turning back. He took a deep breath and rang the bell.

EPILOGUE

The chapel stood in a secluded spot near the fishing village of Kovik on the west side of the island, about five miles south of Gnisvärd.

It was built from Gotland limestone, with a single window like a porthole facing the cow pastures, the windswept boathouses, and the sea. The chapel had been dedicated to the memory of the men who had drowned at sea.

Leif Almlöv came from a family of fishermen who for generations had fished the stormy Baltic along Gotland's coast. That was where he was to be buried, in accordance with his last wishes. Only his immediate family were present.

Knutas sat in the back row of folding chairs that had been set up in the small space. He fixed his eyes on the flower-bedecked coffin in the front of the chapel as he pondered who Leif really was. Or rather, had become.

Everything seemed to have started with Fanny Jansson. Of course Leif had visited the stables on numerous occasions. This was confirmed by his father-in-law, with whom he shared ownership of the horse. That was where he had met the girl.

Then Leif had hired Dahlström to build the sauna out in the country, but the carpenter had discovered what Leif was doing with Fanny. Maybe Dahlström had spent the night there while he was working on the sauna and then saw something that he wasn't supposed to see.

That was the beginning of the end for everyone involved.

No one had any doubts that Leif was the perpetrator. It was his fingerprints that had been found in Dahlström's darkroom, in his apartment, and on the murder weapon. His hair and saliva were on Dahlström's clothes, and on Fanny's.

Several weeks had now passed since that fateful day out at Gnisvärd, which had ended with Leif perishing in the flames. The reason for the powerful explosion was the cylinders of gas that were kept in the storeroom next to the sauna. They could have blown up the boat-house, too; only a few yards separated the two buildings. A nasty chill spread through Knutas's body as he thought that his friend of twenty years might have been planning to blow him up. And what about Karin? The thought was inconceivable, but it was just as unbelievable that Leif could have murdered two people.

Leif's remains had been found in the ashes under the burned-out sauna. Whether he had committed suicide, they would never know. Knutas's thoughts turned again to Ingrid and the children. What sort of life was in store for them after all this? Was it even possible for them to go on?

And Fanny—she was just a child. Knutas felt a deep sorrow when he thought about the fourteen-year-old girl. She hadn't even had a chance to begin her adult life. At the same time he was weighed down by feelings of guilt. He wondered how much his friendship with Leif had interfered, and to what extent it had blinded him. He was fully aware that in his position as head of the homicide team, he was ulti-mately responsible for the investigation.

Outside the chapel the local press had gathered along with a number of curiosity seekers. Knutas declined to answer any questions. He slipped away and stared out at the horizon.

Three seagulls were flying low over the surface of the water. The sea was unusually still, and the new year had begun.

AUTHOR'S ACKNOWLEDGMENTS

This story is entirely a work of fiction. Any similarity between the characters in the book and real individuals is unintentional. Occasionally I've taken the liberty of changing certain things to suit the narrative. This includes the TV news division of Swedish TV on Gotland, which is very much alive, although in the book it has been closed down so that the responsibility for Gotland was moved to Stockholm. I have done this simply in order to tell the story in my own way. I have the greatest admiration for the existing team in Visby and for Swedish TV's regional news program Östnytt, which is responsible for covering Gotland in real life.

Any errors that may have slipped into the book are solely my own.

First and foremost, I want to thank my husband, the journalist Cenneth Niklasson, who is my greatest inspiration, my biggest supporter, and my most persistent critic.

Many thanks also to:

Gösta Svensson, former detective superintendent of the Visby police for his invaluable assistance with the police work.

Johan Gardelius and Bo Ekedahl, crime techs, the Visby police.

Martin Csatlos, the forensic medicine laboratory in Solna.

Neng Wanlayaphol, trotting-horse trainer, Visby Racetrack.

Mats Wihlborg, district prosecutor, Visby.

Jenny Ingårda and Eva Waltré, BRIS—Children's Rights in Society.

Il-nam Kroon, social worker.

Mikaela Säfvenberg, archaeologist and authorized guide, Gotland.

My mother, Kerstin, and my sister Ewa Jungstedt for their assistance on research trips to Gotland.

Tove Wiklander—for her constant positive support during our speed walks.

I would also like to give a warm thank-you to my publisher, Jonas Axelsson, for his faith in me, and to my editor, Ulrika Åkerlund, for all her help with this book.

And to my advance readers for their valuable opinions:

Anna-Maja Persson, journalist, Swedish TV.

Lena Allerstam, journalist, Swedish TV.

Lilian Andersson, editor, Bonniers Educational Books.

Bosse Jungstedt, my brother, and Kerstin Jungstedt, my sister-in-law.

Last, but not least, thanks to my beloved children, Rebecka and Sebastian Jungstedt, for their good humor, love, encouragement, and genuine patience with their mother's writing.

Älta, July 2004
Mari Jungstedt